"Couldn't stop reading—this vividly written comedy would translate well to film." *Vana O'Brien, actress*

"Such a light, enjoyable book about cats, dogs, and their humans! Romantic and realistic at once." *Elizabeth Dossa, author and journalist*

"A charming story in a New England town full of flawed but appealing characters—an outsider perspective on the crazy things humans do." *Nora Long, literary agent*

Second Lives
A novel of humans and other animals

Beatrice Gormley

Cover design: SelfPubBookCovers.com/adventure_frame

In memory of Cool Paw Luke
And Brady the Wonder Dog

[The Cat] went back through the Wet Wild Woods, waving his wild tail and walking by his wild lone.
Rudyard Kipling, *The Just So Stories*

Chapter 1.

The Cat peered out one round hole in the side of the cardboard carrier, then another. The car jerked out of the driveway. He tried to dig his claws into the slick cardboard to keep his balance. A piercing meow caused his heart to beat faster, even though he was making the sound himself.

It wasn't riding in the car that panicked the Cat. He often rode along when the Man drove, for instance to pick up pizza. He liked to stretch out on the shelf behind the back seat, the highest perch in the car, with an ever-changing view. He also rode with the oldest child on her bike, sitting in the basket as she pedaled up and down the cul-de-sac.

The Girl was the one who'd named him "Batman." It was on her bed that he slept at night, in between stints of mouse patrol. But last night, when he'd padded up the stairs for his midnight nap, her bedroom door was shut.

That was not right. The Cat meowed and scratched. Finally he pounded on the door with his front paws, making a racket that even hearing-deficient humans would notice.

The Cat's pounding did wake up the Girl, who woke up the Man and the Woman. There was crying and arguing. But the upshot was not the obvious one, to let the Cat into the Girl's room. Instead, the Man had picked up the Cat and shut him in the laundry room for the night. So the Cat had missed out on not only his nightly naps with the Girl, but also his pre-dawn rounds of the household.

This morning, after the Man and the children had left the house, the Cat jumped onto the sill of the sunny living room window. Licking his white bib while keeping an eye on the fluttering finches at the bird feeder, he purred praises to the Great Cat. Surely he was one of her favored worshippers, for he had lived since kittenhood in this ideal home.

Well—ideal until yesterday. Even before the disturbance last night, there had been an upset involving the Girl. He'd been sitting on her lap, purring as she stroked him and bent down to whisper to him, her breath tickling the long hairs on the inside of his ear.

Then—the Girl's soft, regular breath halted. She made a strangled noise. He glanced up. She began wheezing and choking, and he jumped off her lap in alarm. The Woman came running. She hustled the Girl out of the house and into the car. They were gone until after dark.

This morning the Woman had forgotten, as she sometimes did, to feed the Cat right away. After he groomed himself, he was going to have to annoy her until she remembered.

The Cat heard the Woman's footsteps behind him, but he thought she was coming to water the geraniums at the window. Instead, she grabbed the Cat and stuffed him into the carrier. "I'm sorry, kitty, but my children come first."

The Cat bunched his haunch muscles to leap out, but she shoved the flaps down against the top of his head. As the carrier lifted and swung sickeningly, he lurched from side to side.

Now, in the car, the Cat strained to see, pressing his face against one hole in the cardboard after the other, but the little round openings showed only patches of car upholstery. He poked at the holes with his paws to enlarge them, but the cardboard was too sturdy. He hated not being able to see out the window.

Was the Woman taking him to the vet's? That had been the destination, the other times he'd been crammed into the carrier. The thought of that chemical-smelling place, the cold steel table where he was prodded and stuck, made him yowl again. After the last visit to the vet, the Cat had come home with an unexplained wound in his groin, and it had taken several days to heal.

"It's okay, kitty," the Woman called from the driver's seat. He yowled louder. She turned on the radio, adding a yammer of voices over the Cat's cries.

The Cat was tempted to call on the Great Cat to save him from the vet's. He had learned as a kitten that if a cat was in truly desperate straits, and called upon Her with a pure heart, the Great Cat might come to his rescue. However, the deity should not be bothered for minor problems. As his mother had told him and his litter-mates on the day she weaned them, the Great Cat had more important things to do. Besides, She needed Her sleep.

The Woman's phone rang, and she turned down the radio to answer it. "Hi, Mom. . . . Emma's fine now. She went back to day camp. . . . No, she was fine, as soon as" [*yowl*] "they gave her the epinephrine, even before we left the emergency room. . . . Yes. I'm on my way to the Mattakiset Animal Shelter right now. . . . I didn't" [*yowl*] "ask Scott. If he thinks we can keep a cat in the same house with an allergic child, he's insane. . . ."

The Cat was panting between yowls now. Would they drive on forever, turning corner after corner, his paws slipping as the carrier slid from side to side on the backseat? But no—with one more turn, the car slowed and came to a stop.

From the feeling of the car wheels, this was not the vet's stone parking lot. It was smooth pavement, like the family's driveway. The Cat started to calm down. Maybe the Woman had driven around aimlessly and finally come back home? Humans did stranger things than that.

As the driver's door opened, an overpowering smell rushed into the Cat's nostrils: the reek of dozens of lonely, frightened animals. The air rang with compulsive barking, pierced by yowls.

The back door of the car opened.

The Cat was too horrified to yowl. This was a place much worse than the vet's. A place where animals without patrons sank into despair.

O Great Cat! Save me!

The Woman lifted the carrier out and set it down on the pavement while she locked the car, still talking on the phone. "Look, I'll have Emma call you after her gymnastics class, okay? Gotta go."

O Great Cat, I beg you, help!

The Cat seemed to feel a warm breath on the top of his head. Blue sky appeared between the handles at the top of the carrier. He lunged upward. *Great Cat, give me strength.*

"Damn!" exclaimed the Woman, grabbing at the loose handles. But the Cat's head and shoulders were already out. She tried to push him back down. He raked her arm with his claws. "Damn!"

Cats are small, and humans, even female ones, are large, but the power of the Great Cat was with him. Writhing and scratching, the Cat tumbled onto the pavement. He found his footing and streaked for the trees at the edge of the parking lot.

A throaty voice, like his memory of his mother's purr, only more so, spoke in his ear: *This is the end of your first life.*

It was a doggy-dog world.
Eighth-grade essay on the Dark Ages

Chapter 2.

On a hot, moist July morning in a western suburb of Boston, in a neighborhood where modest houses were out of reach for a teacher's salary, but not for the combined salaries of a teacher and an attorney, Josh Hiller and his friend Carl labored to move most of his worldly goods into a U-Haul truck. The rest of his stuff was already jammed into his Honda Civic, the dusty car waiting at the curb like an overloaded donkey.

Six months ago, Josh's life had seemed difficult but manageable: He and Tanya were not getting along—but considering joint counseling; his dog, Molly, was gray-muzzled and arthritic—but as devoted as ever; and the principal of Josh's middle school was a bitch on wheels—but more important, Josh loved teaching those kids.

Now Tanya had filed for divorce, Molly was a small round carton of ashes and bone fragments on the floor of his car's backseat, and Westham Middle School was Josh's previous employer. Soon his and Tanya's three-bedroom Cape would be on the market, and then it would become someone else's house.

Carl held a wooden-cased clock up to where Josh stood in the back of the U-Haul. "I think this is it, but you'll probably want to take a last look around." Leaning with both hands on the truck, he watched Josh wrap the Seth Thomas clock in a bathmat and wedge it into the seat of an armchair. "Uh, shouldn't you pack that clock in its own box? It looks like an antique."

"No, it'll be fine." Josh wiped his dripping forehead with the sleeve of his T-shirt, briefly disrupting the cloud of gnats around his head. Carl, he noticed, looked like he was going to pass out. "Let's get out of here. Follow me to Liberty Self-Storage? Unit 2B."

That afternoon Josh drove cautiously south on Route 24, having to depend on his side mirrors because the back window was blocked with cartons and bags. Also, the bicycle on the back jiggled whenever he hit a bump. It was generous of Vicky, his sister, to give him the bicycle. Although he didn't like feeling that she was managing him, as if he couldn't manage his own life.

It was Vicky's idea for Josh to spend the summer on the South Coast, healing in the sun and salt air while he looked for a new job. "Not Cape Cod," she told him. "The South Coast is just as nice as the Cape, but closer and less expensive." She set him up with a real estate friend in Mattakiset, a town of farms and summer cottages tucked into the inlets and points around Buzzards Bay.

Josh took the exit for I-195 East, and then the exit for Mattakiset. Suddenly, there was almost no traffic, and the highway was walled in by woods on both sides. Josh followed the directions past stone walls draped with brambles, past a chicken farm, over a creek flowing into a salt marsh, past a field where cows clustered in the shade. "We're in the country, old girl," remarked Josh to the backseat.

Turning off Old Farm Road at a red mailbox, Josh drove between rough-cut stone posts and parked under an ancient mulberry tree. The picture Melissa the real estate agent sent him hadn't lied—in fact, the white-clapboard farmhouse looked even more picturesque in its wider setting, with a barn and the neighboring pasture.

A large, shaggy gray dog bounded out the front door, barking, followed by a tall, sturdy woman. "You must be Josh Hiller. I'm Barbara Schaeffer, and this is Lola."

They shook hands, and Josh held out his fingers for the dog to sniff. English sheep dog mix, he guessed. Barbara and her dog both had straight-cut gray bangs and pale blue eyes.

"Well!" said Barbara. "Let me show you around a bit, and then I'll let you get settled. Here's your key." She watched Josh drop the key into the front pocket of his shorts. "Wouldn't it be a good idea to put that right on your key chain?" Quickly she smiled, as if to soften any impression of bossiness.

Josh smiled, too, to soften any impression of willful disobedience. "Sure, good idea."

Barbara's smile disappeared, but she let the subject drop and beckoned him toward a screened porch on one side of the house. "Now, you're welcome to use this space for relaxing." Opening the screen door, she gestured at the wicker chairs and coffee table. "And to use the washer, of course."

Josh looked from the porch furniture, with the wicker unspooling from its legs, to the top-loading

Kenmore washing machine. He gazed all around the porch. "And the dryer . . .?"

Barbara pointed to an umbrella-style clothesline on the lawn. "I've always preferred to hang laundry out in the sunshine. And now we know how bad dryers are for the environment. And of course terrible fires can start in the lint screen." Josh's dismay must have showed on his face, because she added, "It is stated in our rental agreement: washer, **no** dryer."

Then Barbara cleared her throat, as if to indicate starting over on the right foot. Stepping down from the porch, she explained, "I'm new to this renting business. You see, I've lived in this house for thirty years, but I've never rented the apartment before. We added it on eight years ago, for my mother-in-law." She halted and gestured to the outdoor stairway leading to an apartment over the porch. "Well. I think everything is self-explanatory—I put up some notes around the apartment—but if you have questions, just knock on my door and ask."

Josh smiled wryly. "Or, I could actually read the rental agreement, right?"

Barbara smiled back. "It's really very simple. The important clauses are **No smoking** and **No pets**." She headed back to the house, with her dog ambling after.

Wearily Josh pulled his backpack out of the car and trudged up the outside stairs. It was a little cooler here than in Westham, but just as humid. He was breathing through his mouth, which he'd been doing a lot lately. As if it was hard to get enough oxygen.

There was a hand-lettered notice on the apartment door: PLEASE! LEAVE THE SAND AT THE BEACH! Josh turned the key in the lock, pushed the door open, and headed past the bed for the bathroom. Over the toilet, as he peed, another notice: HOLD HANDLE DOWN THROUGH FLUSH.

Glancing into the kitchenette, he found further instruction over the toaster: TOASTER DOES NOT POP UP—USE TOAST TONGS. Beside the toaster was an implement fashioned from two wooden tongue depressors, a chunk of packing foam, and a rubber band. Barbara must have made this herself. Or maybe the craftsperson was her presumably deceased mother-in-law.

Josh turned to stare at the nubby brown bedspread, struggling against gloom. What had he let his sister do to him? This was a miserable place to spend his summer. Josh had dropped out of middle-class life, down to the level of an aging graduate student.

No. No, that was the wrong way to look at it. Come on, Hiller, pull yourself together. This might be a crappy rental, but he wasn't going to spend much time here, anyway. He was going to spend the summer on the beach. And nothing was stopping him from heading for the surf right now.

"And here come the dogs!" The voice of a woman provoked beyond endurance. "Kids. We are leaving."

Josh must have crashed on the beach, sedated by body-surfing. His towel was damp where he'd drooled a bit in his sleep. Pushing himself to his knees, Josh watched dogs and owners trotting down the path through the dunes. He felt ambushed. Soon enough, he wanted to tell them, *you'll* be holding an empty leash. Then you'll know how it feels.

Josh rolled to a sitting position and settled his Red Sox cap on his head. He glanced westward, down the long sweep of beach to the mouth of the Mattakiset River. Sunlight reflected blindingly from wet sand, and Josh blinked and turned toward the east end of the beach. There, Mattakiset Neck, with its concrete watch tower from World War II, poked into Buzzards Bay.

At the juncture of the causeway and the beach, something was moving: a brown dot, oscillating. Standing up to get a better look, Josh watched the dot grow to a blur of legs and then turn into a dog. A butterscotch brown, medium-large male, galloping like a greyhound along the edge of the surf. Josh wondered for an instant if the dog might be running from fear, but as the dog wheeled to charge a flock of gulls, he caught his expression: pure canine joy.

Josh shook out his towel, still watching. An older man in shorts and a polo shirt stepped forward. "Come here, Tucker!"

Josh could have told him that shouting angrily at a dog wasn't likely to bring him back. Sure enough, the dog, some kind of retriever mix, swerved out of the man's reach. But the dog paused for a split second to poke his black nose into Josh's hand. Then off he galloped toward the west end of the beach. In no time he was a blur with legs again.

Josh laughed before he noticed the older man's reddened face. "Sorry," he said. "Is that dog giving you a bad time?"

"Yes. You might call it a bad time," said the other man. "And it gets worse. The last time we let him run on the beach, he went back and forth for an hour and a half." He checked the L.L. Bean watch on his wrist. "If the son of a bitch takes more than half an hour now, that's the end of his free runs."

Josh smirked at "son of a bitch," but the older man didn't seem to notice the joke. A woman in a wide-brimmed hat and a cover-up tunic appeared at his shoulder, glancing from the direction the dog had taken to the man's face. "Oh, Gardner. Not again." The man snorted.

"The trouble is," the older woman said to Josh, "Tucker's supposed to get free runs to work off his energy, but when we let him off the leash—" She gestured at the dog, shrunk to a brown dot where the waves dwindled into the river.

Pulling down the bill of his baseball hat, Josh watched Tucker disappear around the curve of the shore. "I thought I saw a sign in the parking lot: 'No dogs on beach'?"

"Oh, nobody takes that seriously," said the woman. "The families don't want to stay on the beach after the lifeguards leave, anyway." She pointed to the western end of beach, where the pulsing brown dot had reappeared. "Here he comes."

Something made Josh ask, "Do you want me to grab him, if I get a chance?"

"Good luck with that," said the man.

"That's very kind of you," said his wife.

The dog was now a blur of legs. Josh stepped toward the water, into the dog's path, but didn't look directly at him.

His short ears flapping, the dog skidded to a stop in front of Josh. Josh slipped the fingers of his left hand under the dog's collar at the same time as the dog pushed his nose into Josh's right hand. "Hey, Tucker," said Josh.

The woman hurried forward to give Tucker a treat, and the man snapped the leash on the dog's collar. "About time!" He added, "If it wouldn't mean the end of my fifty-two-year marriage, this mutt would be out the door tomorrow."

The happy, healthy young dog named Tucker grinned at Josh, a loose-jaw doggy grin. Josh felt heavy and sore around the heart. Why had he gotten involved?

"Thank you," the woman said to Josh. "By the way, I'm Carol Harrison, and this is my husband Gardner."

Josh introduced himself, but now he wanted to get off the beach, away from all the frolicking dogs and their owners. Slinging his towel over his shoulder, he raised a hand in farewell. Carol said, "Goodbye, and thank you so much for your help, Josh! Tucker's turned out to be quite a handful."

Her husband looked more angry than grateful, but he said, "Yes, thanks for grabbing him."

"Glad to do it," said Josh. "Sometimes dogs behave better for strangers, because they aren't sure what they can get away with."

Gardner grunted. His wife exclaimed, "Oh, I just thought of something, Josh. I guess you're on vacation, but if you wanted a part-time job, with nice people—Obviously you have a way with dogs, and I know they need help at Coastal Canine. That's where Tucker goes for day care."

"To work off his excess energy, supposedly. Hah." Giving the leash a yank, Gardner stumped off down the beach. Tucker glanced back at Josh, and Josh could almost swear that the dog winked at him.

"Of course, you probably just want to relax." Carol smiled over her shoulder as she followed her husband. "Thanks again!"

By now, a steady stream of canines, licenses jingling, and their people, pockets stuffed with dog treats and poop pickup bags, was flowing onto the beach. Bucking the current, Josh hurried up the path through the dunes to his car.

Back at Barbara Schaeffer's farmhouse, Josh took a shower in the cramped bathroom, which probably had been just right for Barbara's tiny, wizened (he imagined) mother-in-law. Checking his phone, he discovered that it was well after six o'clock. No wonder he was starving.

And it was getting on toward time for the first pitch at Fenway Park. Foresightedly, he'd already set up his TV on a carton of books, plugged it in, and placed a chair in front of it. During the packing this morning, someone—Carl—had thoughtfully taped the remote to the TV.

From one of his grocery bags in the kitchenette Josh pulled a half-full jar of peanut butter and a torn bag of corn chips. Scooping from the jar with a chip, he leaned back in the chair, stretched his legs out, and turned the TV on.

A static buzz, and a screen full of black snow. Oh, shit. It needed a cable connection, of course. Where was it? Not on the wall where he'd set up the TV. Why hadn't Barbara tacked up a little note about *that*?

After searching every inch of wall space in the apartment, Josh climbed down the stairs and walked around the house to Barbara's kitchen door. Through the open window he heard her clanking dishes in the sink and warbling, "If ever I would leave you . . ." Her dog woofed.

"Sorry to bother you," said Josh when Barbara answered his knock, "but I couldn't find the cable connection."

"The *cable* connection?"

"For my TV," said Josh.

"Oh, cable TV!" Barbara was amused at Josh's misunderstanding. She'd never had cable. Didn't miss it at all. She did enjoy her DVD player—did Josh realize how many quality DVD's you could get from the library, free?

Josh took a deep breath, smiled faintly, and went back to the apartment for his car keys.

Fifteen minutes later, he was sitting at a restaurant bar drinking a beer, with an order in for fish and chips. He'd only missed the first two innings of the Red Sox-Mariners game. Josh glanced up and down the bar, noting a young couple, a group of four or five men of different ages, and two women.

Hey, thought Josh, I could hit on someone in a bar! When was the last time he'd done that? Not that he saw any likely women to hit on just now.

There was a *poof* of stale cigarette smoke as someone sat down on the barstool next to Josh. A stringy man in a T-shirt and jeans, with a walrus moustache. He nodded at Josh. "How's it goin'?" He told the bartender, "Jack Daniels on the rocks. And another beer for my friend here."

Josh protested, but the other man, who introduced himself as Rick Johnson, insisted. "No offense, but you look like you could use another drink. You here for the weekend, or what?"

"The summer," said Josh. "I'm renting from Barbara Schaeffer, on Old Farm Road." Why did Rick think Josh needed another drink? Maybe because Josh was hugging himself—he'd been doing that lately. Releasing his arms, Josh placed both elbows on the padded bar.

Rick was nodding. "Mrs. Schaeffer, used to be my math teacher." He raised his glass to Josh and settled himself more comfortably on his stool. "You're lucky you don't own property in this town. I got my tax bill yesterday. Holy shit. I guess Harrison and his buddies expect everyone to just keep paying and paying. *Almost* everybody, that is. Some people get away with murder. 'Agricultural exemption,' what a racket."

Rick went on in this vein, and Josh realized that he didn't need to feel embarrassed about accepting a beer from a stranger. Clearly, the beer was payment for sitting there and listening to Rick's monologue. Or half listening, since Josh had the excuse of watching the game, which was shaping up to be a long one. The pitchers couldn't get strikes, and the batters couldn't get hits, dragging out each inning.

Josh pulled out his phone and checked it. Nothing but a message from his sister, Vicky. He'd get back to her later. This was his summer vacation, after a year from hell, and he was not going to rush to do anything. Except hit the beach again tomorrow.

Thou art the Great Cat, the avenger of the gods, and the judge of words, and the president of the sovereign chiefs and the governor of the holy circle; thou art indeed . . . the Great Cat.

Inscription on the Royal Tombs at Thebes

Chapter 3.

As soon as the racket and smells of the animal shelter faded in the distance, the Cat crept out of the trees. If he'd found himself in his own neighborhood, he would have headed straight for his house and meowed at the back door.

But this territory was nothing like his neighborhood, where the houses were close together and connected by sidewalks, and the yards were fenced. The Cat used to sit on top of the fence on the south side of his house, catching the sunshine and waiting for the spaniel to scramble out of the house next door. It was amusing to watch the little dog running around the lawn, barking at squirrels or digging in the flower beds. Once in a while the Cat would jump down, allow the dog to approach him, and touch noses.

In this new place, he saw no houses at all, and tall weeds edged the road. Even early in the day, heat radiated from the blacktop, which wound on and on without traffic lights, past woods and fields and more fields and more woods. The traffic wasn't as steady as at home, but the occasional motorcycle or truck zoomed past with alarming speed. Here the Cat sniffed at the flattened, bloody corpse of an opossum, there at the flattened, bloody corpse of a squirrel. The Cat sneaked along by starts and stops, shrinking into the weeds each time he heard an engine approaching.

Once the Cat thought he glimpsed a familiar tree back in the woods. It looked like the blue spruce in his back yard, the tree he ran up when he was in high spirits. He pushed through a tangle of underbrush into the woods, willing himself to emerge at home. But when he reached the half-hidden tree, it was only a ragged orphan of a blue spruce, barely staying upright against a leaning dead oak.

The Cat paused in front of the spruce for a moment, mosquitos whining around his head. So many trees, so tall and close together—they oppressed him. As he turned back toward the road, some odd-looking scat caught the Cat's eye, and he paused again to inspect it. This scat smelled something like dog, although it was smaller and drier than dog turds. And—

His fur bristled with sudden horror. This animal had eaten a cat.

A monster that ate cats. The Cat's mother had warned her litter to beware of such a creature, but he had not really believed her.

The Cat backed away, peering all around in case the monster lurked nearby; he whirled; he ran the rest of the way out of the woods.

Back near the road, the Cat continued to sneak along through the weeds. He was afraid of the woods, but he didn't like the road, either. Moving forward, on and on, felt unnatural. The Cat had plenty of patience, but it was a waiting-in-front-of-the-refrigerator kind of patience. In this strange world of unending road and wild woods, there was nowhere to wait.

The Cat was tired. He was hungry. He wanted his own house, with his own patrons. From the day when the Girl had chosen him, he had known that was where he was meant to be.

On that day he and his littermates had been brought outside, without their mother, for the visitors to see. The Cat (the Kitten, at that time) had been dazzled with the sunshine and distracted by the scents of grass and flowers. A buttercup nodded in the breeze, and he pounced on it, just as the striped kitten pounced on his twitching tail.

"I wish we could take all of them," said the Girl, kneeling on the lawn.

"I know, sweetie," said the Man, "but Mom would have kittens herself if we came home with more than one. Just one—your choice."

The Girl sighed. "They're all so cute! I kind of like the striped one . . ."

While the Kitten was tussled with the littermate who'd grabbed his tail, an enormous Presence loomed over him. Mighty jaws fastened on the scruff of his neck, scooted him across the grass, and released him in front of the Girl's knees.

"Oh! Daddy, this one looks like Batman!" She lifted the Kitten gently onto her lap. "See what I mean? The black mask on his face, with pointy black ears?" She stroked the top of his head. "He's purring so loud! I think he likes me."

Yes, the Great Cat had guided him to his ideal home that day. The Cat could not believe that the ideal home was no longer his. He was ready to overlook (although not forget) what the Woman had done. He wanted his own food dish and his own perch in the window by the bird feeder. He began to meow, long, plaintive meows.

There was no one to hear him. The Cat crept into the shade of a milkweed plant and rested, listening to the buzz of insects. Should he go back the way he'd come? But when he stepped onto the dirt shoulder of the road again, he glimpsed a roof beyond the next rise. That was a hopeful sign.

Following the road forward, the Cat came to an unpaved driveway with a chain across the entrance. He slunk under the chain and along the driveway, which looped past a row of sheds.

At the corner of the first shed the Cat shrank back, assaulted by a pungent, hostile scent. To take in its full meaning, he dropped his jaw and lifted his lip, sampling the odor with the roof of his mouth.

Keep out, said the scent. *This means you.* The scent wasn't new, but it wasn't old, either—perhaps from a few days ago.

The Cat was shaken by the warning, but now he also smelled food ahead, somewhere in a landscape of dirt heaps and trenches. He'd eaten nothing since the moth he'd caught in the laundry room last night. He put one cautious paw after the other, sniffing fearfully. More and more deposits of the sharp scent: on weeds, on slabs of sheet rock, on the tires of a bulldozer.

Stealing up to the edge of a trench, the Cat peered over. The food smells came from a sprawling pile of black trash bags. Several cats prowled through the trash, pausing to paw at split bags. One cat, a scrawny calico female, crouched over something edible, while three half-grown kittens shoved her and each other.

The Cat watched them, disturbed and puzzled. Where did these cats live? In the sheds? Then why weren't they eating from their special dishes in the sheds, instead of pawing through garbage?

It didn't seem right, but the Cat was so hungry that he found himself creeping down the slope to join the foragers. He was halfway there when all the cats lifted their heads, ears pricked. An engine paused up on the road.

Next, a battered pickup truck rattled past the sheds, and two men got out. As one of them brought the bulldozer to life with a roar, all the cats leaped out of the trench and fled. The Cat paused at the top of a dirt hill and crouched to watch through a screen of weeds.

The second man stationed himself at the door of the largest shed, and a line of cars formed. First was a bulky black car driven by a gray-haired woman. A shaggy gray dog stuck its muzzle out of a back window.

The black car stopped in front of the shed, where the driver handed a card to the man. He punched the card and handed it back to the woman. Then—the Cat leaned forward to watch more closely—the workman tossed something to the dog, who caught it in the air and gobbled it up.

The next car, driven by a bald man with a smaller dog in the front seat, pulled up to the shed and went through the same routine. And so on, down the line. Some of the cars and trucks had two dogs; some had none. But each dog that rode into the dump received a treat from the workman's hand.

The Cat's mouth watered, although in his first life he'd turned up his nose at dog biscuits. *I* could ride in a car like that, he thought.

As the Cat watched and watched, he found himself creeping down through the weeds. What if he jumped into one of the dog-less cars? Would that be the way to find a new patron?

Near the slope of the hill he came to a row of bins. A woman with blonde hair and freckled skin was walking back and forth in front of the bins, reaching into a bag and tossing cans or bottles into this bin or that. The Cat meowed.

The woman looked up at the weedy slope. The Cat meowed again, and her eyes fastened on his. "Well, hello, black and white kitty." Her voice was low and throaty, like a purr.

Stepping out of the weeds, the Cat meowed once more.

The woman's eyes crinkled. "You look like a panda—did anyone ever tell you that?"

The Cat edged closer. Rubbing against the woman's ankles, he sniffed her sandals. This was a person without a cat! Without even a dog! Could she be his new patron?

"Oh, Panda, you're sweet." She crouched on her heels, rubbing the backs of his ears, then under his chin.

Her hand smelled like coffee, an enticing scent. Now and then, in his first life, he'd found coffee grounds spilled on the kitchen floor; he loved to roll in them.

"You aren't a feral cat, are you?" said the woman. "I wish I could take you home. If Ryan wasn't allergic . . ."

Yes, this must be the new patron the Great Cat intended for him. As the woman stood up and walked to her car, the Cat pattered at her heels.

But at the car door, the blonde woman looked down at the Cat with surprise. "Oh, no. I'm sorry, Panda. I gave you the wrong idea. I can't take you home." She opened the door a crack, and he gathered his haunches to jump in.

"No." She stamped at him. He shrank back. "I'm sorry!" She scrambled in, slammed the door, and started the engine.

As she drove off, the bewildered Cat caught a glimpse of her face in the side mirror. The blonde woman had wanted to take him home—she had *invited* him to be her Cat. Then why—?

Humans! Great Cat, what was the matter with them?

For the rest of that long, hungry day, the Cat lurked in the weeds above the dump. Every time a black bag was hurled into the trench, he caught a whiff of the food mixed with the trash. Food: meat, fish, cheese, eggs. When there was a lull in the traffic entering the dump, all the cats would start to creep toward the trench. And then another string of cars and trucks clanked and rattled past the shed, and the cats would scatter again.

Late in the afternoon the last car drove down the dirt road, unloaded its trash, and left. One of the dump attendants closed the shed and locked the door. The other man got in the bulldozer again and shoveled several loads of dirt into the trench. Then they both drove off in their truck.

The cats reappeared, now trotting confidently to the trench. How they could find anything to eat under all that dirt? But look, some of the trash bags were only half covered. Jumping into the trench, the Cat shoved his head into the nearest split bag.

The Cat tore at a leathery slice of toast. He gobbled an entire blackened hamburger, ignoring the repulsive charred taste. He gulped sour cottage cheese from an open carton. Finally sated, he climbed out of the trench licking his jowls. The Cat retired to the weeds at the top of the dirt pile, cleaned himself, and settled down to sleep.

Later, as daylight faded, the Cat awakened with a sense of unrest in his insides. Apparently his stomach had assessed his trash-bag dinner and judged it inedible, after all. His body heaved. He was violently and thoroughly sick.

My dog digs Mattakiset.

Bone-shaped bumper sticker

Chapter 4.

For the next few days, Josh's plan seemed to be working. The weather turned vacation-perfect. Josh rode his bike in the fresh, bright mornings and spent the hot, bright afternoons on the beach. The surf was free of rip currents, seaweed, and jellyfish, and Josh was careful to leave before five o'clock, when the lifeguards abandoned the beach to the dog people.

Then one morning, Josh woke up to the sound of rain on the roof and a muted, underwater green daylight. Outside the open window, leafy branches swayed like seaweed in the downpour. So—maybe this was the day for another vacation activity: sleeping in.

Last night, back at his apartment after food, beer, and a Red Sox win, Josh had fallen asleep easily. But now his mind refused to return to vacation mode. When he closed his eyes, he seemed to be in a room with several closet doors cracked open, offering him topics it was better not to think about. There was the ex (almost) wife, Tanya, closet. The dead dog, Molly, closet. The last place of employment, Westham Middle School, closet.

Josh rolled over, trying to fool himself into a doze, but he was awake. Not in a ready-to-go, jump-out-of-bed way, but in a state of dull antsiness. Rolling onto his back again, he stared at the dots on the acoustic tile ceiling. He dropped his gaze to the round plastic smoke detector on the opposite wall and the sign underneath it: NO SMOKING IN OUR HOME!

Flinging back the nubby bedspread, Josh swung his feet onto the linoleum floor and padded into the bathroom to brush his teeth. A plywood shelf over the sink jutted out above the faucets. Josh was forced to stoop and twist his head sideways, like a flamingo, to spit.

Still, with clean teeth, Josh felt a little better. Maybe three percent better, as Ron Watanabe's anti-depression list suggested. Ron was a friend from Josh's long-ago MAT program, now teaching in California. At the beginning of the friendship, part of their bond was admitting to spells of paralyzing gloom. Ron had shared his list of gloom-dissipating actions, with the percentages of psychic lift you could expect from each one. One item on the List: *Brush teeth—3%.* Back then Josh had fallen off his chair, laughing.

He smiled now, remembering the first item: *Get up—10%.* Hey, he was already 13 percent ahead of the game. Thinking of Ron and his List made Josh feel even less gloomy—say, 11 percent less? Josh should tell Ron to add his List itself to the list.

Morning coffee must be on the List. If it wasn't, it should be. Coffee implied getting dressed. (*Get dressed—7%.*) Josh could have brewed his own coffee in the kitchenette, but he flinched from spending any time in that dreary little alcove.

A short while later, Josh drove up Main Road, headed for a Cumberland Farms gas station opposite the Mattakiset town hall. He passed a blue sign, Coastal

Canine, sporting a cartoon dog on a surfboard, and he remembered the kennel mentioned to him by the older woman on the beach. In a different state of mind, he might have been tempted to apply for that job.

Inside the Cumby's store, standing in line with his coffee and granola bar, Josh watched the clerk at the register. Her voice was pleasantly husky, with a cheerful note. *And*—he remembered with another uptick in mood—it was now okay for him to flirt.

This clerk, blonde with a dusting of freckles on her face, seemed to know all the other customers, and she kept up a rapid back-and-forth while scanning and ringing up their purchases. Josh was eager for his turn to banter, to make her flash him a smile. But when he set his cup and snack on the counter, all she had to say was, "That it?" and "Have a good one."

Turning away disappointed, Josh took a restorative gulp of coffee. What else was on Ron's damn List?

Just inside the door, a stack of newspapers, the *Mattakiset Mariner*, caught Josh's eye. On the front page a man in a tree reached for a meowing cat. "Department of Good Deeds: Local Hero Saves Kitty by Whisker."

Now Josh remembered another List item: *Do a good deed—20-50%.* What good deed could Josh could accomplish, without climbing up a tree? As he sat in his car munching granola, it came to him. "I'll visit Mom," he called to the backseat.

In March, Martha Hiller had moved into Northport Commons, a senior residence on the North Shore. Vicky had helped their mother with plans and arrangements, and for the move itself, she'd recruited Josh to carry furniture and hang pictures. Josh felt guilty for not being more helpful—but he thought his mother and sister must understand that at this point, he could hardly manage his own life.

After the move, Josh had only seen his mother a few times. They'd talked about once a week. . . . Maybe it was once every two weeks. Their conversations tended to go, "Hi, Mom, how are you?" "I'm fine—how are *you*, dear?" Once she'd lowered her voice, as if she were going to ask whether he had regular bowel movements, and said, "Josh. I don't want to pry into your finances, but if you need something to tide yourself over until you find other . . . work . . ."

"I don't." Josh's answer came out sharper than he intended, and he added quickly, "But thanks, Mom. I'm fine." It got to be more and more of an effort for Josh to pretend he was fine.

But now that Josh was on the upswing, beyond the reach of the psychopathic Westham Middle School principal, almost free from his marriage with Tanya, he could satisfy his mother with a visit. He got out his phone and called to make sure she'd be there today—"I'm always here," she told him—and headed for the North Shore.

After two hours of driving through the rain, Josh signed in at the reception desk at Northport Commons Senior Residence and rode the elevator to the fourth floor. Martha Hiller peered out the door of apartment 421, waving. She was neatly and attractively dressed, as usual, but she looked paler than the last time Josh had seen her, which hadn't been *that* long ago.

Josh hugged her carefully. Didn't she used to be as tall as Vicky? "How are you, Mom?"

"How are *you*, dear? I'm sure you didn't want to drive all this way in the rain. Although it's been several weeks."

"Several?" Josh was sure it hadn't been more than three weeks since he'd seen his mother. Three was "a few," not "several," wasn't it?

Martha beckoned him in. "Sit down for a minute. They don't start serving lunch until 11:15. Tell me about your summer place."

Josh joined her on the love seat in front of the TV. "My new place. Yeah, it's really nice." He gazed around Martha's living room, which actually was nice. The ceiling was high, and French doors opened onto a balcony. "I've got a whole wing of a nineteenth-century farmhouse. No cable TV connection, but that's good; it'll help me concentrate on firming up my plans."

"Yes, I want to hear about your plans."

Shit! Why had he mentioned plans? But Josh plowed on, "Teaching was great for a while, but you know, I got fed up with all the layers of bureaucracy in the school system. . . . I've pretty much decided to go out on my own."

Martha Hiller waited with worried eyes, but Josh had already described the extent of his plans. Reaching into a pocket draped over the arm of the love seat, he fiddled with the TV remote.

"On your own?" asked Martha. "You mean, start a private tutoring service? I guess there's a demand for that, with all the competition over college applications, but—"

"Tutoring—yeah, that's one possibility. Or maybe something entirely different, some other field." Josh saw his mother give an anxious little sigh, and he added, "I'm looking for the right opportunity."

Then they both jumped as the TV blared into life. Josh must have pressed something on the remote. "Sorry!" He grabbed it out of the pocket and pressed what he thought was the power button, but it only changed the channel. "Sorry," Josh repeated.

Pulling the remote from Josh's hand, his mother cut the power. "By the way, Vicky told me that Molly had to be put down. That's too bad, dear. You must miss your dog."

Josh flinched. He started to say that he was sad, but Molly had a good life, etc. Instead, he blurted, "I couldn't believe Tanya did that to me. While I was gone, without even asking me."

"Well, I hate to say this, but I'm not surprised." Gazing down at her knobby-jointed hands, Martha Hiller adjusted her wedding rings. "There was always something . . . *hard* about her."

Josh should have been glad that his mother was taking his side against Tanya, but instead he wished he hadn't given her the chance. Talk about "hard"—look at Martha's expression. It was just as unforgiving as the expression Tanya had turned on him, the last time he saw her.

He glanced at the clock on the cable box. "Look at that, eleven twenty-three. We better go down for lunch."

As soon as they were seated in the dining room, Josh wished they were back in his mother's apartment. The man across the table had a racking, phlegmy cough. A woman next to Josh and the woman on the other side of Martha traded loud complaints about the food. Josh made some attempts at conversation, but his mother seemed to have removed herself mentally from the scene, smiling vaguely as she worked at her food. Maybe that was the best way to deal with mealtimes at Northport Commons.

After dessert Josh escorted Martha to the elevator. He said lightly, "I guess I'll skip the lunch next time." Martha was walking with her face toward the carpet, leaning heavily on her cane, and he wasn't sure she'd heard him. He added, "Mom?"

His mother poked the elevator button, still not looking at him. She said plaintively, "I'm too old and tired to have to worry about my children."

As if he could have mended his unraveling marriage and halted the downward slide of his teaching career, if only he'd considered how much they were going to bother his mother! Escaping to the parking lot, Josh slumped behind his steering wheel. So much for the good deed intended to lift his mood. "I don't know about Mom," he said to the backseat, "but *I* feel 19 percent worse."

Josh felt *old.* As if the two hours at Northport Commons had aged him thirty years. No—it was more as if he could now see all the way down the length of his life. The very end, which before he'd pictured as discretely out of sight, over the horizon, now stopped at a wall.

On top of that, it was still raining, and the distance from the North Shore to the South Coast was still two hours' drive.

Back in Mattakiset, Josh stopped at the library to use their Wi-Fi. The Harrison Library was a quaint brick building with a weathered blue-green copper dome, tucked in between the newer (but not new) structures of the Mattakiset Elementary School and the Mattakiset Middle School. A sign taped to the copy machine in the vestibule read, **Pay at Circulation.** In larger print, it added, **YOU MUST PAY FOR YOUR MISTAKES.** Josh thought, I knew that.

Just inside the main room, Josh stopped to look over a section of books for sale. The bright yellow cover of *Small Business for Dummies* caught his eye, and he pulled it off the shelf. Only two dollars, couldn't hurt. Maybe he *would* start a tutoring service.

You call to a dog and a dog will break its neck to get to you. Dogs just want to please. Call to a cat and its attitude is, What's in it for me?
Lewis Grizzard

Chapter 5.

Days passed, and more days. The Cat learned to hunt through the trash when the dump was quiet, early in the morning and early in the evening, and to distinguish stale food from spoiled food. He was always hungry, and he could feel his ribs now when he licked his sides. Each night the Moon rose later, and each night its shape, like the Cat's, was thinner.

At twilight the rodents appeared, creeping out of their hiding places under the sheds. They puzzled the Cat, because they looked and smelled so much like mice. He knew what to do with mice: pounce, bite, and carry the body to the bathroom rug. But these rodents of the dump were huge! Ten times the size of mice, with nasty-looking yellow teeth. The Cat kept away from them.

If only the Cat could catch an ordinary mouse now, and sink his fangs into its juicy little body . . . There might not be enough left over to drop on the bathroom rug.

Although the Cat was lonely, he did not approach the other cats, all females except for one of the kittens. These cats seemed to be savages. They did not reverence the Moon; they did not praise the Great Cat or petition her with their needs.

As for the Cat, he prayed to the Great Cat every night for a new patron. *She will provide homes for you,* his mother had told her kittens on the day she weaned them. *Humans will caress you and offer you food, toys, and shelter. So has the Great Cat ordered the world.*

One day, for a change, a dog got loose at the dump. The Cat was sitting in the weeds up on a hillock, watching wistfully as dog after dog stuck its head out of its car and snapped up the treat from the man at the shed.

A long gray car paused at the shed. A brown dog with a black nose was already head and front paws out the back window. When the dump attendant tossed him a treat, he snatched it out of the air like the other dogs. But he lunged forward so eagerly that half his body shot out of the car.

The dog hung there for an instant, squealing, his front paws scrabbling at the outside of the rear door, the edge of the window glass scraping his groin. Even as the Cat flinched in sympathy, the dog squirmed all the way out and onto the ground.

"Tucker!" shouted the man in the car. "Get back here!"

The brown dog bounded across the dump, heading for the trench. He paused, sniffed a trash bag or two, and pulled out a bone. By this time the dog's man, an older human with silver hair and a stiff walk, had left his car and was hurrying toward the dog.

As the man came closer, the dog crouched toward him in a play-bow. With the bone still in his mouth, he dashed sideways and ran up the hill.

The Cat froze. He meowed a warning, and the brown dog stopped short in front of the Cat's weed screen. He dropped the bone and raised his muzzle, snuffling intently. The Cat sniffed, too, and his flattened ears came forward a bit. This dog, although he was much larger than the spaniel next door, smelled of a similar disposition. He was out to play, not attack.

"Tucker!" The brown dog's man pushed through the weeds at the bottom of the slope. "I am not going to chase you all over the dump!"

Snatching up his bone, the dog whirled, bounded over a clump of mullein, and scrambled down the back side of the hill. He loped past the recycling bins and paused to sniff the compost pile. Other people at the dump tried to grab him, and the dogs in other cars barked.

The Cat enjoyed watching from his perch on the hill. The dog dragged the game out, but finally he allowed himself to be caught by the dump attendant, holding out a biscuit. Although the gray-haired man scolded, shoving the wayward dog into his car, the Cat couldn't help envying that dog.

Did the brown dog realize how lucky he was? He had a car to ride in, and no doubt a bowl of dog chow and a safe, comfortable place to sleep. Maybe a big, soft towel, like the one the Cat's mother had chosen for her kittens. Maybe the brown dog even shared a bed with his human?

No, the Cat couldn't imagine that man welcoming that dog onto his bed. But still.

The Cat desperately wanted to feel the Girl's small fingers rubbing under his chin. He longed for the lap-naps in front of the TV with the Man. But he tried to put these yearnings for his first life out of his mind, for the Great Cat had spoken. Now the Cat must search for the patron of his second life.

That evening, as the Cat pawed through banana peels and plastic wrap toward a promising chicken smell, an unholy yowl split the air over the dump. The Cat crouched with his ears flattened. He'd heard that kind of yowl before, but only from the safety of the Girl's bed.

The other cats, too, paused in their foraging and looked fearfully toward a nearby hillock, lit orange by a street lamp. Spotlighted on the crest, glaring down at the other cats, was a large, tiger-striped male with ragged ears. He began stalking down the slope, pausing every so often to snarl.

The Cat backed away from his trash bag and the chicken. Scrambling out of the trench, he slunk off at an angle from the tiger cat's path with ears tucked down and tail low.

Glancing over his shoulder, the Cat saw that his submissive signals were not pacifying the other cat. The pupils of the tom's eyes contracted to hostile slits, and his tail thrashed. With another ear-piercing yowl, he bounded onto the Cat and dug claws into his flank.

Screaming, the Cat rolled away and streaked for the refuge of the bulldozer. He scrambled into the cab and whirled to defend himself.

But the tom seemed to consider the Cat defeated. He turned his attention back to the trench. The other cats—all except for the mother and her kittens—backed off from the trash bags and crept away. The mother cat was signaling her kittens to retreat with her, but they were deep in a squabble over a bit of garbage.

The tomcat swaggered down into the trench. The mother placed herself in front of her kittens, hissing and puffing out her scrawny tail. Ignoring her, he bore down upon the kittens, his tail thrashing again, as if they were chipmunks.

Taking heed at last, the kittens crouched. The male kitten opened his mouth, spitting and showing baby fangs.

Knocking aside the mother, the tiger cat sprang. His jaws closed on the male kitten's neck. The small paws flailed for a moment and then went limp.

Standing over the kitten's body, the tom stared around the trash heaps as if to say, Who else wants a fight? The mother and her remaining kittens, as well as the other cats, had vanished.

As for the Cat, he only wanted to be gone from this goddess-forsaken place. Creeping down the other side of the bulldozer, he stole behind the sheds to the road. He followed the sliver of the setting moon west until he couldn't even smell the dump.

Every dog must have his day [care].
Jonathan Swift

Chapter 6.

Josh peered into the dim mirror over the bathroom sink in his apartment. (Where did his landlady even *find* fifteen-watt bulbs?) He wasn't sure how well-groomed you had to be to apply for a kennel job, but it couldn't hurt to shave.

Josh used to consider himself a not-bad-looking guy, but sometime this spring he'd begun to dislike his reflection. There were grooves on either side of his mouth, pulling it down. That must be why his face ached. The grooves also made it harder to shave.

After reading and highlighting Chapter 1 of *Small Business for Dummies*, Josh had decided that doing some low-key work would have a steadying influence on him, help him to concentrate on plans for his new career. It was even on Ron's List: *Do useful work—21%.* When the woman on the beach suggested the kennel job, Josh had rejected it out of hand, but the idea had grown on him. He'd liked volunteering at a dog shelter in Westham. And actually taking care of dogs would be different from watching dogs on the beach with a sore heart, wouldn't it?

Out in the driveway, Josh met Barbara loading black trash bags into the back of her SUV.

Lola, her English shepherd mix, sat behind the car, sniffing each bag as if doing quality control.

"Morning," said Josh, holding out a hand to the dog. "Today must be dump day."

“Well, good early morning!” Barbara’s wrinkled face, peering from under the tailgate, was flushed. She looked him over. “Aren’t you all spruced up! Going somewhere special?”

Josh felt a tweak of annoyance. Was it a big deal that he’d gotten out of bed this morning at eight o’clock, shaved, and put on a clean shirt? But he told her about the job opening at Coastal Canine.

“Oh, yes, I’d heard they were looking for someone.” Straightening, she put her hands on her hips. “By the way, I’ve been meaning to mention: Would you make sure to put the trash barrel lid on tight? I’m afraid a raccoon got into the trash last night, and I had to pick it up.”

“Oh, sorry,” said Josh. “I didn’t—”

“See, the handles lock down over the lid.” Barbara demonstrated. “And then you re-fasten it with the bungee cord.”

Josh drove away from the farmhouse tingling with irritation. Maybe coffee, a doughnut, and an exchange of pleasantries at the Cumberland Farms store would have a soothing effect.

In the store, the blonde clerk was deep in conversation with a man in uniform—a security guard? Josh watched them from the coffee station. The man leaned on the counter, talking soberly, as she rang up each customer and gave them change.

Josh thought that Danielle—according to her name tag—might recognize him from the other morning. “Nice morning, huh? It was pouring cats and dogs, the last time I was in here.”

"Cats and dogs," she repeated. To the man in the uniform—a fireman, Josh saw now—she said, "I owe you, Neil. You saved Ryan's butt—again." She rang up Josh's coffee and doughnut.

Josh started to say, "Cats and dogs, that's an expression," but the fireman spoke first, with a modest shrug, "Better us than the cops, right?"

To Josh, Danielle said, "Have a good one," dropping the change into his hand. She was smiling, but at Neil, not Josh.

Oh, well. Returning to his car, Josh said to the backseat, "Maybe Barbara had a point, you think? Maybe I do look different this morning." Sipping and chewing, Josh followed the winding road past a dairy farm and a cat shelter (Fur-Ever) to Coastal Canine.

A chorus of barking burst out as Josh parked by the stockade fence, and the racket continued as he passed a whimsical fire hydrant in a flower bed and climbed the steps to the office door. Inside, the office was lined with racks of collars and leashes, shelves of dog toys and treats.

A woman with a cap of severely cropped hair and an outdoor worker's tan sat behind the counter, the phone to her ear. Her Coastal Canine T-shirt was apple green, with the surfer dog logo outlined in dark green. Catching sight of Josh, she held up a finger in a be-with-you-in-just-a-minute gesture.

While he waited, Josh imagined Molly cringing beside him, pressing against his legs. When he first started to volunteer at the Westham dog shelter, he'd naively assumed that all dogs liked palling around with their kind. He was puzzled by one dog at the shelter, a Labrador retriever, who hugged the fence of the exercise pen, keeping a fearful eye on her fellow dogs.

Thinking to reassure the shy dog, Josh had sat down on his heels and held out his hand. She crawled right into his lap, tipping both of them over onto the ground. The shelter supervisor had laughed and said, "Did you want a dog? Looks like you just got one."

Putting down the phone, the Coastal Canine woman squinted at Josh as if she was trying to place him. "Hi, can I help you? You're picking up—?" She waited for him to fill in his dog's name.

Molly, thought Josh. *I wish.* He explained that he'd heard about a possible job. "Can I talk to the manager?"

"That would be me," she said evenly. "Erica LeClerq, owner and manager."

Great, thought Josh as he introduced himself. I've pissed off another touchy woman.

Pressing a button on the phone, Erica shouted into it. "Uncle George, will you come and cover the desk?" She went on to Josh, "I'll show you around while you tell me about your experience working with dogs."

A man with white hair, short on the sides and long and thin on top, pushed open a door at the back of the office. He was bent over, and he walked with a quick shuffle. He nodded to Josh and saluted Erica. "Just don't expect *me* to handle the dogs," he said as he took her seat behind the counter. "Maybe a Chihuahua, in a pinch."

With a patient smile, Erica unlatched the wooden gate beside the counter and beckoned Josh through. "You know this job is a temporary fill-in, right?"

"That could work for me," said Josh, following her into the kennel. "I'm in between things." He noted to himself that this kennel smelled clean—that was a good sign. "You asked about my experience with dogs: I volunteered at a dog shelter in Westham for several years."

Erica nodded in a neutral way. "And your job at the shelter was—?"

"I did a lot of different jobs there: feeding and cleaning up, exercising. The last year I did some evaluating and basic training."

"That would be a plus," said Erica. "I've been thinking of starting an obedience class." As she went on to explain her day care procedures, Josh began to wonder if he was going to measure up to her standards. From the serious way she talked, the kennel was total commitment.

In back of the kennel they stepped into a spacious lot covered with wood chips and sectioned by chain-link fencing. The ten or twelve good-sized dogs in the nearest pen charged toward them, barking. "This is the Large Dogs play yard," said Erica unnecessarily. She unlatched the gate and held it while Josh squeezed through, careful to block the crowd of dogs from the exit.

As the Large Dogs milled around Josh, one familiar-looking light brown animal shoved his way through the pack. Before Josh could remember where he'd seen this dog, his front paws were on Josh's chest and his tongue swiped Josh's chin.

"You don't need to let them jump up on you," said Erica. "Just turn aside when they try; they'll get the idea."

Josh had an impulse to say, Show some respect—I was a runner-up for Massachusetts Teacher of the Year. Instead, he said, "I know. Dog obedience training 101. I guess I was off guard, surprised to find a dog I'd seen before. Tucker, right?" But he was also pleased that Tucker remembered him. "His owners—I can't remember *their* name—are the ones who told me you had an opening."

Erica smiled slightly. "Gardner and Carol Harrison. If you stay in Mattakiset for long, you'll know Gardner's name, all right." She turned and pointed at a youth filling a water bucket at the other end of the pen. "And that's Ryan. He's going to be starting at U. Mass Dartmouth, so he's cutting back his hours."

Josh was more interested in a woman with long, loose hair on the far side of the exercise yard, lobbing tennis balls for a pack of retrievers. But Erica was looking at her watch. "Excuse me for a minute," she said. "Ryan," she yelled across the pen, "want to show Josh around?"

Ryan up close was younger than he'd looked from a distance, thought Josh, with the adult bone structure struggling against the childlike softness of his face. "Erica says you're starting at U. Mass Dartmouth?"

"Yep." Ryan tugged self-consciously at the bill of his yellow Coastal Canine cap. "I'm majoring in marine biology."

As Ryan detailed the outdoor kennel duties, Josh watched the dogs, now dissolved into smaller units. Tucker and a brown and white pit bull terrier played keep-away with a well-gnawed toy; a pair of Akitas chased each other up the ramp and down the ladder of a plastic deck; an English shepherd, a boxer mix, and a Doberman played King of the Mountain on a low platform. A gray-muzzled Great Dane watched them all benevolently from inside a plastic igloo, like an elderly gentleman on the porch of a retirement home.

If Molly were here now . . . If Molly were here now, the other dogs would be picking on her. She seemed to have the canine equivalent of a KICK ME sign on her back.

Last year there'd been a girl in Josh's third period class, Kaylee, who reminded him of Molly. So shy that she could hardly speak. Josh had worked all fall semester on getting her to participate in class in small, non-threatening ways, while discouraging the other kids from picking on her.

Among the many things Josh hated his former principal for, he hated her for ruining a chance for Kaylee to come out of her shell. That morning, Josh had asked the class how they would vote on a local issue: whether to fund a designated dog park in Westham, and why. He'd called on a couple of other kids, and then he noticed Kaylee.

She'd pushed her hair out of her eyes, and her lips were quivering; she wanted to speak. She'd actually raised her hand. Josh nodded toward her, careful not to alarm her by saying her name out loud.

But at the same time, the classroom door opened and Principal Voss stepped in, smiling her public smile. "Good morning, Mr. Hiller! Good morning, people. Don't mind me, I'll just be part of the woodwork." She pointed at Kaylee. "Go ahead there, speak up!" She took a seat in the back, pen poised over the clipboard on her lap.

The other students turned to stare at the principal, whispering. As for Kaylee, she shrank back in her seat, shaking her head.

Reliving that moment, Josh felt his hatred for Charlene Voss glow hotter. There'd been no reason for her to observe his class, except to punish him for pointing out the grammatical and factual errors in her recent memo to the faculty. And that was only one of many unwarranted visitations by the principal, always followed by a memo critiquing his teaching methods in vague educationese.

Josh pulled himself back to the dogs' exercise pen, where Ryan had stopped talking and was watching him with a puzzled frown.

"Sorry, I lost concentration," said Josh. He reached into the part of his brain that was supposed to record conversations while he was thinking about something else. "You were saying, it's better to pick up poop as soon as you see it, so nobody steps in it."

"Right," said Ryan. "But *then* I was saying, the big thing here is to watch out for fights. The dogs get along pretty well, but sometimes fights break out of nowhere."

Josh nodded. "That's dogs. . . . Do you like working here?"

"Yeah, it's an okay summer job. My mom thinks it keeps me out of trouble." Ryan's smile revealed an overbite, just enough to be charming.

Josh wondered what kind of trouble Ryan got into. He seemed mature and polite. But that didn't mean he wasn't one of the kids who gathered at the deserted guard tower on Mattakiset Neck and smoked pot.

"I like dogs," Ryan went on. "A lot better than I like cats, for sure." He made a face and then laughed uneasily, as if he'd given away too much. He added, "The only thing, Erica doesn't want you to text while you're watching the dogs. So it gets kind of boring—if you follow that rule all the time." He glanced sideways at Josh, as if to check whether Josh was going to be a fellow conspirator or another authority figure.

Sometimes Josh, also, wondered which he was. . . . Erica seemed to be taking a long time. He wished he hadn't set himself up to become a doggie day care supervisor reject. "Thanks for the rundown," he told Ryan. "Why don't I get a tour of the other side from—what's her name?"

"Rune," said Ryan, with a roll of his eyes. Was that was about the name, or about Rune herself?

The pen adjoining the Large Dogs playground was the same size, but flat instead of hilly, and empty of equipment. As Josh came up to the gate, Rune threw one more ball for the dogs to chase. She hung up the throwing stick and strolled to the gate, a crystal pendant sparkling against her red Coastal Canine T-shirt.

"Hello, I'm Rune. Are you going to fill in for Ryan?" As she spoke, Rune pulled a hair clasp from her pocket and gathered her long, rippling hair into a twist.

"If I measure up to Erica's standards." The retrievers had returned, led by an Irish setter with the ball, and they were looking hopefully at Josh.

Rune nodded toward someone behind him, and Josh turned to see Erica beckoning from the back door of the kennel. Did it really matter whether Erica wanted to hire him or not? Yes.

As Josh joined her, Erica said, "The Westham shelter gave you high marks. Can you start tomorrow?"

Over the next few days, Josh settled into a new routine. Up at six, shower, pull on clothes, jump in the car, pause at the Cumberland Farms store on his way to the kennel.

Josh noticed that on the mornings when the blonde clerk, Danielle, was on duty, the same fireman was hanging around: a stocky man with short, dark hair. Could he be doubling as a security guard? When Josh accidentally caught his eye, the other man scowled, as if he suspected Josh of slipping an extra granola bar into his pocket.

By the third day Josh had learned where to park at Cumby's in order to exit quickly. This early, the parking lot was humming with customers arriving and leaving: landscapers, construction workers, fishermen. One of the landscapers, filling his truck at the gas pumps, nodded at Josh. "How's it going?" He was a stringy, dour man, with a walrus moustache. A Jack Russell terrier watched him from the cab of the truck.

Skinny Walrus looked familiar. "I'm good," said Josh. "It's Rick, right? I never forget a guy who buys me a beer."

Rick nodded, pointing at Josh. "Right!" He focused on Josh's Coastal Canine T-shirt. "You working at the kennel now? Tell Erica I'll get her that load of wood chips later today."

At Coastal Canine, Erica received Rick's message without comment, except for a raised eyebrow. She sent Josh into the back of the kennel to transfer the boarding dogs into the exercise pens. A card in a slot on each cage door told the dog's name, the owner's name, and vital information. Some had notes: "Aodh—hates cats." "Buster—special diet (ORGANIC BISCUITS ONLY)." "Tucker—thunderstorm phobic."

Tucker was boarding at Coastal Canine for a few days, and he greeted Josh by throwing his weight against the barred door of his cage. "How do you expect me to open it?" asked Josh. "Let's do this right." Leaving the door shut, he put his forefinger in front of his nose. "Tucker." The dog dropped down on all fours, his eyes on Josh. "Tucker, *sit*." Josh gestured upward with all fingers together. The dog's hindquarters sank toward the floor. "Good sit! Now *wait*." Josh opened the door—and Tucker burst out, leaping up to lick Josh's face.

Josh laughed and made Tucker sit again. "Good sit! Practice, practice, practice." He fondled the dog's muzzle, remembering the way Gardner Harrison had looked at Tucker. It reminded Josh of a stepfather looking at an eighth-grade stepson.

Today, Rune didn't show until after the morning rush. She burst out the back door of the kennel, long wet hair flapping like the ears of a spaniel fresh from a pond. "I'm here," she panted. "Sorry, Josh!"

The dogs mobbed the gate, barking. "*Namaste*, guys." Rune slipped through the gate and bent down to kiss the nearest dogs.

"Not a big deal," said Josh, handing her the rake. "Although Erica might think it is."

"I know." Smiling ruefully, she pushed the damp strands away from her face. "I didn't tell Erica, because she wouldn't understand, but I'm trying to make a commitment to spiritual discipline. So I meditated first thing this morning and lost track of time, and then I had to take a shower . . ." She rolled her eyes at her own transgression. "I guess spiritual discipline isn't so good for job discipline."

"Well, I could provide discipline," said Josh. "*Bad* Rune. *No* biscuit."

Rune flicked her long eyelashes at him. "I guess you could." In a more business-like tone, she added, "So, I'll spread wood chips and scoop poop, and you'll get the rest of the dogs from the office?"

Josh headed for the office, feeling very positive about his new job.

Cats here, cats there, cats and kittens everywhere. Hundreds of cats, thousands of cats, millions and billions and trillions of cats.

Wanda Gág, *Millions of Cats*

Chapter 7.

The Cat crawled out of the culvert where he'd spent the night, brushing spider webs from his ears. His left flank stung where the tiger tom had scratched him. Climbing onto a stone wall, he licked the wound clean and then wearily groomed the rest of himself.

Where was he? He was on the road again. Across the road, a battered mailbox on a post marked the head of a lane.

The Cat trotted across the pavement, barely dodging a rattling landscaping truck. A white dog stuck its brown and white head out the truck window to bark at him. As if the Cat cared that a dog barked! Dogs had no idea.

The lane was paved with crushed shells, which gave off a faint aroma that might have once been food. The Cat also sniffed recent traces of car tires. *Does my new patron live here?* he asked the Great Cat.

No answer. Uneasily, the Cat realized that he had forgotten to send praises to the Great Cat this morning. Still, he decided to investigate the lane. Perhaps not his new patron, but there were humans of some sort not far off. He would settle for a safe place to nap.

The lane passed a field dotted with baled hay, and swung around an orchard fragrant with fallen peaches. The Cat glimpsed a shingled roof through the branches.

Did he detect fresh human scent? He thought so, although that scent was almost overpowered by the reek of cats.

So many cats, all in one house? Placing one cautious paw after the other, the Cat crept past the orchard. He halted on a stretch of scruffy grass and stared, his whiskers quivering.

Cats! He had never seen so many cats in one place. They lounged in the open windows of the one-story house; they crouched on the mossy roof; they perched on old tires planted with scraggly petunias. Under an upside-down wheelbarrow with a missing wheel, a mother cat and her litter of kittens sprawled. There were several times as many cats here as in the feral colony at the dump.

This place was wrong, wrong, *wrong*. All these cats together—and none of them behaving as if there was anything unnatural about it! The scene made the Cat's gorge rise, as if he had a hairball. The Great Cat did not mean for her people to live in swarms, like gnats or ants.

At the same time, the Cat was curious, in a horrified way. What strange circumstance would bring so many cats—not even from the same litter, judging from their scents—together? This house wasn't like the animal shelter where the Woman had tried to leave him. There was no harsh smell of disinfectant, no scent of panicked animals. He heard cats meowing, but in a demanding rather than a desperate tone.

The Cat's nausea faded, and he crept closer to the house. The deck, too, swarmed with cats: longhair and shorthair, large and small, white cats, gray cats, striped cats, calico cats. There was a slim brown cat with dark ears, a cat with tufted ears and a thick striped tail, and two fluffy cats with pushed-in faces.

Jumping onto the edge of the deck, the Cat saw plates of cat chow scattered across the splintering boards. The nearest plate lured him toward its chicken-ish aroma. The other cats were uncomfortably close, but none of them were feeding at that plate.

The Cat sneaked along the railing, ready to dash back at any moment. A couple of the nearest felines noticed him and hissed, but without much feeling. Slinking up to the plate, he began to snatch mouthfuls of chow, raising his head after each bite to stare around.

The sliding door to the deck opened, and a plump young woman in a tank top and pajama bottoms stepped out. "Oh my god, look who's here—a tuxedo kitty!" She flip-flopped across the boards and squatted to pet the Cat. He edged away from her hand, but kept on eating.

The young woman spoke in a high, nasal voice as she ran her hand over his back. "Ryan says I shouldn't take in any more cats, it's starting to smell." She sighed. "But you just keep showing up. *Somebody* has to take care of you. How can I turn you away?"

The Cat kept on crunching cat chow, while the young woman shooed away another cat trying to sniff his tail. "It's not Ryan's house," she went on defiantly. "It belongs to *my* grandmother. And if Ryan wants to come see me (I *think* he does!), he can just breathe through his mouth."

Finishing the last bite of chow, the Cat turned away and looked for a place to sit while he washed his face.

But with a quick motion, the young woman scooped him up. She stepped back into the house and pushed the sliding door shut. “Don’t you want a nap, Mr. Tux?” she murmured. “No one’s using my sock drawer right now.”

As the young woman carried him through the front room, the Cat tried to escape in spasms of struggle. Twisting suddenly to scratch and bite used to work with the Woman in his first life, but this new person had a practiced way of holding a cat. One hand gripped the scruff of his neck, while her elbow wedged his body against her solid hip. He couldn’t turn his head to bite, and his claws only flailed the air.

They entered a room with yet more cats. Pulling out the top drawer of the dresser, she released him into a jumble of socks. “Here’s your bed, Mr. Tux.”

The Cat jumped right back out of the drawer, but the young woman—quicker on her plump feet than she looked—swung out of the bedroom and shut the door. The Cat stared around the room, ready to bristle his fur if anyone signaled aggression. Two tabbies lolled on the crumpled sheets, one of them sleeping with the tip of its tongue protruding, the other regarding him in a bored way. He sniffed the presence of more cats, probably under the bed or behind the TV stand. And he could certainly smell their well-used litter box in the closet.

Turning back to the door, the Cat poked a paw underneath. Sometimes doors could be opened that way. Or a human on the other side would notice the paw and open the door for him.

This door remained shut. The Cat poked more vigorously, meowing at the same time. It could take a while for a human to notice.

A fluffy female crawled out from under the bed, sniffed the Cat's tail, and hissed at him. Throwing a responding hiss over his shoulder, he kept on scratching and meowing at the door.

Out, out! He wanted out of this perverted house!

The fluffy cat, having expressed her opinion of the Cat, bent over a platter near the bed and quietly crunched cat chow.

Gradually the Cat calmed down. He stopped meowing and gave the door one last scratch. After all, his stomach was full, and he was weary.

Returning to the dresser, the Cat jumped back into the open drawer. He sniffed and kneaded the mat of socks and tights, turning around and around, and started to curl up. Then a cat under the bed sneezed, and he sat up again.

The fluffy cat was now crouching on the floor with her paws tucked in and her eyes closed. The alert tabby on the bed vigorously groomed the face of the sleeping one, who tried to push her away with a languid paw. The Cat's own inner eyelids slid shut, and he stretched out among the socks.

Just as the Cat was sliding into a doze, the *braaaAAaa* roar of an engine jolted him awake. He jumped out of the drawer and up on a window sill to see a car in the driveway. The driver, a youth in a T-shirt and baggy shorts, pushed open the car door. "Hey, Jor," he called out. "I got what you wanted."

"Hey, Ryan," called the young woman. "Get your muffler fixed! It sounds like a chain saw." She came into the Cat's view, holding a match to a paper twist. She walked down the steps from the deck with a sway of her hips. "But you got the cat chow? Good boy!"

Ryan hefted a large sack from the trunk of his car to his shoulder. She held the twist to his lips, and he took a drag. The aromatic smoke drifted in the Cat's window, tickling his nose.

"Where do you want me to put this?" Ryan asked, tapping the bag of chow on his shoulder.

The young woman giggled. "Do you really need me to tell you?"

Ryan laughed. "Come on, where should I put the cat chow?"

Tipping her head back, she let a stream of smoke escape her lips. "Just put it . . ." She slid a hand into his back pocket. "Put it in the . . ." She pushed him toward the steps. "Just put it in the . . . kitchen." Their footsteps crunched on the crushed-shell driveway as they moved out of the Cat's view, and there was the sound of a sliding door opening.

The two tabbies on the bed sat up now, and an elderly longhaired calico crept out of the closet. They seemed watchful, but not alarmed. As for the Cat, he jumped down from the sill, pattered to the door, and stood ready. *O Great Cat, aid me!*

The human noises were approaching. Not words now, but loud, uneven breathing. Then the young woman cried, "Oh my god! Not the bedroom—I just remembered, I've got a new—"

The bedroom door swung open, yanked by a furry paw as big as a ping-pong paddle—or was it only the youth's oversized hand?

The Cat dove between the humans' legs. He streaked through the living room, out the open slider. He flew off the deck and bounded past the tire planters. Far behind him a voice wailed, "You *asshole*, Ryan!"

The Cat squeezed under a wire fence. He heard the young woman calling, "Come back, Mr. Tux," and the distant rattle of cat chow in a jug. He didn't stop.

Praises be to Thee, Great Cat!

Dogs are wise. They crawl away into a quiet corner and lick their wounds and do not rejoin the world until they are whole once more.

Agatha Christie

Chapter 8.

By afternoon it was hot and muggy in the Large Dogs exercise yard, worse than the day Josh had left Westham for Mattakiset. Josh began to fixate on what he was going to do come closing time: head for the beach and fall into the surf. Meanwhile, he helped Rune bring out a wading pool for the dogs to play in.

Josh joined Rune at a bench in the shade. He hadn't sweated this much since . . . Since last Labor Day, a steam-bath day like this, when Josh and Tanya had hosted a cookout.

Whose stupid idea had it been to throw a Labor Day cookout? In fact, as Josh remembered, he and Tanya had agreed it would be fun, and not too much trouble. They'd provide the grill, the drinks, the ice, the backyard. Everyone else—Tanya's law office friends, Josh's teacher friends, etc.—would bring side dishes.

Fun, hah.

That day Josh had thought, for the first time, Maybe this is just not going to work out. "This" being his marriage. Was it the first time for Tanya, too? Or had she already been thinking that?

Josh dragged himself out of the past to focus on Rune beside him, bending forward to wipe sweat from her face with her T-shirt. She was asking, "Would you say that the Dog is your totem animal? Not for me. I have a psychic connection with all living things, of course, but the Cat is definitely my totem. I'm on the board of Fur-Ever. That's the cat shelter, up the street?"

Josh's eyes were on her back, where the pulled-up T-shirt revealed bare skin. He wanted to put his hand right *there*. "Uh, yeah, I'd say I was a dog person. But cats are—cats are great, too. Fur-Ever, that's a cute name."

Rune straightened, and the gap between T-shirt and shorts disappeared. "Our name means we're committed to placing every cat in their forever home."

Rune intrigued Josh. He'd never known anyone who talked seriously, and openly, about totem animals and psychic forces. She evidently believed in that crystal she wore, too; he'd seen her holding it above a dog that was getting out of line. Was she simply deluded, or did the New Age way of looking at the world actually work for her? Hey—now Josh was free to get to know another woman, without worrying about where a friendship might lead.

At the end of the day, when all the dogs had either been picked up by their owners or stowed in their overnight kennels, Josh asked Rune, "Want to go for a swim, and then a glass of wine?"

Rune considered. "Mm— Not tonight, I'm doing TNR. That's Trap, Neuter, Release. There's a colony of feral cats at the dump. Well, not just feral—there's at least one tame lost cat. According to Danielle at Cumby's." She made an exasperated face. "Why Danielle didn't just *bring* that cat into Fur-Ever herself, instead of *telling* me about it— People don't realize all the work we do, and the least they could do is help a little."

Josh wondered if this was leading up to how *he* could help Fur-Ever. Sure enough, Rune gave him an inviting smile. "Want to come along tonight?"

As Josh hesitated, caught between not wanting a date with feral cats at the dump and not wanting to discourage a possible relationship with Rune, she spoke again. "But I wasn't thinking—you probably aren't immunized for rabies, are you? No, never mind."

"Maybe some other time," said Josh. "I mean, the glass of wine, not the TNR." Then it occurred to him that hanging out in a bar might not be Rune's style. "Or, do you want to go somewhere for dinner?"

"Mm. Tomorrow night? Where do you want to go? The problem is, the places to eat around here are sort of mainstream. There's the Sincere Garden up on Route 6, next to the Dreamland Motel, they have some vegetarian dishes, but I hate to say, I think they throw a little pork into them. . . ." She gave him a thoughtful look. Her eyes, Josh noticed, were actually green. "I have a better idea: Why don't you come to my place tomorrow for omelets? I get these incredible eggs from my neighbor's free-range chickens. Or how about stir-fry? Gaia's Organic Garden has truly harmonic kale."

Josh showed up at Rune's the next evening with a bottle of awesome (the clerk at Soule's Liquor had assured him) organic wine. This was him, out on a date! With a pagan!

No one answered the front door of the small frame house on the Old Fall River Road, but he found Rune in her back garden, a profusion of blossoms and humming insects with cats lurking here and there. Barefoot, dressed in a loose shift, Rune was turning over a mound with a garden fork. "Come look at this," she urged. She held out a handful of black soil. "Have you ever seen such rich compost?"

"No—I haven't." Josh hoped that Rune was going to wash her hands before she cooked dinner. Then he noticed scratches on her upper arm. "Whoa, someone got you bad. One of the dogs?"

Rune looked surprised. "Our dogs? Haven't you noticed their special respect for me? They wouldn't think of hurting me. This—" she nodded at the scratches— "is from TNR, trap-neuter-release, at the dump last night. Usually even feral cats understand that I'm helping them, but this one tiger male, whoa, he went into a kind of Viking rage."

"I can see how a tomcat might not like the 'neuter' part," said Josh.

After strolling around the garden, drinking a glass or two of wine (not quite awesome, but not bad), Josh forgot about the compost. Rune served dinner at a picnic table on her screened porch. The kale stir-fry she'd promised was tastier than Josh expected—there must have been some redeeming ingredient, like local, uncured, apple wood-smoked bacon—and there was also a platter of steamed corn on the cob. Rolling her corn on a stick of butter, Rune closed her eyes as she sank her teeth in. "Mm."

Josh followed suit. "Mm." The plump, sweet kernels were the best thing he'd ever tasted. He grinned at Rune over his ear of corn, and she smiled back, her mouth shiny with butter. Josh swallowed and paused. "You know what they say about corn."

"What they say about corn?"

Josh took another big bite before answering. "They say, 'People have tried and they have tried, but sweet corn is better than sex.'"

Rune frowned slightly. Had Josh put her off with his stupid joke? Gazing at her ear of corn, she shook her head. "I don't think you can compare. No, I wouldn't compare them."

How to interpret that? Best to change the subject, so Josh mentioned that he was renting from Barbara Schaeffer. "Do you know her?"

"Mm, Mrs. Schaeffer—she used to teach math at the high school. Her intuitive side wasn't very well developed, but I thought she was a good teacher. I mean, she expected a lot, but she really cared about the kids."

With a pang, Josh wondered if his former students would say that about him. *He really cared about the kids.* Then—why had he left them in the lurch before the end of the school year?

Never mind. Josh continued with more first-date information: He was a former teacher himself, now exploring business opportunities, and he was separated and scheduled for divorce. In exchange, Rune revealed that she was not currently in a committed relationship. She'd grown up in Mattakiset, spent a stretch of her early adulthood in Vermont, and returned to Mattakiset to "nurture an alternate community here."

"An alternate community?" asked Josh.

"You know, like they had in the lost civilization of Atlantis, or before the Druids."

"You're joking," said Josh.

"No, I'm not." Her uncanny green eyes were perfectly serious. "I'm talking about the time when wise women led the community on the principle of harmony, and the People were in tune with Nature."

"Look, I don't want to argue," said Josh, "but this is kind of my field—I'm a social studies teacher. I have a master's in history." Rune looked unimpressed, but he went on, "As for Nature, it can be pretty savage. Actually being in tune with Nature would have to include infanticide. And periodic famines." Josh stopped, afraid he might have offended Rune and ruined the evening.

But she only gave him a pitying smile. "That's such a reductionist view of humankind."

Josh opened his mouth to cite authoritative sources, then thought better of it. "Well. Who really knows about back then? So . . . tell me more about Fur-Ever."

While Rune described how hard the volunteers worked, and how much joy was experienced by cat adopters, Josh munched another ear of corn and half-listened. The light faded. The thick, warm air that had seemed oppressive at the kennel now felt tropical in a good way. A breeze pulsed through the screens.

Rune was leaning forward, eyebrows raised as if she expected a response. "Before you say yes or no, you've got to meet Pansy. She's so sweet. And she's already seventeen years old, so it wouldn't be that long-term a commitment." Her voice turned sad. "The owner's moving into assisted living—it breaks her heart to give up Pansy."

Suddenly alert, Josh gathered what Rune must be asking. "I—I wish I could help out, but—"

"Oh, just take a look at her. She's so pretty, a black and white longhair. You'd have to commit to brushing her regularly, but you know, grooming is very relaxing for the person, too." Rune talked faster as she went on, "The poor thing has arthritis, but she'd come with her memory-foam pillow with the built-in heating pad, and a supply of meds. You know you can't give cats the same pain-killers as people. I'd take her myself, but I already have three cats, and I have to keep Orion separated from the others as it is, or he'd bully them. So I thought you—"

"Wait," Josh interrupted. "*I* thought your cat shelter took really, really good care of the cats." A vision of his mother's Northport Commons, only with cats in little wheelchairs and walkers, flashed in his mind. "This cat should live out its last days there."

Rune shook her head. "I was just saying, the Fur-Ever shelter's so strained right now. We do have some volunteers who foster cats in their homes, but everybody reliable is full up. Yesterday I checked out this girl, she's related to the Harrisons—'girl'? Actually, she's twenty-two, but she didn't seem very mature—who'd said we could place cats at her house. Well, no way I'd leave any animals there! She reached her limit a long time ago. She was feeding them, I guess, but that was about it. I saw at least three mother cats with litters, and some longhairs with matted fur. More or less a hoarding situation. I warned her, she's going to get a visit from Animal Control if she doesn't shape up."

"But as far as—" started Josh.

"And then she tried to bribe me with her unregistered weed," Rune went on. "Decent quality, but still . . . Anyway, you don't have to make up your mind right this minute about Pansy."

Josh realized what he should have said to begin with. "Rune. I don't like cats. And my landlady doesn't allow pets. I'm sorry."

As if these were pathetically flimsy excuses, Rune gazed silently into his eyes. She rose and began lighting candles around the screened porch. Bringing out a small package wrapped in black silk, she uncovered a pack of cards. "Josh," she said, "I get the feeling you're . . . adrift."

"Adrift?" Josh was taken aback; hadn't he presented himself as confidently in control of his future?

"Do you want me to do a reading for you?" Rune went on. "It might help orient you to where you are on your journey."

"A reading?" Josh peered at the top card. The Hanged Man. "You mean Tarot cards? I thought Tarot readings went out with the 1970s."

"Tarot is not a fad," she said. "It's ancient wisdom. And by the way, I'm offering you a free gift. People pay me fifty dollars for a reading."

"I'm sorry," said Josh. He *was* sorry that he and Rune had gotten sidetracked from a promising beginning. But she had cooked him dinner; he should be able to put up with some New Age nonsense. "Sure, please go ahead."

Rune looked at him severely for a moment before she nodded and spread out the black cloth. "Now. This first card I'm putting down is the querent," she said. "That stands for you, your recent or present situation. The Fool."

"That's flattering," said Josh. He was trying for a light tone, but the words came out bitter.

In any case, Rune didn't smile. "The characteristics of the Fool are, he's naïve, feather-headed, unaware of danger. See, he's about to step off a cliff. But some animal instinct (that's this dog) is trying to pull him back."

Josh had resolved to listen to the Tarot reading with polite amusement, but the idea of a dog trying to save him blindsided him. "I don't have a dog," he snapped.

"The dog is a symbol, of course," said Rune. "Now, the next card—"

Without meaning to, Josh burst out, "I used to have a dog. A black Lab. Molly." He made an effort at irony: "She was a good old dog, but I can't say that she would have pulled me back from a cliff. . . . I couldn't pull her back from the cliff, either."

Josh stopped talking before his voice broke. He fingered the edge of the black silk. Molly's ears had been black and silky.

"The next card," said Rune, "shows the immediate influences on the querent."

Josh was mesmerized by the candle flame, and by the chorus of insects chanting outside the porch. "I got her eleven years ago," he went on. "Or actually it was more like *she* picked *me*. That was before I got married." It felt dangerous to be talking about Molly like this, but at the same time, it was a relief.

"The Two of Cups," said Rune, tapping the edge of the second card. It showed a young man and a young woman, offering each other large goblets. Rune unpinned her hair, which slithered over her bare shoulders.

"And then it was ten years later," Josh rushed on. "How did she get old so fast? Tanya (my ex-wife) started complaining about Molly's breath. I thought it was just normal doggy breath. But when I took her to the vet for a checkup, it turned out she had cancer of the mouth." Josh put a hand to his own mouth. "So she had surgery. Then she was okay for another year, except for some arthritis, you could tell that bothered her."

"Then she started to lose it. She started peeing inside if I didn't take her out every so often. I guess she was pretty sick, but still . . . My wife decided— I wasn't there—" Josh choked. "My dog— A carton of ashes."

Josh stopped talking. Finally focusing on Rune, he saw that she was frowning. Did she think he was pathetic, crying over his dog to someone he hardly knew? If she had such a psychic gift, she should be more understanding. "What?"

Rune shook her head. "It's no wonder you're so far off your path. You need to release Molly. Did you do a farewell ceremony with her ashes?"

"No." Josh did not add that he'd been driving around talking to the ashes in his backseat.

"Well, there's your problem." Rune gathered the cards, wrapped them deftly in the silk, and set the package aside. "There's no point in going through a whole reading. Molly needs to move on, and you're trying to hold her back, so you aren't moving on, either."

Josh felt his face heat up. He pulled his legs out from under the picnic table. "Right. Time for me to move on." He stood up. "Thanks for dinner. Thanks for the free advice."

"Josh!" Rune seemed to have lost patience. "Didn't you see the second card, the Two of Cups? It signifies Nature's blessing for romantic passion." She slid off her bench and around the table in a fluid movement. "In this moment." Her arms slipped under his.

Josh's anger drained away, leaving him feeling as foolish as the Fool, and as much off balance. He let his face sink into the hair rippling over Rune's shoulder. "Mm."

"Mm," Rune echoed, letting her breath out on his neck.

For the first time this evening, Josh felt in tune with her, and maybe with Nature, too. His lips brushed over her face; his hands slid down her back.

Rune leaned away from him, but only to pick up a candle. She led him through the house, into her bedroom. As Josh pulled his T-shirt over his head, she said, "Wait a minute."

"I've got a condom," said Josh helpfully.

Rune bent over the bed, scooping something up. "I have to put this daddy long-legs out."

"Oh. How do you know its journey doesn't end right here, getting squished?" Josh asked, but Rune had disappeared.

He lay down, remembering Tanya reacting to a daddy long-legs on her towel as she stepped out of the shower: "Josh! Ee-yew! Kill it!" Josh had tried to reason with her. "A daddy long-legs isn't like a spider. It won't bite you. Unless you're an aphid."

Rune was back. Josh wondered if the Two of Cups moment might have passed. But apparently removing an arachnid from the bed was no mood-breaker for Rune.

I'm a happy dog in a car.
Flying Leming

Chapter 9.

Driving along the winding road to the kennel, Josh had all four windows open to the morning breeze. With each change of scenery along the route, fresh smells blew into the car, and Josh called them out to the backseat. Passing the campground: "Pine trees!" The long bramble-covered stone wall: "Roses!" As the road crossed a creek: "Cattails!"

Josh thought fondly of his sister, Vicky, giving her full credit for bringing him to Mattakiset. He'd rejected her idea at first, mainly because (as he told himself at the time) he could fucking well run his own life without help from his older sister. Wasn't it enough satisfaction, that she'd been right about Tanya? Vicky (he'd added snidely to himself) evidently didn't have enough to do, now that both her kids were away at college.

And Josh had been unfairly critical of Vicky's real estate friend, Melissa, burbling about the attractions of Mattakiset. "It's just an *unsung gem,*" she'd assured him. Unsung gem? He'd snickered to himself.

How perversely ungrateful he'd been. Josh was lucky to land in Barbara Schaeffer's apartment. Yeah, Barbara could be a pain, but she meant well.

In the Cumberland Farms parking lot, the air was scented with gasoline and Dumpster, but that was okay, for a little contrast. "Cumby's!" Josh called to the backseat.

Josh felt a warm kinship with the other early risers at the gas pumps and in the parking spaces. They were the people who did the real work of the world: lobstermen, landscapers, dog day care attendants. In the store he waved to the blonde clerk, and she waved back.

Outside again, savoring his first sip of the roasty-toasty Cumby's special blend with half and half, Josh had an insight. The List. He shouldn't drop the List just because he felt good. He could stretch *beyond* 100 percent, leveraging his well-being for someone else's benefit.

Rune, for instance. Even if she'd enjoyed the end of the evening as much as Josh had—and he was pretty sure she had—it would be gallant to show his appreciation. She might be dwelling on a different planet, but they'd intersected where it mattered most. A dozen red roses would be appropriate, damn the expense. He had time to swing by Soule's Market.

The kennel was already busy when Josh checked in, and no one except Uncle George remarked on the large bunch of roses. "For me?" asked the old man. "Aw, you shouldn't have."

Josh stowed the bouquet in the staff room until he could present them properly to Rune. As he hurried back to the office, a black nose poked through the front doorway. Tucker panted hoarsely, straining against his collar with his front paws in the air. Behind him, leaning backward on the leash with a grim expression, was Gardner Harrison.

"Tucker!" said Josh. The dog gave an extra leap toward Josh, and Harrison gritted his teeth.

Uncle George, setting down the phone, opened his mouth in alarm. "That mutt'll jerk you off your feet before you can say 'pelvic fracture'."

Grabbing the leash, Josh turned his shoulder to keep Tucker from jumping up, then bent down to reward the dog with a kiss. To Harrison he said, "You know, when a dog pulls on the leash like that, you can discourage the behavior by standing still. That teaches him that if he pulls, he doesn't go anywhere. Right, Tuck?"

Tucker dodged Josh's hands to shove his nose into Josh's crotch. Harrison said, "Shouldn't you discourage *that* behavior?"

Tucker gave a thoughtful snort. Uncle George smiled to himself. Gardner Harrison was out the door with a *Good riddance* glance.

At the other end of the kennel, Tucker tried to leap toward the back door, but Josh didn't move. "Whoa. Tucker. *Wait.*" The dog turned to look at Josh. "Tucker, *sit.*" As the dog's hindquarters touched the floor, Josh exclaimed, "Good job!" and gave him a pat. It occurred to him that he was doing Gardner and Carol Harrison a big favor, training their dog for them. On the scale of the List, the good deed of dog training for free made Josh feel 20 percent better, so now he was at, what—140 percent?

Josh let Tucker into the exercise yard, where Rune was raking wood chips around the playground equipment. "Hey, Rune!" he called.

Tucker skidded to a stop at Rune's feet, and she greeted him with a kiss. "Hey, Josh. Did Erica say when

Rick was going to deliver more wood chips? We're running low." She continued raking.

Josh felt uncertain. He started to call, "I brought you something!" but changed his mind. Maybe he should tend to business and let Rune discover the bouquet on her break.

It was a busy morning, with the full number of dogs in day care. Erica asked Josh to take some shots of the Large Dogs with his phone. "I'm revamping our Facebook page," she said. "Customers like to see pictures of their dogs." She added, "Maybe this will stir up business."

Josh found taking the pictures more difficult than he expected, partly because he was laughing the whole time. The ones of Tucker playing with Buster were blurred. The one of Lola digging in the wood chips was basically a picture of flying wood chips, obscuring a shaggy animal that might or might not be Lola. And just when Josh thought he had a fetching angle on Tucker, the dog lunged at the phone and almost knocked Josh over.

At last Josh had a decent collection of dog shots to download onto the office computer. Erica watched, nodding approval. "Yes, yes, and yes. I can use all of those . . . except maybe that." She pointed to a shot of a Doberman politely sniffing Tucker's butt. "By the way, are you interested in teaching a Beginning Obedience class? If so, I'll send our customers an email blast and see how much of a response I get."

"Sure, great." That might be fun. Josh had taught kids, and he'd taught dogs, but he'd never taught adults.

They'd be smarter than dogs, and more respectful than kids, right? A piece of cake.

In the staff room, Josh noticed that his red roses were looking tired. You idiot, Josh told himself. Of course flowers needed to be in water. He picked up his "World's Best Teacher" coffee mug, then put it down—too small.

Finding an empty coffee can, Josh filled it at the sink and stuck the rose stems in. That should revive them. After Rune took her break and discovered the bouquet, he could admit that he'd brought them for her. Although it would be classier if she could discover them in a vase, instead of a coffee can.

But after her break, Rune showed no sign of having discovered anything. She must not have made the connection between the red roses in the staff room and last night. Or, was she mad at him? Mad at him for what?

Tanya had expressed anger at Josh by becoming remote, but Rune seemed to be merely going about the doggie day care tasks while thinking of something else. But then, he didn't know Rune very well, and he'd never known anyone quite so . . . New Age.

At noon, when the dogs were settled in their private kennels, Josh caught up with Rune in the staff room. Her back turned to him, she was examining the bouquet in the coffee can, tilting it this way and that. Shit. There was a price tag on the cellophane wrap.

"I brought those for you," he said. "But I forgot to take the price tag off. Uncool, Josh!" He laughed uneasily.

"You brought these flowers for me?" Rune's tone of voice might have been saying, You brought these used tampons for me?

Josh was taken aback. "I—I thought you liked flowers, so . . ."

With a heavy sigh, Rune launched into a lecture. Did he not realize that these were non-native flowers? Grown in Latin American countries by exploited workers? Flown to the United States on an airplane that generated fifty-three pounds of carbon dioxide per mile? "You have a lot to learn, Josh," she finished. "Too bad you didn't just donate the money to Fur-Ever."

"All right," said Josh slowly, his face warm. "I'll give you a check for the cat shelter." He unzipped his backpack.

"By the way," Rune went on, watching Josh write in his checkbook, "I did a reading for me and you."

"A reading. A Tarot card reading, you mean?" Josh was startled at her serious tone. Was she, against his assumptions, about to demand a deeper commitment?

Rune nodded. "So . . . it looks like we should just be friends from now on." She spoke regretfully, as if Josh were a dog she was culling from the Large Dogs Play Group.

"What? Why?"

"Don't get upset—there's nothing wrong, really. It's just that the Chariot kept coming up for you, like you should concentrate on your own goals right now."

"That's ridiculous," said Josh. "I mean, I appreciate the advice, but I think I can handle my goals."

Rune sighed, looking down at the limp roses. To herself she muttered, "Not even good for compost—they're grown with all those toxic poisons." To Josh she went on, "And not only that, but what turned up for *me* was the Three of Swords. In other words, there's probably a third party involved, and it'll only lead to trouble. So . . . a dead end, you and me romantically."

Smiling reassuringly, she plucked the check for Fur-Ever from his hand. "But no problem with staying friends."

"The Three of Swords. The Chariot." Josh meant his tone of voice to sound ironic and detached, but it came out petulant. "Well. This is the first time I've ever been dumped with a Tarot reading."

Rune tucked his check into her hemp tote bag.

A short while later, Josh arrived at Soule's Market and Deli, stewing. What was going on with Rune? Did she sense that he was also attracted to Danielle? Did she think he was too needy? Or was that Tarot talk just an inventive way to blow him off?

Josh ordered his lunch at the deli counter and carried it out to one of the wobbly cast-iron tables on Soule's patio. Smarting from Rune's rejection, he could think of several other things to feel resentful about. The tone his sister took with him, as if he were eight years old again and she was sixteen, telling him when to go to bed. Barbara's helpful infuriating instructions. And most enormously of all, Principal Charlotte Voss signing him up for a sensitivity workshop.

Whoa! Don't go there.

"Mind if I join you?" It was Rick Johnson, setting down a cardboard clamshell and pulling out a chair opposite Josh with a metallic scrape. His T-shirt was streaked with green, and grass clippings clung to the bill of his Red Sox cap.

"Sure," said Josh, glad for a distraction. Even as he spoke, he realized that "Sure" was a potentially confusing response, but then he realized further that Rick was not tuned in to such nuances. He was already in the chair, destabilizing the table with his elbows, chomping on a Buffalo wing. Josh regretted his own tofu salad and pomegranate juice, chosen to balance last night's butter and wine.

Rick nodded at Josh's Coastal Canine T-shirt. "How d'you like working at the kennel?"

"It's good. I like the dogs," said Josh.

"Yeah, I'll take them over people any time." Rick gestured toward his truck in the Pooch Park carports at the far end of the parking lot. "I've got a Jack Russell terrier, Pepper, goes everywhere with me." Rick's normally dour expression softened. "Smart! That dog could do my bookkeeping for me. She—"

Rick broke off to glare at someone behind Josh. "Asshole. I never should have rented from him." Josh turned and saw Gardner Harrison pushing a shopping cart out of the market. Josh raised his eyebrows, and Rick went on, "But it was the only place I could find, when my wife threw me out."

Josh gave a short laugh. "Tell me about it."

Rick grunted sympathetically. "You too, huh? Bitches, all of 'em." He cleared chicken from his teeth with his forefinger and sucked Buffalo sauce from his mustache. "Yeah, I'm staying in one of Harrison's cottages. The deal is, instead of paying rent, I do landscaping for him. I must have planted forty fucking hydrangeas around his house, and I'm not through yet. Worth a lot more than the rent of that shitbox cottage. He must have got his appliances at the dump."

Rick went on to detail the decrepitude of the clothes dryer in his cottage. "Every time it starts up, it goes *Whoop! Whoop! Whoop!"*

"Be thankful you have a dryer," said Josh. "Barbara Schaeffer wants to make everyone hang their wash on clotheslines."

"Oh, yeah, you're renting from Mrs. Schaeffer." Rick smiled slyly. "She gave me a D in algebra. How much is she clipping you for that apartment?"

Josh told him, and Rick shook his head, still smiling. "Unbelievable."

"Believe it," said Josh curtly. "Anyway, it was only half as much as the ones on Cape Cod."

Rick leaned back, tilting his head to the side. "What if you sub-rented from me, for half of that? There's an extra bedroom in my cottage."

Josh laughed. "Why would I want to move into Harrison's 'shitbox'?"

Rick laughed, too. "Yeah, I did say that, didn't I? It's not so bad. At least it's got a dish for TV. Come by and take a look. You know the Camp Seaside sign on Old Farm Road? Turn in there, watch out you don't bust your axle on the potholes. It's the first cottage on the left."

Josh didn't want to room with Rick Johnson, but it bothered him to think he was paying too much for Barbara's apartment. Driving along Old Farm Road after work, he had an idea: He could leverage Rick's offer to get Barbara to reduce his rent.

At the farmhouse Josh found his landlady sitting on her doorstep, brushing Lola's shaggy coat. She waved at Josh, and she nodded approvingly as he parked on the gravel, not on the stretch of lawn she was pampering. But when he mentioned that he'd been offered a cheaper rental, she seemed bewildered, then hurt, then offended.

"I need to watch my expenses," said Josh. He was looking at the dog as he spoke, but he could feel Barbara's direct pale blue gaze on him.

"You do realize that I couldn't give you a rebate on the rest of this month's rent," said Barbara. She picked a burr out of Lola's coat. "May I ask where this other rental is?"

"It's off of Old Farm Road, farther up. Camp Seaside?"

"Oh, yes," said Barbara. "One of those shacks on concrete blocks. It used to be a summer camp, and Gardner Harrison bought it up. People call it 'Mosquito Village'."

"This other place has a satellite dish," said Josh. "TV sports reception." Trying to lighten up the discussion, he added, "Hey, I can't help it—I'm a Red Sox addict."

"Of course the choice is up to you," said Barbara. "But as far as the money goes, another expense, if you leave, would be repairs to my apartment. I was going to speak to you about the damage to the floor. The window must have been left open in the rain, because the linoleum there is curling up." She stood and turned to go in the house, followed by her dog. Lola paused in the kitchen doorway to regard Josh with reproachful pale eyes.

Josh climbed back into his car, remarking to the backseat, "Well, that was a total flop." To top it off, the Sox weren't playing tonight. He might as well try that Chinese place on Route 6 that Rune had mentioned. Any restaurant that threw pork into dishes indiscriminately couldn't be all bad.

"I am the Cat who walks by himself, and I wish to come into your Cave."

Rudyard Kipling, *Just So Stories*

Chapter 10.

The Cat hurried through a grove of beech trees, down a slope, across a creek, up the opposite slope, and under the branches of pine trees, urged on by the threat of the cat-hoarding house. The trees thinned to open sky above a pasture, with a road beside, and the Cat jumped onto a stone wall. As he rested and groomed himself, he tried to remember what his mother had told him and the other kittens on the day she weaned them. *Pay attention!* Then, what had she said? Something about choosing the right patron. Not settling for second best.

The Cat needed to redouble his efforts to find a patron. He thought wistfully of the coffee woman at the dump. Where was she? Poor Cat! *Meow.*

Stop that. Jumping to his feet, the Cat shook himself and looked all around. On the other side of the pasture, a white house showed through a screen of evergreens.

Wait! The breeze shifted, and the Cat opened his nostrils wide to a tantalizing bird-scent. It came from some distance off, across the road. It reminded the Cat of food that came from special cans, and even more of a food that humans ate. The Girl used to slip him shreds of it under the table.

The breeze shifted again, overwhelming the delectable bird-scent with some aromatic weed.

Dropping down from the wall, the Cat pushed through Queen Anne's lace and milkweed toward the row of evergreens. He climbed another stone wall, leaped across a ditch, and crawled under the thick hedge to a lawn. There was the white house he'd glimpsed, a spread-out structure with an outdoor stairway on one side.

The Cat crossed the grass to an old tree, its sagging limbs propped up on posts. Underneath the tree there was a marrow bone that had recently been chewed by a dog—too thoroughly to tempt the Cat. On the lawn beside the house, towels and shirts flapped on a clothesline tree. The Cat sniffed a low-hanging sleeve, detecting a woman.

As the Cat explored the scene, he heard an engine approaching on the road. A small yellow car paused at the stone posts and turned in the driveway. The Cat crouched behind a laundry basket to watch.

The driver, a woman with wavy brown hair, drove around to the outside stairway, got out with a paper bag, and placed the bag on the first step. While the Cat tried to decide whether to approach her, the woman lifted a glinting stone from around her neck, held it over the bag, and murmured. Then she got back in her car and drove away.

It was too late to approach the woman as a possible patron, but at least she'd left the paper bag. The Cat loved paper bags, and he crept up to the stairway to inspect this one. Whew, what an overpowering fragrance! It almost obscured the fresh scent of a man around the stairs.

The Cat pattered up the stairs and meowed several times, in case the man was in the house now. He pattered down and rubbed his jowls against the folded edges of the bag. Even a perfumed bag was irresistible, especially lined with crinkly tissue paper.

Would the man, or the woman of the shirt on the clothesline, show up sooner or later? The Cat sat down and wrapped his black tail around his white paws to wait.

Sure enough, before long a green car with a man drove through the stone posts. He, too, climbed out with a bag, a plastic grocery bag. As he closed the car door, the man noticed the Cat on the stairs. His face contracted. "Rune! What the—?"

The man's eyes shifted from the Cat to the paper bag and back again, and his frown deepened.

This was not a promising beginning for a patron, but the Cat, withholding judgment, stepped down and rubbed against his ankle. This was the man who lived in the house; he could tell by the smell. The man leaned down, and the Cat raised his head to be petted.

But the man only picked up the paper bag and stared at a note stuck to it. "Rune," he growled at the sheet of paper, "did you not read my lips? I said *No.* No, I will *not* take that black and white cat. Why are you doing this to me? I just want to eat my comfort food and crash." He parted the tissue paper and looked inside the bag. "And a lavender-scented candle. Sheesh! Did she think I was going to go into some kind of Christmas Tree Shop trance and suddenly want to adopt a cat?"

The Cat had just realized the most interesting thing about this man: the plastic bag hanging from his other hand. The bag swung gently back and forth, teasing him with a meaty aroma. The Cat sniffed and meowed, glancing meaningfully at the man.

Setting the candle down, the man squinted at him. "But just a minute—you aren't fluffy. Didn't Rune mention long hair, brushing? So maybe she didn't leave you. Although I wouldn't put it past Rune to pull a switcheroo."

The Cat wasn't sure if this man would be willing to share, but the smell of warm meat overpowered his caution. Balancing on his haunches, he reached up a paw to snag the bottom of the takeout bag. The plastic ripped, but not enough to release the contents.

The man jerked the bag up. "Shit! Get out of there!" The Cat backed away and meowed.

Pulling a key from his pocket, the man started up the stairs. But then he stopped and looked back. "I guess you're hungry."

The Cat meowed.

The man sighed. "Okay, I lied to Rune. I don't actually dislike cats." Pulling a box out of his bag, he lifted the lid and dropped a few pieces of meat onto the step.

Meat! The Cat fell upon it, purring as he gulped a succulent strip.

"But this is a one-off deal, understand?" said the man, licking his fingers. "Don't expect to settle in here."

As the Cat gobbled and purred, the man climbed the stairs and disappeared. The Cat licked the last traces of oily sauce from the wooden step. Perhaps the man would return with more food. Or invite the Cat in.

While the Cat waited, he pawed carefully around the spot where the meat had fallen, as if to cover it. He stretched his tongue from side to side to clean his whiskers. He licked his right paw and rubbed the right side of his face, then licked his left paw and rubbed the left side.

Well. That done, the Cat felt himself sinking into a stupor as the sun sank behind the evergreen hedge. But it wasn't safe to sleep out here. Leaving the doorstep, the Cat padded across the driveway to inspect the green car. Sometimes cars were left open.

As the Cat sniffed the tires of the man's car, headlights from another car poked into the driveway. A shaggy dog was hanging from its back window. "There you go, Lola," said a woman's voice. The Cat darted under the first car, in case the dog was hostile.

The dog shambled across the lawn and squatted to pee. Had the Cat seen that dog, in that car, before?

The dog stood up again, sniffing in the direction of the Cat. She whined and took a step toward the man's car.

"Come on, Lola," said the woman, opening the front door of the house. "We're going to watch *Nature*, remember? About wolves." The door shut behind them.

Dogs and their humans. It was pathetic, the way dogs let humans order them around. Humans, as the Cat's mother had pointed out to her kittens, didn't hear very well, could hardly smell anything, and couldn't see in the dark. Why would you allow such creatures to make the rules?

In the distance a creature yip-howled, and the fur on the back of the Cat's neck bristled. Shelter, he needed shelter. Crawling out from under the green car, he found a front window open. He leaped up and into the seat. Recent smells: the man, with overtones of many dogs. And a deep old smell, coming from the backseat: one particular dog.

Squeezing between the front seats, onto the back floor, the Cat nosed through a clutter of newspapers, foam coffee cups, dog toys, leashes, and flip-flops. Sometimes food was left in cars, and here was a round cardboard carton, like an ice cream carton. Only it smelled like ashes.

The Cat climbed onto the backseat, which was covered with a towel. The feel of the rough cloth under his paw pads, together with its old dog smell, triggered a kittenhood memory.

The Cat kneaded and purred and kneaded and purred until he had the towel rumpled just right.

Somewhere the wild creature yipped again, and the Cat's ear twitched. But he was safely wrapped in a dream of his mother's nest in the laundry room.

Must be a dogged cat.
Uncle George

Chapter 11.

Loping across the gravel to his car the next morning, Josh noticed something black and white moving through the dew-fogged back windows. A skunk? Oh shit.

Meowing, the black and white animal leaped from the backseat to the front seat to the open window. Purring urgently, it butted its head into Josh's T-shirt.

Oh, the cat. Josh had fed this cat last night, and now it seemed to think they were friends. Lifting the cat from the window, Josh set it on the gravel driveway. He opened the car door. But before he got so much as his foot inside, the cat had jumped in again and slipped into the backseat.

Josh glanced at his watch. "You aren't going to like this," he warned the cat. He sat down, felt moisture soak into his shorts, and realized too late that there was dew on the front seat as well as on the back windows. "Shit." He rolled down the back windows and turned the key in the ignition, bringing the engine to life with a series of coughs. Josh waited for the cat to fly out of the car.

Instead, the cat leaped onto the shelf above the backseat. Josh stared at the cat in the rear view mirror. The cat regarded him calmly from its black Batman mask with white antennae-like eyebrows.

Josh turned slowly, cautiously onto Old Farm Road, waiting for the black and white cat to panic and exit. But it stayed put, swaying slightly as the car rounded the curves, blinking placidly out the window.

"I'll be damned," said Josh. "Or, as Uncle George puts it, 'Butter my butt and call me a biscuit.'"

Stepping out of the car at Cumby's, Josh felt again that cool dampness on the back of his shorts. He helped himself to a wad of napkins at the coffee station, patted the seat of his pants ineffectually, and pushed the napkins into an overflowing trash bin. Glancing over his shoulder, he caught Danielle watching him.

Josh set his coffee and granola bar down at the cash register, deciding to make the best of it. "If you really want to know why my pants are wet," he told her with mock annoyance, "I left my car window down last night. And this morning I didn't dry the seat before I got in, because I found a cat in my car."

Danielle gave a surprised laugh. "Now *that* makes perfect sense. Except you left out the part where you stuffed our trash so full with all those napkins that now someone has to empty it." She handed Josh his change and turned to the next customer. "Scott will help you at the other register."

Josh assumed that was the end of flirting while wet, but Danielle followed him out of the store with a full trash bag over her shoulder and heaved it into a Dumpster. Instead of hurrying back inside, she walked over to his car. "You do have a cat in there." A big smile spread over her face. "Oh my god. It's Panda."

The cat seemed to recognize her, too, because it hurried to the back window. "*Mrr?*" It rubbed its head against her neck.

"Wow, this is your cat?" asked Josh. "Lucky day! Can you take it right now?"

"No, I can't." Danielle looked at him as if he were teasing her unkindly. "I can't have cats in my house. My son's allergic. Do you know how much Epi-pens cost?"

"Oh. That's too bad," said Josh. He meant it, and not just because he wanted to get rid of the cat. He'd really like to do something to make Danielle smile like that again.

Danielle sighed, scratching behind the cat's ears. "I thought Rune's crew was going to pick him up at the dump. You know what? You should take Panda to Fur-Ever, the cat shelter down the street." She stepped back from the car. "Have a good one."

Of course the cat shelter was full, according to Rune. But as Josh drove away from Cumby's, it occurred to him that he could drop the black and white cat off outside the shelter anyway. The cat people would figure something out.

However, before Josh reached Fur-Ever, he spotted Rune's car, a yellow VW, ahead of him, and it turned in at the cat shelter sign. Josh wasn't quite brave enough to leave the cat if Rune was watching. Josh thought indignantly that Rune had some gall, stopping at Fur-Ever when she was supposed to be at work. Never mind—later, Josh would just transfer the cat to Rune's car.

At Coastal Canine, a Lexus with an Irish setter in the passenger seat was already waiting. The driver rolled down her window and pushed up her sunglasses. "Thank god! The door's locked—I thought I was going to have to sit here forever." The young woman jumped out, pulling the dog after her by his leash. She wore a stylish suit and high-heeled shoes, and she had silky auburn hair, feathered at the ends, as if she and her dog had gone to the same hairdresser.

Josh had expected a few minutes to finish his coffee before starting work, and he glanced at his watch. "We're not actually open until 7:00."

"Oh, Erica wouldn't mind if I drop Aodh off a few minutes early." Handing him the leash, she patted the Irish setter's glossy back, swept a hand over her own glossy hair, and swung back into the car.

Josh looked at the leash handle, one of those damn retractable things. How did they work? While he was trying to remember, the Irish setter made a dash up the steps to the office, yanking the leash out to its full twenty feet. "Wait!" he told the dog.

Whirling, the setter galloped toward Josh. The slack in the leash whipped back into the handle, snapping against Josh's fingernail. "Oh shit!" The setter crouched with his feathery tail wagging, as if they were playing.

Now Josh remembered how to control the leash, but the nail of his ring finger (currently ringless) hurt like hell. He knocked on the office door with his other hand.

Unbolting the door for Josh, Uncle George looked at the setter and smiled knowingly. "Tricia got you to bring Murphy in early, huh?" He shook his head. "A piece of work, that girl. She thinks the rules are for everyone else, and Erica lets her get away with it."

"Well, in my humble opinion," said Josh, "it's a mistake to make a rule and then give in to rule-breaking." He'd never do that in a middle-school classroom.

The old man shrugged. "Erica's the boss."

"Uh-huh." Josh led Murphy to the back of the kennel and popped him into a cage to await the actual start of the Large Dogs play group. Then he paused in the staff room to run cold water on his throbbing ring finger.

By the time Josh returned to the office, Uncle George had the phone pressed to his leathery ear. "No insurance on the barn, huh? I guess it went up like tinder." The old man lifted a forefinger to Josh and then pointed to the front door.

A brawny brown dog leaped through the doorway, dragging Carol Harrison after him. "No, Tucker . . . Stop, I can't keep up!" She bumped against a rack of dog toys, dislodging a rubber Kong.

Hastening to take Tucker's leash, Josh also picked up the dog toy, while Carol massaged her shoulder. "I should work on my upper body strength," she said ruefully. "Say, Josh, is that your green Honda Civic parked by the fence? Did you know there's a cat in your car? Tucker barked at it, but your cat didn't twitch a whisker."

"Yeah, I know," said Josh. "But it's not my cat," he added quickly.

Uncle George had hung up the phone and was leaning back in his chair, smirking as if he'd thought of a good one. "A cat that rides in the car? Doesn't mind dogs? That must be a *dogged* cat! Heh-heh."

Ducking into the hall with Tucker, Josh wondered why the Harrisons, who weren't exactly spring chickens, had chosen such a large, muscular, willful young dog. Carol seemed genuinely fond of Tucker, but Josh would peg her as more of a King Charles spaniel person. Maybe Tucker had been chosen as a surrogate for Gardner's lost youthful vigor?

After Rune took her morning break, she reappeared in the exercise yard with an odd look on her face. "Josh! So you 'don't like cats'? Uncle George told me about the cat in your car—why didn't *you* tell me you already had a cat? He's a sweetie. And handsome, or he could be, if he weren't so skinny."

"Oh, the cat in my car?" Josh kicked himself mentally. He'd missed his chance to shift the cat to the yellow VW for Rune to find, without connecting it to Josh. "Wait, just a damn minute! Didn't you leave that cat for me? With that candle?"

Rune looked sincerely surprised. "I did leave you a candle yesterday," she said. "I thought it would help you mellow out." Then she stiffened. "You thought I'd— I would never, ever just dump a cat on someone's doorstep! How could you think that?"

Rune grew more and more indignant. Josh found himself not only apologizing, but thanking her profusely for the unwanted scented candle. "Anyway," he finished, "can't you squeeze the cat into a corner of Fur-Ever? It sure can't stay in my car."

"Him," said Rune. " 'Him,' not 'it.' If you'd noticed *he's* a neutered male, you wouldn't have thought he was Pansy."

"Yeah, silly me—I didn't inspect its—"

Rune interrupted, a beatific look coming over her face. "Josh, I'm the one who's silly for trying to get you to adopt Pansy. Obviously *this* is the cat meant for you!" Leaning toward him, she spoke in a soft, impressive voice. "I have such a strong intuition that he was guided to you by your black Lab who passed on. The cat was revealing that to you by sleeping on the towel in the backseat. That was where your dog used to lie, wasn't it?"

"That's . . . ridiculous," said Josh weakly. It was far beyond ridiculous. Yeah, Molly used to lie in the backseat, on that old towel. Still, obviously the cat wouldn't know, or care. Besides! Rune was way out of line, trying to play on his grief for Molly.

"Anyway," Rune was saying, "I thought he might be hungry, and I happened to have a bag of organic cat chow in my car, so I gave him some. Oh—I just thought of the perfect name for him! Uncle George said he must be a 'dogged' cat. So you could call him 'Ged.' For his psychic powers."

"Psychic powers, uh-huh," said Josh. The other day, Rune had informed him that it had been "proven again and again that animals are in touch with their psychic powers." He'd tried rational argument with her. "It might *seem* as if animals are psychic, but actually they're only paying attention to other information, since they don't understand what we're saying. It's like my mother: She doesn't hear that well, so she misses some of what I tell her, but she picks up on how I'm really feeling, even when I'm trying to hide it from her."

Rune had squinted as if *she* was straining to understand *him*. "But that's not like an animal, if your mother can't hear you. Cats and dogs can hear even better than we can."

Now Rune was looking at Josh as if he was slow on the uptake. "Like Ged, the Wizard of Earthsea, you know?"

Josh shrugged. "I never watched those Harry Potter movies."

Rune began to explain that Ged had nothing to do with Harry Potter. Josh broke in, "I'm not naming it, anyway. Because I'm not keeping it. Even if I wanted to have a cat—which I don't—it's in my rental agreement: *no pets.*" Before Rune could open her mouth again, he added, "Time for *my* break."

Before getting coffee from the staff room, Josh went out to check on the cat. Maybe it had left, in which case Josh's argument with Rune would have been a stupid waste of energy. Hope flared as Josh neared his car, where the black and white cat had disappeared from the back shelf.

He hurried forward to roll up the windows, in case the cat returned. Then he saw that it had merely moved from the back shelf to the car floor. It was pawing at the top of Molly's carton.

"Get out of there!" Josh leaned in to thump his fist against the backseat.

The cat gave him a *What's the big deal?* look, but it climbed out of the clutter and jumped onto the back shelf again.

Josh was not responsible for this cat. If it was still in his car after work, he'd make a stop at the Mattakiset Animal Shelter.

A man who carries a cat by the tail learns something he can learn in no other way.
Mark Twain

Chapter 12.

After the man parked the car beside a low building and left, the Cat settled down for a nap on the towel. Just as his inner eyelids closed, a parade of cars with dogs began in the half-circle driveway. The Cat returned to the back shelf, a safer place to watch from, in case he had to dive under a seat. But the dogs and their owners seemed intent on hurrying into the building.

To the Cat's surprise, he recognized one of the dogs: a large brown male with a black nose—yes, the dog he'd met at the place of trash, only this time he was with a woman. The dog dragged her over to the green car, gave the Cat a greeting bark, and pulled her away toward the door of the building.

The stream of cars and dogs dwindled off. Curling up on the towel again, the Cat wondered dreamily if there was a Great Dog—like the Great Cat, but of course a lesser deity—who arranged patrons for those creatures.

Sometime later the Cat was roused by a woman with long brown hair—the same woman who had placed the paper bag on the man's doorstep yesterday evening. The Cat had a sudden intuition: She must have left that bag as a shy offering for *him*! Why else would she now be stroking him, speaking in such a high, sweet tone of voice? And her eyes, he saw, were a cat-like green.

But then the Cat was confused. Sniffing the woman's hands, he identified the fresh smells of three other cats. Surely the Great Cat did not intend for him to share his patron. The woman left, and he did not try to follow her.

The Cat did appreciate the handful of kibbles she left on his towel, though. It was an unfamiliar kind of cat chow, with a grassy undertone beneath the dominant bird and rice flavors. As he crunched the food, he speculated that the Great Cat might have guided this woman to him simply to supply nourishment.

Late in the afternoon the long-haired woman reappeared, running after the man. "Josh? You weren't serious about the Mattakiset shelter! *They aren't a no-kill shelter*. If you could just foster Ged for a few days . . . I put a bag of organic cat chow in your trunk, so you don't have to buy food."

"Thanks, Rune, but I'm not going to need it," said the man, jingling his key ring. "As I told you, Barbara doesn't allow pets in her apartment, a.k.a. the place where I live and don't want to get thrown out of. Why don't *you* 'foster Ged for a few days'?"

"I can't! If I *could* have another cat, even for a few days, I would have taken Pansy. But I know my limits— I am not a hoarder, like Jordan Harrison, trying to tell me she could do foster care for Fur-Ever, and meanwhile she wasn't even spaying and neutering the cats she already had. If you ask me, that girl needs help."

"Okay, okay." The man called Josh held up a hand. "You can't take the cat—I can't take the cat."

Their voices, sharper with each exchange, made the Cat's ears twitch. He didn't like to be around quarreling humans. They were so big, and when they became upset, they forgot to be careful.

The woman called Rune leaned her back against the front door of the car, one hand on her crystal pendant. "I'm sure Barbara would understand, if you explained to her it was just for a few— Look, *I'll* call her."

"Excuse me," said Josh, reaching behind her to open the door. As he swung into the driver's seat he muttered, "I am so fed up with women telling me what to do." He backed the car away from the fence.

Rune shouted, "So, you're okay with Ged being *executed*?" The man's tires squealed as he pulled onto the road.

The Cat was relieved that the shouting had stopped. Watching the passing scenery from the backseat shelf, he noted that they were retracing this morning's route. But at the next corner, the car swung in a different direction. They passed a pond where ducks floated and a long-legged white bird waded, its neck tilted forward. The road climbed a hill. The car turned off the road into a paved parking lot.

Before the Cat could fully take in where he was, his ears flattened and his fur puffed out. He'd only glimpsed this building once before, but he remembered well its stench and racket. A horrified howl burst out of his throat: *Worlworl!*

The man Josh opened the back door of the car. The Cat shrank into a corner of the shelf, trying to contract himself into invisibility. As the man leaned into the backseat, the Cat gave a warning growl.

The man Josh drew back his hands. "Calm down—it's okay, kitty. Let's do this the easy way." Slowly he reached for the Cat again.

The Cat nipped at his fingers, and the man jerked them back, although the Cat had been careful not to break the man's skin.

"Oh, shit." The man seemed to get the message; he backed out and shut the door. The Cat watched him walk across the parking lot to the building.

After a short while the man Josh returned, accompanied by a younger man with greased hair and an earring. He gave the man Josh a disapproving look as he pulled on a pair of heavy gloves. "You know, you should never try to transport a cat loose in a car. They get freaked just from the motion of the vehicle."

"Well, this cat doesn't," said Josh. "It likes riding in the car."

"Yeah?" said the other man. "See how his ears and whiskers are pulled back, and he keeps licking his lips? When a cat does that, it means they're upset."

The man Josh answered, "Thanks; I know something about animal expressions. He's upset now, but he was fine until we pulled in here. He's been riding around with me all day, happy as a clam."

"I guess you know a lot about clam expressions, too." The younger man snickered to himself as he opened the car door. He put a knee on the back seat. "Here, dude."

Watching the leather gloves approach, the Cat hissed and growled and shrank back even farther. *O Great Cat!*

Just as the gloves closed around the Cat, a vision appeared outside. Eyes like yellow headlights shone on the back of the man Josh's head. Fangs the size of knives gripped his shoulder.

"Wait!" said the man Josh. "Wait. I . . . changed my mind."

Let sleeping dogs lie.
Proverb

Chapter 13.

Josh gripped the wheel as he drove out of the shelter parking lot onto Meeting House Road. Great, just great, he told himself. Then what do you plan on doing with this fucking cat?

In the rear view mirror Josh watched the cat lick its paws and run them over its black mask.

"I hope you're happy," said Josh. The cat met Josh's eyes briefly in the mirror, licked its white bib, and crouched down on the shelf again.

The trouble was, there was a room in the Mattakiset Animal Shelter where un-adopted cats and dogs were injected with lethal fluid. Josh had managed for a long time *not* to imagine such a scene, but now the assistant's leather gloves, the steel table, and the vet's medical green scrubs filled the screen in his mind.

Maybe if Josh had actually been present during Molly's last moments, he wouldn't be obsessed with them now. But he'd been out of town, leading the eighth-grade field trip to Washington, D.C. That was in May, when the new leaves on the trees around the Westham Middle School parking lot were as soft and floppy as a puppy's ears. The first morning, checking off each student on his clipboard list, Josh boarded the bus after them with a resigned resentment. God, how he loathed field trips.

Two days later, Josh stood outside the field trip bus under the portico of the Holiday Inn Express in

Alexandria, Virginia, breathing humid, exhaust-laden air. Setting his iced coffee on the edge of a planter, he once again checked off the names on his clipboard list.

Who was missing? Kaylee, and one of the parent chaperones, Sarah Rothman. Josh had learned to count the heads of the parents as well as the kids, because one year a father had overslept and almost got left behind at the motel. Parent chaperones were often more trouble than they were worth, in Josh's opinion; their children hated having them along on the trip, and the other kids didn't necessarily accept their authority.

It would be so wonderful, thought Josh, to climb onto this bus and sink into his seat. From the moment they'd boarded the bus to head for D.C., he'd been on edge. Josh knew how to handle twenty-some kids as long as they were in a classroom, but he'd spent the field trip to Washington feeling totally responsible for all the disasters that could happen—and at the same time, helpless to prevent them.

On a three-day field trip, the eighth graders' obsession with social relationships popped to the fore. In various ways. For instance, on the bus ride south, Siobhan kept dropping her stretch-jeaned rear end into a boy's lap, then bouncing up in pretended surprise. What if she got pregnant on this trip?

Sarah Rothman had finally ordered Siobhan to sit next to her, in the window seat. Siobhan merely flicked her blue-streaked hair over her shoulder as she changed seats, but Sarah's daughter Margaret, watching from across the aisle, rolled her eyes and turned away with a hopeless expression.

Then there was the son of the second chaperone, Amanda Gill. Curtis Gill had proved that he could be cool, in spite of his mother's presence, by bringing along a box-cutter. Fortunately, Josh caught him showing it off to another boy and made him hand it over.

But Josh thought about the box-cutter the next day, as his group waited for their docent in a domed hall of the National Gallery. Herding them into the space behind a pillar, Josh put on his sternest face. He reminded them, in a low, intense voice, how privileged they were to visit the nation's capital, how respectful they should be of the national treasures they were about to view, and what dire consequences would result if any of them damaged said treasures.

"Any student who breaks the rules that *you all agreed to* will be immediately sent home with a chaperone. Is that clear?" Josh glowered around the group.

Who was listening? Maybe half the group. With some kids, it was hard to tell—Margaret Rothman, for instance, was gazing at her reflection in the polished stone floor. The chaperones, Sarah Rothman and Amanda Gill, *were* paying attention to Josh, and they looked alarmed. Perhaps more about having to escort a student home, than about national treasures being mutilated.

As the docent led the group into the American Art tour, Josh noticed that Kaylee was trailing behind. She seemed different this morning—yesterday afternoon, at the Washington Monument, she'd been almost peppy.

Josh, at the end of the line behind Kaylee, had called to the group, "Onward and upward!"

Climbing the first step, Kaylee had turned to Josh with a little smile and said, almost audibly, "Only 896 more steps to go."

"Right!" said Josh. His cell phone buzzed. He pulled it out of his pocket, saw that Tanya was calling—probably about whether he'd paid a disputed bill, which he refused to do—and dropped the phone back in his pocket. He called up the stairwell to his group, "Only 896 more steps!"

But this morning, at the National Gallery, Kaylee seemed to be trying to avoid finding out whether anyone wanted to walk with her. "Pick up the pace, Kaylee," said Josh. "We don't want to lose anyone." Kaylee brushed her hair aside, showing a glimpse of her unhappy face. Josh almost asked her what the matter was, but he didn't have time.

The docent finished explaining about the French and Indian War, and the eighth graders of Westham Middle School ambled from the hall of battle scenes into a portrait gallery: men wearing knee breeches and powdered wigs, ladies in corseted silk. Josh's trouble-sensing antennae went up as a cluster of girls, led by Margaret Rothman, headed for the bench in the middle of the room. They sat down with much pushing and indignant squeals, although there was room for one or two more. Then as Kaylee trudged toward them, the other girls spread out to fill the space.

Josh recognized one of those moments of middle-school aggression that *could* be only friendly teasing, but wasn't. Kaylee paused for an instant, looking at the girls' feet, then turned and plodded past Josh, toward a chair against the wall. It was a lyre-backed side chair of polished wood, with an embroidered design on the seat cover.

Poor Kaylee. She seemed really tired for some reason. Josh thought she'd realize, as she came closer to the chair, that it was an item on exhibit, not public seating.

But Kaylee was right in front of the chair, and she wasn't hesitating. She turned and sank down heavily on the fancy needlework.

Immediately a whistle shrilled. "Look what she's doing!" exclaimed Margaret. A uniformed gallery guard bore down on Kaylee, who stared at him blankly.

Josh sprinted across the room. "So sorry; she's in my group," he told the grim-faced guard. "Kaylee, what were you thinking, sitting on a museum piece? What did I just tell you guys?"

"I'm afraid you'll have to leave," said the guard.

"I'm sorry, I'm sorry." Kaylee crept out of the chair, shrinking away from the guard. "I just wanted to sit down."

She looked so miserable. Josh wished he hadn't snapped at her. Putting an arm around her, he patted her head as if she were a dog. A sob shook her hunched shoulders. "Hey, it's not so bad, Kaylee. It's all right."

Sarah Rothman appeared at Kaylee's side, pulling the girl away from Josh. "Come on, Kaylee. We'll go wait in the café."

“Good idea,” said Josh with a nod. But why was Sarah giving him that cold look? Maybe she felt, as Josh did himself, that he’d been too hard on Kaylee.

Josh turned to scowl at the girls on the bench. Margaret Rothman whispered loudly to Siobhan, “That’s Kaylee—always on the *spot*!”

The girl next to her added in a faux-British accent, “You might say she was *spot* on!”

Josh didn’t know what they were talking about—pimples? and he didn’t really care. “I don’t appreciate *your* part in this scene,” he told the girls.

Siobhan gazed wide-eyed at Josh as she stifled a giggle with her hand. “What? We were going to let her sit down here.” She nudged Margaret, opening up a space on the bench.

Josh continued to glare at them for another moment before he turned away. You can get through this, he promised himself. The rest of today, one more night, then back on the bus.

On the final morning, Josh could have worried that the bus would have an accident on the way home, and all the kids would be killed or crippled for life. But he was too tired to work up any more worry. The eighth graders were worn out, too. The same kids who’d bounced around screaming during the ride south climbed into the bus almost meekly, plopped into their seats, and began texting on their phones. After two sleepless nights, everyone, including Josh, would soon be snoozing.

At last, here came Sarah Rothman and Kaylee. Sarah had a hand on the girl's shoulder and was talking quietly to her as they walked a few feet, paused, and then walked another few feet. Josh couldn't see Kaylee's expression—her hair hung over her face as usual—but Sarah looked grave.

Josh decided not to chide them for holding up the group. "Kaylee, check," he called, making a mark on his clipboard. "Ms. Rothman, check. We're good to go."

Kaylee skirted Josh, not meeting his eyes as she climbed into the bus. Sarah said, "Mr. Hiller, can we talk a minute?"

"Sure," said Josh, "but let's talk on the bus. We're a little behind schedule."

"No, let's talk over here." She motioned him away from the bus with her head. "It's about what happened yesterday."

Josh signaled the bus driver to wait a minute, and also to close the doors to prevent any kids from getting off. Then he followed Sarah into the shade of the portico.

Sarah took a deep breath. "I just thought I should let you know that I'm going to mention your inappropriate action in my report."

"My— What!" Josh almost choked.

Sarah looked aside. "I just found it very disturbing that you would put Kaylee in that position, when the poor girl is so shy, and she was suffering from cramps, and apparently Siobhan was teasing her—"

Cramps, so that was why Kaylee had been dragging herself around. "Oh shit," muttered Josh.

Immediately he added, "Excuse me. But I don't see how I—"

"Fortunately I had some Advil in my purse to give her, so I think she felt better after lunch. But then last night, Margaret told me, the girls started teasing her about her crush on you, telling her she should send you some *pictures . . .*"

As Josh fumbled for words, a beep from the bus driver made them both jump. "All right," said Josh, "we'd better—" He turned toward the bus, then turned back to Sarah. "This is a really unfortunate misunderstanding. I'll sit with Kaylee and straighten it out with her, at least."

"I'm going to sit with her," said Sarah, pushing ahead of him.

Under the circumstances, Josh realized immediately, it was probably better for him *not* to sit with Kaylee in front of the whole gossiping group. But he couldn't let Sarah Rothman get away with her outrageous assumptions, her righteousness. "I hope you also find it 'disturbing' that Margaret, *your daughter*, is the ringleader of the Mean Girls."

Sarah didn't answer, but her back stiffened, and she climbed into the bus with forceful steps.

As the bus pulled away from the Holiday Inn Express, Josh felt ill. His mouth was dry, and his head was beginning to throb. He became aware of the empty cup holder on his arm rest. He'd left his fucking iced coffee on the planter outside the motel.

What Josh needed even more than coffee was his dog Molly beside him, slumped against his shoulder, the way she did when they watched TV on the sofa. He remembered Molly as he'd last seen her, wagging her arthritic tail in the kitchen. After Molly's surgery last fall for cancer of the mouth, the stitches had pulled her lip into a lopsided smile.

"It isn't fair, is it?" Josh had asked Molly that morning. The one leading the group to D.C. this year should have been the other social studies teacher. That would have been fair, since Josh had led the year before.

Molly had gazed up at Josh, seeming to agree, with her cynical expression, that Principal Charlene Voss was not interested in fairness. Voss was interested in punishing Josh for his persistent wisecracks during faculty meetings. For his confidence that he didn't need her guidance in order to do his job well.

Voss. Oh shit. The bus jolted over a rough patch in the road, and Josh hunched his shoulders. The principal would gleefully seize on Sarah Rothman's version of what happened to Kaylee.

Josh wanted badly to talk to someone, but not anyone on this bus. He took out his phone and checked the messages. Tanya's just said "Please call me back." He hadn't, because they'd had another fight before he left, and he needed to concentrate all his energy on getting through the field trip.

But now that the field trip was essentially over, Josh wished that he could call Tanya and *talk*, the way they used to. She used to give him pep talks, whenever he felt discouraged about teaching. She'd act the part of his defense attorney. *They should be grateful to have a dedicated teacher like you. You really know history, you really connect with the kids. They should pay you twice as much.*

Maybe Josh could have that kind of support now, if he called Tanya back and started out by apologizing for their fight two days ago. Josh *was* sorry, and no need to add that Tanya was 75 percent to blame. He pulled out his phone.

Tanya picked up right away. "I've been trying to get hold of you! Why didn't you call back?"

Josh was startled at her tone. "I've been straight out on this field trip," he said. "Have a little imagination." He waited for a retort, or maybe—just maybe—some sympathy. There was silence.

Josh tried to lighten up. "Listen, is Molly there? Would you put her on?" More silence. "It's just that I'd appreciate a sympathetic ear. A black, floppy ear."

"Molly's— She's gone," blurted Tanya.

For a moment Josh thought that Tanya was playing the game he'd started. Only she should have said something like, "I'm afraid Molly is away from her desk for the moment."

"Molly was twelve years old," Tanya had shifted into the remote tone she used to talk about unpleasant things.

Was. The word felt like a straight-arm in Josh's chest.

"The poor dog was suffering. I asked you to do something about it before you left."

"*What did you do*?" Josh was aware of heads turning toward him on the bus, but he couldn't lower his tone. "You . . . put Molly down?"

"I tried to call you," said Tanya. "You didn't pick up, and you didn't call back. Finally . . . frankly, I thought it might be easier for you if I made the decision."

"You thought . . . you thought . . ." Josh started to say, *Well, don't do me any more favors.* But that was too mild.

"Josh!" Tanya dropped the objective tone. "You should have seen her. The cancer must have gotten to her brain. She couldn't even find the back door in the morning." Her voice trembled. "I had to lead her out into the backyard. Even then, she didn't pee right away. She just wandered across the lawn, totally out of it, until her nose touched the back fence." When Josh didn't say anything, she added, "I tried to call you from the vet's."

Tanya was upset about putting *his* dog down. The idea made Josh even angrier than her detached tone of a moment ago. "I guess it's a good thing we didn't have kids. It would have been really tough for you to put one down if they didn't turn out right."

Tanya was silent for a moment, and then she said, "Yes. It is a good thing we didn't have kids. Because then you would have had to grow up."

"So, maybe you should find a Big Daddy to have children with before it's too late."

"Good idea." Tanya ended the call.

The bus paused at a red light, and Josh slumped back. He stared out the window at green highway signs. The light changed, and the bus lumbered onto the ramp.

"Mr. Hiller?"

Josh was shivering. Maybe the bus's AC was turned up too high; maybe it was just him, because his head was throbbing. Maybe it was caffeine withdrawal. He folded his arms for warmth.

"Dude. Mr. Hiller, you okay?" Curtis Gill was leaning out of the seat opposite Josh's, a licorice whip hanging from one corner of his mouth.

Josh forced a smile. "Yes. I'm fine. Thanks for asking, Curtis." Glancing up at the driver's rear view mirror, he realized that everyone on the bus was watching him. Maybe Amanda Gill or Sarah Rothman would describe his outburst to Principal Voss.

Remembering that moment on the bus, what struck Josh now was Curtis's kind concern. One clueless thirteen-year-old kid, at least, had offered him sympathy. As Josh drove away from the animal shelter, grief flooded him. It was as physical as an attack of nausea. His eyes streamed, and sobs rippled up through his throat.

Pulling to the side of the road, Josh leaned against the steering wheel. Molly's chew marks in the plastic were rough against his forehead. He bawled.

Josh was beginning to wonder if he could stop crying, now that he'd started, when he heard a car engine approaching. His sobs trailed off abruptly. Pull yourself together, Hiller. If someone in the other car saw a man slumped over the steering wheel, they were likely to stop and see if he was in cardiac arrest.

Josh pushed himself upright, grabbed a Cumby's napkin from the floor, and blew his nose. Glancing over his shoulder, he noticed the black and white cat gazing at him. Its yellow eyes met his eyes, and then the cat looked down, as if to allow him privacy for his emotional outburst.

Josh let out a long, ragged sigh. "All right," he said aloud, putting the car back in gear. He would make a serious effort to return this cat to its owners. Barbara wouldn't even have to know about the cat, if it slept in the car as it had last night, and Josh found it a home tomorrow.

It was the black kitten's fault entirely.
Lewis Carroll, *Alice Through the Looking-Glass*

Chapter 14.

"**J**osh, I *told* Jennifer very clearly, I cannot make any exceptions. No pets." The woman of the large white house had been hanging up laundry when the man Josh drove between the stone posts. She marched across the lawn still holding a pair of damp underpants.

The Cat, watching from the car window, thought she had the posture of a mother cat about to cuff a naughty kitten. The woman's shaggy dog, on the other hand, ambled over and greeted the Cat with a play-bow. Maybe the Cat would play with the dog. Maybe he wouldn't.

"I know, I know." The man sounded tired, perhaps from his recent convulsions. "No pets. This cat isn't my pet. I'm just keeping it—"

"Jennifer admitted you've been feeding it," said the woman. "That's always a mistake. You know, I'd rather you'd approached me about this directly, instead of—"

"Just a minute," said the man Josh. "Who's 'Jennifer'?"

The woman frowned. "Jennifer Borden, of course, your colleague at the kennel." Then she gave a little laugh. "Oh—I suppose she's gotten you to call her 'Rune.' She likes to think she's some kind of psychic. She said you were 'at a vulnerable point in your journey' and needed 'animal companionship'."

"Rune was way out of line," said the man. He pushed himself wearily out of the car. "Anyway,

Barbara, I wasn't going to bring the cat into the house. If it could just stay in my *car* overnight . . ."

The woman Barbara pressed her lips together. "I don't want to be hard-hearted, but this is Lola's home (and my home, of course), and she won't tolerate—"

All right, the Cat decided, he would play with the dog. He reached a paw out to bat at the dog's plumy tail. The dog whirled, barking joyfully.

"Lola! Come here." The dog's ear flicked back at her person, but she didn't obey. The Cat jumped down, let the dog chase him to the mulberry tree, and leaped onto a low branch.

The woman turned on the man. "I don't know why I should have to argue. You signed my lease, didn't you? The lease says NO PETS."

"I know, I get it," said the man. "But it's not my cat—I'm just— I've had a really hard day. If you could just—"

"If you won't remove the cat, that would be a violation of your lease."

"You mean, you're going to throw me out just for having a cat in my car overnight?" The man's voice was louder.

The woman raised her voice, too. "I mean, if you insist on violating the terms of the lease . . ." She took a deep breath. "Well, then I have no choice but to have to ask you to vacate the apartment."

The Cat leaned from the branch to bat at the dog's tail again, but now the dog was distracted by the bickering humans. Trotting over to the woman, the dog nudged her hand. The Cat was a little uneasy about the humans, too. If they were cats, their tails would be puffed out.

"So that's the way it is," said the man. "Okay. Thanks a lot for your understanding. I am *vacating*." He headed for the apartment stairs. Barbara headed for the Cat, who jumped out of the tree and scampered back to the safety of the car.

In a few minutes the man Josh reappeared with a stack of cartons. Watching him, the woman gave a deep sigh. "You know, Josh, it's too bad for us to quarrel. . . . I've had a hard day myself. I thought I had just enough cash to pay for having the septic tank pumped, and now they're telling me the system won't pass Title V—I have to put in a new tank and leaching field, to the tune of twenty thousand dollars."

The man didn't look at her. As he shoved cartons into the car, the Cat crept up onto the back shelf.

The man Josh carried another load of his belongings down from the apartment, and then another, working so fast that he panted as he lugged out the third load. Cramming it all in his car, he swung back into the front seat and started the engine.

I am not a cat man, but a dog man, and all felines can tell this at a glance—a sharp, vindictive glance.
James Thurber

Chapter 15.

"Barbara's a pain in the ass," Josh muttered to the backseat as he turned off Old Farm Road at the Camp Seaside sign. No one could blame him for being fed up. And since Barbara seemed to view him as such an undesirable tenant, she should be grateful to get rid of him. Getting rid of the cat, now, might not be so easy—good luck to her!

The car swerved, and Josh gripped the wheel. Whoa, Rick hadn't been kidding about breaking his axle on the ruts. And overgrown bushes scraped the sides of the car as he jolted down the lane. He was beginning to regret his hasty decision when a cottage came into view through a stand of pines. Rick's pickup truck was parked outside, and yes, there was a satellite dish. Josh stopped in a bare space among the weeds.

The cottage rested on concrete blocks, as Barbara had described, and mosquitos floated through the open car windows, whining eagerly. One sank its tiny needle into his left earlobe. Mosquitos, Josh told himself as he slapped, were nothing as annoying as Barbara's little observations and admonitions.

As Josh pulled his backpack out of the car, there was a burst of yipping from the cottage. A small brown and white dog bumped the screen door open, dashed down the splintery steps, and raced around Josh, still barking.

"Pepper, shut up!" called Rick from the doorway. The dog swallowed its last yip and sat down. To Josh, Rick said, "Hey, don't just stand there, slapping bugs—come on in."

Josh stepped into a living room with two lumpy armchairs and a TV. "Barbara finally got to me," he confessed. "You still looking for a roommate?"

Rick grinned. "Welcome to your new home, sweet home." He and Pepper led Josh on a tour over floors gritty with sand. Beyond the living room: "Kitchen. Mud room, with world's oldest washer and dryer." In the back of the house: "My room." An open sleeping bag on a mattress, and a dirty window. "And your room." Exactly like Rick's room, only without the sleeping bag.

As Josh dropped his backpack on the mattress, Pepper rushed back to the living room, yipping urgently again. "Someone else looking for a room?" suggested Josh.

"Maybe we should have a bidding war," said Rick, following his dog. "Oh shit. It's a cat."

Over Rick's shoulder, Josh caught sight of the cat's black mask and ears, and its front paws stretched up on the outside of the screen door. "How the hell—" It was the same cat he thought he'd left behind at Barbara's. It plucked the screen like a harpist, accompanying the *pings* with meows.

"Get outta there!" The cat dropped off the screen as Rick opened the door for Pepper. "Run 'em off, girl."

Pepper launched herself at the black and white cat. Instead of fleeing, the cat made what looked like a casual swipe with its paw. The dog shrank back, whimpering and rubbing her snout. Josh laughed.

Rick turned on him. “What’s so funny?” Without waiting for an answer, he went on, “Is that *your* fucking cat?”

“Not really,” said Josh. “It just showed up in—”

“Who said you could bring a cat? Look what it did to Pepper!” Rick scooped up his dog, bending over the red line on her white muzzle. “Poor little Peps, little sweetie-pie, *sh-sh-sh.*”

“That doesn’t look too serious,” said Josh. The cat sat calmly on the doorstep, as if waiting for the dog and humans to stop fussing and let him in.

Rick carried Pepper back in the cottage, aiming a harmless kick at the black and white cat. He dropped into one of the lumpy armchairs in front of the TV and took a gulp of beer from the can on the floor, cuddling the terrier with his other hand.

Stepping back inside, Josh started to say “Sorry,” then changed his mind. Rick was making a big fuss about a simple communication between a cat and a dog. The dog had tried to intimidate the cat; the cat had put the dog in its place; and now the two animals had an understanding.

“You wanna make a takeout run?” growled Rick, aiming the remote at the TV. “I could go for fish and chips. Extra tartar.”

“Okay.” Josh shrugged and fetched his wallet from his backpack. The black and white cat followed him out to his car, jumped in, and squeezed over the cartons and bags to the back shelf. No wonder Josh hadn’t noticed the cat in the car when he left Barbara's—in the rear view mirror, it was completely hidden by his stuff.

Half an hour later, when Josh returned from Ahab's Clam Shack, the black and white cat squirmed over the crowded back seat to exit the car along with Josh. Josh made only a halfhearted effort to beat the cat to Rick's door, and the cat slipped into the cottage ahead of him, disregarding a barrage of yaps from the living room.

The terrier jumped out of Rick's armchair, made a wide circle around the cat to sniff Josh's sneakers, and jumped back beside Rick. "What the fuck?" said Rick, glaring from the cat to Josh.

"Pepper doesn't seem to see a problem," said Josh. "The cat doesn't seem to see a problem." Setting the fish and chips bag on the second armchair, he pulled out the box labeled "X TAR" and handed it to Rick. "I don't see a problem, either."

Looking unhappy, Rick let his dog nibble a French fry. "If you'd told me you had a fucking cat . . ."

"If you're going to pull the No Pets clause on me," said Josh through a mouthful of batter-coated fish, "I might as well go back to Barbara's."

Rick sat glaring at the TV, where the Red Sox announcers were chatting, pre-game. "The minute it starts spraying inside," he muttered at the screen, "you both go."

Josh went to the kitchen to help himself to a beer, feeling that he'd stood up for his rights today. Nobody—not Barbara, not Rick—was going to tell him what to do. Wasn't standing up for your rights an item on Ron

Watanabe's famous anti-depression List? It had lifted Josh's spirits a good 32 percent.

The black and white cat ducked under his arm, meowing pointedly at the open refrigerator. Josh considered feeding it from an open can of dog food, but that seemed like it might be pushing Rick too far. And that bag of Rune's donated cat chow was in his trunk.

Barbara had called feeding the cat a mistake. But actually, Josh argued to himself as he fetched the cat chow, poured a bowlful, and set the cat's dinner on the floor, it was only part of a major good deed (high on the List), since Josh was going to place the cat in someone else's loving home. Tomorrow he would put up Found Cat posters around town.

Settling into his armchair with the takeout box on his lap, Josh dug in. By now Rick was cleaning up his last stray fries, and he seemed pacified. As he muted an advertisement, he told Josh, "You gotta see this trick of Pepper's." The dog sat up, her brown ears cocked, her eyes on Rick. "Watch this: Pepper, fetch cigs." The dog jumped from the chair, trotted into Rick's bedroom, and reappeared with a pack of cigarettes in her jaws. Rick took the pack from Pepper, fed her a last crumb of batter, and grinned at Josh as he lit up.

"That's a nice trick," Josh admitted. "But—you smoke in the house?"

Shrugging, Rick blew out a stream of smoke. "You have a problem with that?"

Josh decided not to have a problem. The facts were that a) Josh had known, before he moved in, that Rick smoked; b) Josh had not negotiated the house rules with

Rick, and c) Josh had already used his political capital to let the black and white cat stay. Josh sighed and sipped his beer. There was a smoke alarm on the wall opposite Rick, he noticed. He wondered if Rick ever set it off. Maybe not in the summer, with all the windows open.

The mattress in the cottage's second bedroom was more comfortable than it looked, and Josh quickly put himself to sleep, reading chapter 2 of *Small Business for Dummies*. He slept well except that when he shifted position, the bedframe wobbled on a short leg. The *Dummies* book was just the right thickness to prop it up, until he could find something better.

In the morning, it seemed clear that the black and white cat had not sprayed piss inside the cottage, apparently satisfied that it had dominated the dog. Josh fed the cat again, with the sense that he was banking a respectable number of good deeds.

On his route to Cumby's and then Coastal Canine, Josh reflected with satisfaction that he had achieved important closure yesterday. Yes, after the triple catharsis of grieving for his dog, his marriage, and his teaching career, Josh was now ready to move on. "I mean, really moving on," he explained to the back seat.

For one thing, Josh already had a plan to upgrade his relationship with his mother. He would take action to improve her life, instead of just showing up and suffering through a visit. He'd spirit her away from the Commons for a really nice lunch. He'd order her a glass of sauvignon blanc; they'd celebrate his late-onset maturity.

Glancing in the rear view mirror, Josh noticed the cat crawling through boxes and bundles onto the back shelf, which was now visible, since Josh had brought his bag of sheets and towels into the cottage. Hmm. He hadn't planned to take the cat to work again, but maybe it would be handy to have it in the car, in case he got a quick response to his Found Cat posters.

At the kennel, Josh took a picture of the cat on the back shelf. Then he sought out Erica in the grooming room, shampooing a cocker-poo. She gave Josh permission to print a FOUND CAT poster and tack it on the Coastal Canine bulletin board, but the frown line between her eyebrows deepened. "Just so you don't bring the cat into the kennel, even in a carrier. Some of our dogs would go berserk."

"Like Murphy, for instance?" asked Josh, thinking of the Irish setter.

" 'Murphy.' Did Uncle George tell you to call him that?" Erica paused in the middle of rinsing the little dog to look directly at Josh. "The Irish setter's name is Aodh. And Tricia, the owner, is very touchy about it. She says it means "fire" in Gaelic."

"Okay," said Josh, "but a name pronounced "ay-ee" isn't practical for a dog. It's all vowels." Erica continued to stare at him, so he shrugged in compliance, sort of. Turning toward the door, he muttered under his breath, "Dogs need to hear some consonants."

"Josh," Erica called after him. "By the way, I got a lot of interest from my email blast about a Beginning Obedience class. How about starting on Friday?"

They agreed on the day and time for the class, and Erica gave Josh a set of obedience lesson plans to look over. Obedience class would be fun and easy, thought Josh as he returned to his duties. Dogs might not be as smart as eighth graders, but they were a whole lot more eager to do what you wanted them to. "Right, Tucker?" Josh made the gesture for "Sit," and Tucker sank into a sit, looking pleased with himself.

Back in the exercise pens, Josh dragged the wading pool out of the shed. As he began filling it for the Large Dogs, Tucker tried to drink from the hose. Josh noticed movement at the gate out of the corner of his eye, and he turned to see Rune bearing down on him, looking as dangerous as the Queen of Swords in her Tarot pack.

"I did not leave the cat at the shelter, if that's what you're thinking," said Josh. "Didn't you see it in my car? Or see my poster in the office?"

The Queen of Swords turned into the benevolent Tarot Empress. "Oh. That's cool." Rune side-stepped the spray as Tucker and Buster leaped in and out of the pool, splashing and shaking.

For lunch, Josh ate a ready-made turkey sandwich from Soule's Market while he drove to the Mattakiset library. Rick's cabin didn't have an internet connection, any more than Barbara did, and the kennel's Wi-Fi was not for employees. So Josh would use his lunch hour to put up another Found Cat poster and check his email. "We're killing two birds with one stone," he remarked to the backseat. He wasn't talking to the cat, but he saw it blink its yellow eyes, as if uninterested in figurative birds.

An impatient Lexus passed Josh on the two-lane road, causing him to brake and drop a shred of mustard-soaked lettuce from his sandwich onto the front of his blue T-shirt. "Thanks, Tricia," said Josh, recognizing the driver.

Just inside the library, a brass plaque above the bulletin board stated that the building had been a generous gift from Gardner Harrison to the town in 1908. Nineteen-oh-eight? Tucker's owner was old and pompous, but not nearly *that* old. His family must have been big players in this town for generations.

The clerk behind the circulation counter gave Josh four push-pins for his notice and nodded back toward the bulletin board in the vestibule. "Just don't cover up anything that's still current," she instructed. "Especially of people looking for work."

"I'm not out of work," said Josh, suddenly aware of her eyes on his mustard-stained T-shirt. "I'm just putting up a 'found cat' notice."

"No, of course not," said the clerk soothingly, as if she was used to dealing with touchy unemployed people. "Yes, of course." She began busily scanning a pile of returned books.

Annoyed with himself for being defensive, Josh looked over the postings on the board. They were all sort of current. Josh started to pin "FOUND: Black and white neutered male" (he trusted Rune about the gender) over a notice with a decorative Celtic pattern. "Tarot readings. Gifted sensitive, 20 years' experience." Then he realized that the decorative Celtic pattern actually spelled out "Ask for Rune." He decided instead to cover up a "Tea 'n' Scrapbooking" event at the Tufted Duck Gift Shop.

It occurred to Josh that he could put a Found Cat announcement on Craig's List, too. He'd better do it now, while he had the Internet connection. Heading back into the library, past the newspaper racks, he noticed the *Mattakiset Mariner.* It wouldn't hurt to check their classifieds for lost cats, either.

As Josh perched on the corner of a table with the local paper, a headline caught his eye: **Selectmen Veto Wind Turbine Study**. "Board of Selectmen chair Gardner Harrison . . ."

A town governed by selectmen, with the direct democracy of a town meeting. Wouldn't that make a good unit for the Colonial era segment of Josh's American History class? New England
kids, especially, ought to know that there was a time when the town fathers (sorry, no town mothers then) ruled on public use of the herring run, and granted licenses for ferries—for instance, across the Mattakiset River, where the bridges stood now.

Maybe Josh could take a class on a field trip to study local government. Or—Josh's lips twitched in amusement—maybe not. He himself had attended a few school committee meetings in Westham, monitoring for the teachers' union, and he'd been bored out of his mind. Why did the committee members have to speak exclusively in stale figures of speech? They spent most of the meeting time cautioning each other not to "compare apples with oranges," "reinvent the wheel," or "put the cart before the horse."

Josh shook himself. Talk about putting the cart before the horse! He was planning a unit for a class he didn't have. For a career he'd left behind. Raising his head, Josh looked across the room at the library's row of public computers. The heads bent over keyboards were all men—were they all out of work?

Turning to the back pages of the *Mariner,* Josh scanned the classifieds. There were a couple of "Lost Cats," but no black and white ones.

His eyes wandered over to "Jobs." Some jobs in education, but for positions like "preschool teacher" or "part-time cheer coach." One ad for a "floating teacher," whatever that might mean. Josh was not a floating teacher. He was going to launch his own business, or maybe buy a going concern.

"Business Opportunities." Several restaurants for sale. Everyone knew *that* was risky business.

"Owner of established, thriving pet services seeks investor/partner." Wait, the phone number was . . . Josh checked his phone contacts. It was the phone number for Coastal Canine. Well, well.

One thing at a time. Josh returned the newspaper to the rack, pulled out his phone, and brought up Craig's List. He posted his Found Cat notice, then checked his email. A couple of weeks ago he'd sent a message to Ron Watanabe, his old friend in California. Ron was teaching in a middle school, too, and Josh had thought he might be sympathetic to—or at least tolerant of—a self-pitying rant from a colleague.

There was no reply from Ron. Aside from the usual spam, there was a message from Josh's college class president, urging him to come to their twentieth reunion. *Right. I'll hang a nametag with my senior year picture around my neck and regale my classmates with tales of my failed marriage.* Although maybe he'd feel different about the reunion, if his new business was underway.

There was also another terse note from Tanya. Her last message had requested the return of the nineteenth-century Seth Thomas clock. "You must have accidentally put it in the truck when you moved out," she'd written. "Remember, your father gave it to me as a birthday present."

Josh did remember how fond the old man had been of Tanya, but he was sure his father hadn't meant for the antique clock to leave the family. Josh had written back, with what he thought was exquisite self-control, "The clock's in the middle of my storage unit. I'll deal with it when I get a new place."

So, what now, Tanya? Josh's stomach tightened as he scrolled down to her name. This time, she was asking if he wanted to come get the dog bed. Otherwise, she was going to put it out at the curb.

The dog bed! Actually, the way Tanya felt about it, Josh was surprised that she hadn't stuffed the dog bed into his U-Haul truck with her own hands. But Josh could have sworn he'd put it in the truck himself. He must have been in a worse state than he'd realized.

Of course he didn't want Tanya to throw out Molly's dog bed. It was a high-end Orvis model, with a puffy rim, a separate central cushion, and washable covers. It wasn't even that used, since he'd bought the bed for Molly's late middle age, when her Labrador retriever joints had started to bother her.

Tanya's email also seemed like an unsympathetic way of saying, What are your plans? Where will you live? What will you do?

Poor Tanya, Josh told himself. She obviously hadn't achieved closure, and was having a hard time moving on to the next phase of her life. He needed to be patient with her.

After sending Tanya a message listing the days and times when he could pick up the dog bed, Josh turned to his Sent mail to review his unanswered message to Ron. It was even more of a self-pitying rant than he remembered. He started a new message:

Hey Ron, delete my last email from your files and your brain. I was in the grip of a narcissistic and paranoid state. Didn't Winston Churchill say, "Never attribute to malice what can be explained by incompetence"? Btw, how are you, buddy? I seem to remember that Diana was pregnant. Hope everything's OK. . . .

Dogs who learn to soil their dens can be extremely difficult... to housetrain.

Pat B. Miller, *Positive Perspectives: Love Your Dog, Train Your Dog*

Chapter 16.

During his first week at Rick's cottage, Josh began riding the bike Vicky had given him. He'd hardly used it while he was staying at Barbara's, in spite of Vicky's suggestion that he should ride it to the beach, improving his fitness at the same time that he healed his psyche. In fact, this suggestion/instruction was so annoying that Josh had driven his car to the beach instead, and left the bike out in the rain.

But now, to prove that he'd achieved closure and moved on to a better stage of life, Josh decided to oil his bike and ride it to work. Pedaling past a field on Old Farm Road that first morning, breathing in the fragrance of new-mown hay, he felt justly rewarded. At the end of the day, he felt tired but virtuous.

The second day it rained. Obviously he couldn't be expected to bike in the rain.

The third day he rode the bike again, but he was beginning to think he didn't need to be so rigid about doing this all the time. Today the air was heavy, even early in the morning—and he had to leave the cottage earlier than usual if he biked. Probably it wasn't healthy to bike in humid weather. Also, feeling every rock and rut in the lane through bicycle tires made the ride seem twice as long.

Furthermore, after his stop at Cumby's, Josh had coffee to hold while balancing on the bike. Back when he was in graduate school, he'd done that trick easily. Maybe with practice, the knack would come back to him.

As Josh pedaled past the dairy farm, slopping coffee, the phone in his shorts pocket sounded its generic ring. He kept meaning to replace it with something distinctive, like the opening bars of "Ring of Fire."

Josh swerved onto the shoulder, set the cup on a fence post, and dug his phone out. It was his sister again—why, at this time of day? He felt a flicker of worry about their mother. He should have called Vicky back before now. "Hey, Vic."

"Finally!" said his sister. "I'm sorry if I woke you up, but not too sorry, because you didn't return my calls." She spoke against a background of rattling and talking—she must be on a commuter train.

"I'm sorry," said Josh, gazing over the pasture, where cows ambled and a wind turbine spun. "The trouble is, I can't get a signal where I'm staying. And I'm not supposed to make personal calls at work."

"Never mind," said Vicky. "How's your rental working out? Melissa said she had to hunt to find a place for you."

"Yeah, I *really* appreciated that," said Josh, trying for a sincere tone. Should he tell Vicky he'd left Barbara's, and why? Vicky would probably think his landlady's bossy rules were perfectly reasonable. Or no;

Vicky would take Josh's side, but instruct Josh on how he should deal with Barbara.

While Josh hesitated, Vicky went on, "The reason I'm calling is, can we have dinner this weekend? Friday night? I'll take you out for your birthday."

His birthday. Josh had forgotten that was coming up. This was a chance to show Vicky how much he'd matured. "Sure, let's have dinner," he said, "but let me take you out. You already gave me the bike."

"Good, it's a date! Um—" She paused. "Listen, I'm a little concerned about something. Mom says you're thinking of starting your own business."

"Yeah." Josh wished he hadn't told his mother that. "I'm exploring some opportunities."

"Oh, Josh." Another pause. "Before you get financially involved in anything, I have to tell you—"

"Excuse me, sorry, thanks for calling, but I have to get to work," said Josh. "Talk to you—"

"Work?" Vicky interrupted. "You mentioned work before. What work?"

"At a doggie day care kennel."

"*Doggie day care?*"

"Vic? Vic? I can't hear you. You're breaking up." Josh pushed the phone into his pocket and swung back onto the road.

At Coastal Canine, the black Lexus was lurking in the parking lot, early again. Josh's ring finger was still swollen from his first encounter with the retractable leash, and he did not return Tricia's smile as she handed over the Irish setter. Not that she cared. Not that she even said "Thank you" as she drove away.

Finding Erica in the office, Josh opened his mouth to protest about Tricia, but Erica spoke first. "Josh. You know that the Beginning Obedience class starts this Friday? I'm so pleased this is getting off the ground. Come in when you take your break, and I'll show you the setup."

"Okay, great." Josh stowed his complaints for the moment, but he muttered to the Irish setter as he ushered him through the back rooms. "And furthermore, Tricia shouldn't be allowed to own a perfectly good dog—maybe a little hyper—like you."

Later that morning, Josh took a mugful of coffee and followed Erica to the exercise shed. She pointed out the whiteboard, the folding chairs, and the spray cleaner and paper towels. Reading the Beginning Obedience flyer she'd sent out to customers, Josh was impressed with her detail. "You really have to spell it out for them, don't you?" he remarked. "I mean, things like 'All dogs must be on leash' and 'bring treats to motivate your dog.' "

"Yep, you really do. Keep it simple. Repeat as necessary." Closing up the shed again, Erica smiled and nodded at Josh's coffee mug. "The 'World's Best Teacher' shouldn't have any trouble."

At noontime Josh pedaled up the road to Soule's Market & Deli, sweating and looking forward to the AC in the market. Rolling his bike into the bicycle rack, he glanced over at the Pooch Park, the set of carports providing shade for customers' dogs. He realized now what had been bothering him from the first day he rode his bike: it meant leaving his car, with Molly's ashes in the backseat, unattended all day. But what could happen? He didn't know; it just bothered him.

In the market, Josh added a Found Cat poster to the Soule's bulletin board. With luck, this would be his last day as a cat host. Joining a checkout line a short while later, he pulled out his phone and found a text message from Vicky: *Meant to remind you: call Mom.* Yeah, yeah.

Where to eat lunch today? Josh liked sitting out on Soule's patio, but he might be joined by Rick Johnson again, and he saw plenty of Rick these days. As Josh set his bottle and cardboard clamshell on the conveyer belt, he heard a husky voice behind him. "Hey, Coastal Canine?"

"Hey, Danielle!" Josh watched her put down a divider and place her own clamshell and bottle on the belt. "I'm Josh, by the way. Are you eating here?" He nodded toward the patio outside the doors. "Be my guest." He lifted the divider and set it down behind her order.

"Oh—thanks!" Danielle seemed sincerely glad to see him.

Now that Josh thought of it, she'd looked as if she wanted to say something to him, earlier this morning. Paying for both of them, he remarked jokingly, "I know how to show a girl a good time."

They found a free table with a strip of shade, although it was pretty warm even in the shade. As Danielle opened her mac and cheese, she asked, "Do you know if the shelter placed that cat, the one who looks like a panda? I hope he finds a good home."

Josh started to explain that he still had the cat, and if Danielle knew of anyone who was interested—

Peering suddenly at Josh's lunch, Danielle interrupted him. "What're you *eating*, guinea pig feed?"

"Tabouli," said Josh, "but I have to admit your lunch looks better than mine." He lifted his bottle of acai berry juice. "So, here's to summertime."

Danielle lifted her iced tea bottle in response, but her smile faded. "To tell you the truth, I'm not such a big fan of summertime these days, because—"

"Really? I feel like I'm just beginning to enjoy it. After nine months of teaching middle school kids—"

"You're a teacher?" Danielle brightened. "That's even better. I'm glad I ran into you, because what I wanted to ask you—"

"But I'm not a teacher anymore." Were some women especially attracted to teachers? Josh doubted it. "I'm, um, in transition to a new career."

Danielle waved a hand. "Okay, but you're used to dealing with teenagers." She smiled apologetically. "I hope you don't think I'm one of those helicopter moms, but I feel like Ryan is at a turning point, you know what I mean? Just a little nudge one way or the other could make all the difference. And you working at the kennel with him . . ."

"Oh, Ryan." Josh connected Danielle with the youth he'd met at Coastal Canine.

"He's super-smart in some ways," she went on. "He does really well in math and science, and he has a scholarship to U. Mass. Dartmouth. But in other ways, he doesn't have the sense of a stump." She laughed unhappily. "Like about girls."

"That sounds like some of the kids I teach—I used to teach," said Josh. "Sometimes they amazed me, though." He started to tell her about Curtis Gill.

"I think he's been spending time with this older girl, Jordan." Danielle poked at her mac and cheese. "I'm afraid she'll get him to do something stupid, like dealing weed to high school kids." She looked up at Josh. "So if you could just give him a word to the wise . . ."

"Well, okay." Josh doubted that Ryan would listen to any warning from him about the dangers of wild women. Would a good deed that didn't work count on the List? Maybe only 10 percent. "When I get a chance. But I don't see Ryan every day." In fact, Josh hadn't seen Ryan since the day he was hired.

"Thank you. I know it's not your problem, but—" Danielle leaned forward earnestly. "I just figure, the more people looking out for him, the better. A couple of times, the fire department brought him home."

"The *fire* department?"

"I know; he's lucky it wasn't the police! Well, it's not just luck. The police don't really want to deal with kids who light bonfires on the Neck, they've got stuff like break-ins and drug busts to worry about. So they call the firemen—it is a fire hazard, after all—and the firemen go chase the kids off. Neil—that's one of the firemen—has been really nice to Ryan and his brain-dead friends. Not that they appreciate it." Danielle took a deep breath, let it out, and glanced at her watch. "I have to go."

Josh felt an opportunity slipping away. "Hey, this was fun." To be honest, Danielle was turning out to be more complicated than he'd expected, but still more relatable than Rune. "Want to go out for a glass of wine or whatever sometime?"

"Like tomorrow night? Let me look at my schedule, and I'll tell you for sure." They traded phone numbers, and Danielle cast him a smile. "Don't forget, next time you see Ryan . . ."

As Josh dropped his clamshell box into the trash barrel, he reflected that dating was a lot of effort for what might not be much return on investment. ROI, as they said in the business world, which he planned to enter as soon as he found the right opportunity.

The next morning Josh woke up late, after an interrupted night's sleep. He confronted Rick in the kitchenette. "What the hell were you doing last night?"

"Pepper had a nightmare, didn't you, Peps." Rick spooned premium dog pâté into a dish labeled "Pepper." "Had to let her out and then walk her around the house for a while, calm her down." He nudged away the black and white cat, which was showing too much interest in the dog's food.

"Uh-huh," growled Josh. "Did you have to smoke a pack of cigarettes in the process and blow the smoke under my door?"

"Sheesh, I didn't know you were such a princess." Stopping in mid-snicker, Rick pointed the spoon at Josh.

"You know what your problem is? Same as my problem: working for a living."

"Oh? What's your solution? Marry for money? Win the lottery?"

"I heard about a opportunity," said Rick coolly. "Gonna meet a guy tonight."

"Uh-huh." Josh stalked out the door. He was *not* going to let Rick's screwed-up way of life keep him from following his new program. But in order to get to the kennel in time, Josh would have to drive instead of biking, plus he was going to have to skip Cumby's.

To top it off, as Josh rounded the last curve in the road to Coastal Canine, he spotted Tricia's black Lexus. Again. This was so wrong. Behavior modification 101: When an animal behaves badly, it's getting some kind of reward for that behavior. To change the behavior, remove the reward.

Before Tricia could open her car door, Josh was out of his car and headed for the back of the kennel grounds.

"Excuse me!" called Tricia, holding up the handle of her leash.

"Open at seven," Josh called over his shoulder, tapping his watch. "Coastal Canine rules, no exceptions." He ducked around the fence and into the pen, bolting the gate from the inside, in case she tried to follow. Instead, he heard a scream from the parking lot.

Peering through a crack in the fence, Josh saw the Irish setter pawing at the open back window of the Honda Civic, while the black and white cat watched its would-be attacker from the back shelf. Tricia stumbled across the gravel, hanging onto the retractable leash.

Josh smiled. Maybe the leash would snap painfully against her finger.

In the exercise yard, Josh began working industriously at wood-chip raking and water-bucket filling. A few minutes later, he turned a bland face to Rune as she appeared at the back door of the kennel.

Rune released the Irish setter into the Large Dogs pen, where he raced back and forth between Josh and the retrievers' section. "Tricia's in the office, complaining to Erica about you. She said you wouldn't take her dog in for her."

"She tried to drop him off before seven," Josh said. "Don't we open at seven?"

"I guess Tricia was under a lot of pressure to get to work early," said Rune. She added primly, "For Erica, it's not worth offending a regular customer over five minutes. She's running a business, you know."

Josh snorted. Now Ms. Wicca was giving out business advice? "I'd say that depends on the customer."

"Furthermore," said Rune, "you've gotten poor Murphy all agitated. You'd better start throwing balls."

Late that afternoon a red landscaping truck rattled into the back of the kennel grounds. "Finally," said Erica, watching the wood chips pour onto a pile beside the exercise shed.

But it turned out that Rick had brought less than half a load. "The chipper's broken," he explained to a dissatisfied Erica. "I can get the rest first thing tomorrow." As Rick fastened the tailgate of his truck, he spoke to Josh in a lower voice. "You interested in a free meal? That guy wants to talk to me about a investment, going to meet him at the Moby Dick. He said to bring a friend if I want."

A friend? What a joke. Josh, shoveling wood chips into the wheelbarrow, started to say no. But then he thought, What was wrong with enjoying a free drink, while he let Rick's "guy" pitch a deal? For the last several days Josh had proved that he could lead a disciplined life, and now he was tired and thirsty. He deserved to get something for nothing, even if it was only a bottle of Buzzards Bay craft-brewed golden ale.

As every cat owner knows, nobody owns a cat.
Ellen Perry Berkeley

Chapter 17.

The Cat was not satisfied with the man Josh. He had allowed the Cat into his new dwelling and fed him, but that was about it. This man didn't pet the Cat, or murmur soft high-pitched words to him. Much of the time, he seemed to forget about the Cat entirely.

And then the man began going off for the day on his *bicycle*. How was the Cat supposed to ride along, on a bicycle without even a basket? To top it off, one morning the man pedaled away from the cabin without even refilling the Cat's bowl. That did it. The Great Cat must have a better patron in mind for him, and it was up to the Cat to start looking again.

Pushing open the loose screen door, the Cat followed the dirt lane to the road, and the road to the edge of a highway. The highway was empty of cars for the moment, and on the yellow lines, a large black bird with a naked neck hunched over a carcass. A breeze from across the road carried the road kill and vulture odors, but also another scent, hauntingly familiar. It was a mixture of tomato, garlic, and herbs, laced with oil and cheese.

The Cat pictured a fragrant flat cardboard box like the one that the Man used to pick up from the pizza store, and his heart ached for his first life. Giving the vulture a wide berth, he trotted across the highway. The enticing fragrance led him to a large white building surrounded by pavement.

The building did not seem to be a pizza store, but it didn't look like a house, either. The front was a huge garage with bays for long, shiny trucks. Circling the building, the Cat found the source of the pizza smell: an open window—and men's voices. The Cat positioned himself under the window and meowed.

A face appeared at the window, a man with dark eyes under bristly dark hair. His eyes focused on the Cat. "Check this out," he said to someone behind him. "A black and white cat—a fire station cat. You know, like a Dalmatian?"

"Really, a white cat with black spots?" Another face, redder and bonier, peered over his shoulder. "Hah. Yeah, it has *one* black spot, all over his back."

The Cat meowed again, and the first man drew back from the window. The second man said, "Neil. You're not going to feed him, are you? We'll have all the stray cats from the dump moving here."

A door opened, and the man called Neil reappeared. He was stocky, medium height for a human male, wearing jeans and a navy blue T-shirt. He carried a paper plate. "You hungry, buddy?" He set down the plate and stroked the Cat, who sniffed the pizza crusts. "You could be our mascot, Spot."

The bony-faced man scowled from the window. "It's bad enough that we keep getting calls: 'My cat's up a tree—can you send out that guy?' Calls from Fall River—New Bedford—even Fairhaven."

"I'm a cat magnet," said Neil modestly. "What can I say?"

"Personally, I'd rather be a babe magnet."

Although the smell of pizza roused a yearning in the Cat, he was not eager to actually eat it. A substance with so much bread and tomato sauce and so little meat was not real food. In his former life, the only part of pizza he would eat was a glob of pure cheese, dropped under the table by the Girl.

On the other hand, he was very hungry. He began to gnaw at the crusts, concentrating on hard-baked strands of cheese.

The twilight deepened, the firemen disappeared inside the station, and the Cat wandered onto a nearby expanse of lawn. The grass was set with rows of stone slabs, some of them thick enough to serve as pedestals for a cat, and dotted with flowers crawling with edible insects.

The Cat was not the only creature hunting moths. At first he thought the others were some kind of night bird, because they appeared overhead, flitting here and there above the lawn. But weirdly, they squeaked like mice, only in even higher tones. One of the creatures swooped low over the Cat, and he glimpsed its pointed teeth, and the leathery webs of its wings.

Great Cat! It was a *flying mouse*. Trembling with excitement, the Cat leaped high, claws outstretched. But his paws clapped on empty air.

In the morning the Cat returned to the fire station, where he was glad to find the man of compact build with dark brown eyes. The man Neil sat outside the back door of the station, scribbling on a clipboard pad. Glancing up, he seemed to recognize the Cat. "Hey, Spot."

As he paused to rub the Cat under the chin, a small blue car drove into the parking lot. "Hey, Danielle!" called Neil, standing up.

The driver, a blonde woman, waved. "Hey, Neil."

The Cat stared. His heart leaped. This woman looked like the one he'd seen in the place of dirt hills and trash bags.

The woman climbed out of her car, took a large white box from the backseat, and presented it to Neil. "I was stopping at the cemetery anyway, to put some flowers on my grandma's grave, and I thought you guys might enjoy some donuts."

Great Cat! That throaty voice . . . Yes. His intended patron had found him again.

Neil took the box. "Nope. No one at the station likes donuts."

The woman laughed as she sat down beside him. "Right. Silly me." Then her face turned serious. "Neil. I know you saved Ryan's butt the other night. He didn't deserve it, but I sure appreciated it."

"No problem," said Neil, looking aside. He lifted the lid, grinning from the open box to Danielle's face. "Oh, no! Not coconut-frosted donuts. I personally can't stand coconut-frosted donuts." He looked down at the Cat. "How about you, Spot?"

The Cat meowed, but his eyes were fixed on the blonde woman.

At last, Danielle's gaze fell on the Cat. Her mouth dropped open. "Holy guacamole! This might be—I think this *is* the same cat that I saw at the dump." She reached over to stroke his head with her fingertips. "And then Josh had him riding around in his car. I'm sure it's the same cat."

"Josh. Who's Josh?" asked Neil. "That guy that's been hanging around Cumby's?"

"Mm-hm, I think he's here for the summer. Ryan says he's working at the kennel." Danielle petted the Cat from the top of his head to the tip of his tail. The Cat rubbed against her knees with one shoulder, then the other, inhaling her coffee scent. The Great Cat was surely with him.

"My grandma used to have a black and white cat like this, Panda, that would turn off the light for her," Danielle told Neil. "Seriously. When she went to bed, she'd say, 'Good night, Panda,' and he'd jump at the light switch—you know, the big flat kind—and hit it with his paw."

"No kidding?" said Neil. "Well, Spot seems pretty smart—you could probably teach him to do that, too."

Danielle lifted her hand from the Cat's fur. "Except I can't have a cat," she sighed, standing up. "I'm sure I told you, Ryan's allergic. We found that out when he was a little kid, because every time I left him at my mom's with her Persians, he'd start sneezing and wheezing." Pulling keys from her pocket, she gave Neil a brief wave. "Gotta go. Thanks again. Take it easy."

What went wrong? As the Cat watched in disbelief, the blonde woman swung into her car and backed out of the parking space. She was leaving him behind. For the second time.

“Well, thanks for the donuts,” said Neil to the disappearing blue car.

Later in the day, the Cat managed to slip in the fire station door with Neil. The unfriendly man noticed the Cat and stamped at him. “Neil! Get that fleabag outta here.”

“Spot isn’t hurting anything,” retorted Neil. “All right, come on, Spot.” But the Cat had already scooted out of sight. Slinking into one of the bays, he crouched between the back tires of a long truck.

This seemed like a quiet part of the building, a good place for a nap. The Cat crept around the enormous metal body, gazing with his pupils wide and round and working his nostrils. There was a low platform in front, wide enough for a small animal to perch on, and two more platforms on the sides, but they were cold, hard metal. Spotting an open window, the Cat leaped up to explore.

This was more inviting. Like the cars the Cat rode in, the truck had two cushioned seats in front. One smelled like the man who tried to chase the Cat away, but the driver’s seat had Neil’s scent. The Cat settled himself behind the steering wheel, humming praise to the Great Cat, and groomed himself in preparation for slumber.

Hideous clanging! The Cat leaped into the back seat, and then farther back onto on a coil of hose, as firefighters dove into the truck. The door of the bay rose with a grinding noise. Howling and flashing its lights, the truck roared onto the road.

Even in his distress, the Cat had to wonder why none of the men seemed upset by the unbearable noise. They smelled excited, as if they were going after prey. As they passed a street light, one of the crew twisted to stretch his neck muscles, and he caught sight of the Cat crouching on the hose. The Cat stared back, too petrified to blink.

The firefighter nudged the man next to him, and he, too, looked over his shoulder. "I don't believe it! Hey, Neil!" he shouted over the siren. "Spot's in the truck."

"He doesn't look too happy," the other firefighter added. "Neil shouldn't have convinced the cat that he's a Dalmatian."

The crew laughed, except for Neil. "Poor Spot!" he shouted. "I've gotta let him out!" The fire truck pulled to the side of the road and stopped, its wail dying away as the other men protested: "You can't just stop!" "Neil, what the fuck?" Then gloved hands scooped the Cat off the hose and dropped him onto the dirt shoulder. "I didn't say *throw* him out!" shouted Neil.

The Cat slunk into the weeds. The fire truck swung back onto the road, gathered speed, and disappeared around a curve, its unholy din trailing behind. Badly shaken, the Cat crouched beside a stone wall and waited for his balance to return.

As the Cat reflected on what a mistake it had been, to even consider the man Neil for a patron, a small beady-eyed head poked out of a crevice in the wall. It stared into the Cat's eyes for one terrified instant, and then it was gone.

The Cat began to feel more like himself. He stretched, peered through the weeds, and jumped onto the wall to look around. Across the road, the scene seemed familiar. There was a wooden sign with chipped paint, and a rutted lane leading into pine trees. Yes, this was the way the Cat had set out when he left the man Josh yesterday evening. Was he fated to accept such an unsatisfactory person as his patron?

The Cat sat on the wall, waiting for an answer. At last his stomach spoke up with a growl. The Cat would return to the cabin, just to see if the man Josh would feed him now. Once he had a solid meal, he could take up the quest for a patron again.

At the cabin, the small green car was parked outside and Josh was visible through the screen door. The Cat meowed and plucked the wires until Josh exclaimed, "Shut up!" pushed himself out of his armchair, and opened the door.

The man plopped back in his chair, but the Cat continued to meow. "Oh, for Chrissakes," said Josh. He let the Cat lead him to the kitchen, where he poured cat chow into the bowl on the floor.

The Cat tore into the crunchy bits of food before Josh finished pouring. Food. So good.

By the time the Cat had finished his meal, his feelings toward the man had softened. Did he really need to look for another patron? Maybe, with a little more effort, the man Josh could be trained.

People and dogs are species that continue to play into adulthood.

Jennifer Arnold, *Through a Dog's Eyes*

Chapter 18.

Josh was prepared for Rick's "guy" to be a slicker version of Rick himself. But Ollie, as Oliver Griffith introduced himself, was casually but neatly dressed, with a mild, confident manner. They chatted about the weather and the Red Sox as Ollie ordered a round of drinks. Rick went on at length about local politics, especially as corrupted by Gardner Harrison—no surprise—but Josh also found himself talking more than he expected. Ollie seemed sincerely interested in Josh's observations about the under-compensation of teachers and the cost of divorce.

The conversation turned naturally from divorce to real estate, as Josh complained about the current downturn in the Boston-area market. "It's a shame, isn't it?" Ollie agreed. He ordered another round of drinks.

"Still, my house is in a good school district," said Josh. Except that the middle school isn't as good as it used to be before Principal Voss, he added to himself.

Ollie nodded respectfully. "It sounds like you have a fair amount of savvy about the real estate market, Josh."

"Not really," said Josh modestly. "Maybe just west of Boston."

"So you probably know about the legislation pending on Beacon Hill." Josh didn't admit that he had no idea what legislation was pending on Beacon Hill, and Ollie went on to talk about state subsidies, riding out waves of market fluctuations, and flipping properties. It seemed that an associate of Ollie's, a developer, was in a position to get in on the ground floor, if he only had the initial backing.

At "initial backing" Josh's guard went up. Sure enough, the next thing Ollie said was, "Once in a long while, an opportunity comes along that has the potential to leverage a minor investment off the charts." He signaled the barkeeper for another round.

"Sounds like a Silicon Valley startup," said Josh, accepting a fresh beer. "How about a new social media platform—maybe call it Facebook?"

Ollie pointed at Josh, chuckling. "Good one, Josh. Don't we all wish we'd gotten in on the ground floor there? Who knew?" He went on seriously, "To tell you the truth, I'd never invest in tech, because I don't know anything about it. What I do know is real estate."

Josh, feeling that he should be more amiable with a guy who was buying him drinks, remarked, "And you know what Mark Twain said: 'Buy land. They aren't making any more of it.'

Ollie chuckled again. "So true." He went on to cite examples of how a big opportunity had come along, but only one person had been smart enough to seize it.

And then, as Josh was waiting for Ollie to pressure him to produce cash for his developer, Ollie stood up and shook hands with Rick. He turned to Josh. "It's been a real pleasure, Josh. A shame you don't have access to the funds from the sale of your house yet—I'd love to see you take advantage of this opportunity. But anyway, good luck with your house."

So there hadn't been any hard sell, after all. Just a free drink or three, as Rick had promised, and some conversation. Josh liked Ollie, and he felt slightly guilty about accepting the invitation under false pretenses, since he didn't have any money to invest.

Driving to work the next morning, Josh wondered if he was missing an opportunity. Although he didn't have bundles of cash lying around, he might be able to come up with the funds to invest. Wasn't his mother always asking him if he needed "something to tide yourself over"? How about something to *turn* the tide?

At the kennel, the dogs shoved each other in their eagerness to greet Josh, their beloved day-care attendant. But Rune only frowned at him from across the exercise yard. "You're late again. What time is it? It must be almost eight o'clock. I had to bring in all the drop-offs for day care at the same time I was setting up the yard."

"Sorry," said Josh, closing the gate behind him. He thought of something and laughed. "Oh, I guess I was *meditating* too long."

"You don't meditate," said Rune, ignoring the sarcasm. She stepped closer to Josh, putting up a hand to squint at him against the sun. "What's the matter with you?"

"Maybe you should do another reading on me," said Josh. "The answer's in the cards, isn't it?"

"Actually the answer is obvious: rooming with Rick. He was supposed to deliver the rest of the wood chips—look at the bare spots in the yard! He's a perfect example of a Sagittarius gone wrong. If you'd asked me, I would have advised you to stay at Barbara Schaeffer's."

A group of dogs waiting at the entrance to the next pen began to whine. Those were the six or seven dogs with retriever inclinations, including the Irish setter. Murphy/Aodh escalated his whines to impatient yips.

"What do you know about Rick?" asked Josh. "Or what's good for me?" He started toward the ball-throwing section, then turned on Rune. "Not only that—you're the one who got me thrown out of Barbara's, *Jennifer*."

Strolling away from Rune's indignant stare, Josh found himself smiling. Life was a lot simpler, living at Rick's level. Sort of like being a dog. Days filled with a no-brainer job, topped off with a refreshing plunge in the surf, followed by evenings of beer and baseball. Maybe the purpose-driven life was overrated.

As Josh lifted the throwing stick from its hook on the fence, Tucker materialized in front of him. "You going to do the retriever thing today?" Josh asked. "Wait, I have to get the bucket of balls." Then Josh noticed a tennis ball, so grimy that it had been missed in yesterday's pickup, in the dog's jaws. Tucker dropped it in front of Josh and nudged it with his nose. "Okay, if you say so. We'll start with that ball."

With each swing of Josh's arm, the dogs raced to the far end of the yard, wood chips scattering under their paws. Tucker reached the ball first every time, which seemed to annoy the Irish setter. But instead of snatching the ball from under Murphy/Aodh's nose, Tucker let the other dog grab it. Then Tucker led the whole pack back to Josh.

"You goof," said Josh to Tucker. "You just want to be first, huh?" Lobbing the ball toward the front fence, Josh began to whistle, "Dogs Just Wanna Have Fun."

Early that afternoon, Josh walked Smitty, a German shepherd that needed exercise but didn't like play groups. Josh led the dog down the street and into a shady path through the woods, one of the dozens of walking trails scattered around Mattakiset. Technically, dogs were supposed to be on leash, but that was a silly rule, especially for a reasonable dog like Smitty. It wasn't as if Smitty was going to run away. As Josh released the catch on the dog's leash, he felt his phone vibrate.

Erica had been very clear about the day care attendants not using their phones while they were on duty—but Erica wasn't anywhere in sight, was she? Josh paused to read the text: *Thought we had a date last night?*

Danielle. Oh, yeah. They'd agreed to meet for a glass of wine at the Stone Ledge, 6 p.m. It must have slipped his mind. *Sorry,* he texted. *How about tonite?*

While Josh waited for an answer, he heard barking farther into the trees. Smitty must have treed a squirrel, or something. He pocketed his phone and followed the trail around a bend and across a creek.

At a narrow place in the trail, a young man in workout gear, gripping a heavy stick, blocked the way.

Smitty made motions to go around the man on one side or the other, but the man brandished the stick at him, and each time the dog shrank back.

"What are you doing?" shouted Josh. "That dog won't hurt you."

"Damn right he won't." Keeping his eyes on Smitty, the man went on, "Are you from the kennel?"

"No," said Josh, although of course he was wearing a Coastal Canine T-shirt. Whistling to Smitty, he snapped the leash on his collar. "Get a grip," he advised the jogger.

"There's a leash law," the young man called after him. "I'm reporting this!"

"Oh, I'm scared," Josh muttered over his shoulder. But he led the dog back out of the woods. He'd have to walk Smitty along the street today.

Josh checked his phone, but Danielle hadn't answered him yet. She must be pissed. Sheesh. Everyone was pissy today. It must be the steam-bath weather.

Back in the office, Josh paused to look over Uncle George's shoulder. The old man was streaming a Mattakiset selectmen's meeting on the office computer. Josh caught the phrase "low-hanging fruit" from Selectman Harrison, and Uncle George's comment, "Low-hanging nuts."

Erica appeared from the back of the kennel, and the old man closed the video. "Josh," said Erica, "it looks like you have one more in your class tomorrow afternoon: Tricia Harrison."

"Good news/bad news, huh?" said Josh. "Good news: another paying member in the class. Bad news—"

"Bad news," interrupted Uncle George, "it's Princess Tricia!"

Erica looked from her uncle to Josh. "If you two were dogs," she said, "I'd put you in separate pens." Josh went to run off another copy of his handout for the class, snickering.

Toward the end of afternoon day care, Rick Johnson showed up, and Erica came out to meet him in back. "We could have used the wood chips this morning," she said pointedly. Then she focused on the empty bed of his truck. "*Still* no chips?"

"Yeah . . . you know how it is." Rick smiled insincerely. "Had to cut all the lawns first thing, plus, Harrison was after me to finish planting his hydrangeas, because it was supposed to rain tonight. But I can probably get them for you—"

"I'm going to order from Bayview Garden Supply."

As Erica stalked away, Rick shrugged at Josh from the cab of his truck. "What're you gonna do?"

"For one thing," said Josh with a grin, "you could stay away from here until you have wood chips in the truck. You just got her more pissed."

"Everyone's pissed," said Rick. "Get this: Harrison found out you're living with me, and he says now you owe him rent." Before Josh could react to this, Rick leaned out of the cab, jerking his head in a come-closer gesture. "Hey. What'd you think, last night? Are you in, or what? I'm in."

"You're in. On Ollie's real estate deal?" Josh wondered where Rick would get his hands on that amount of cash.

"Can't lose," said Rick. "Waterfront property? Can't get more solid than waterfront. And the owner's desperate to sell."

"I have to think about it," said Josh. "I'm not sure—"

"I can put up half. If you're in, I'm in." Rick started his engine. "But we better move on it."

For the rest of the day, Josh's mind kept returning to Rick's proposal. Was it too easy, more like gambling than like a business deal? Borrow to invest in real estate that was about to balloon in value, make a pile of money quickly, enough to live on the interest? People actually did that, though. You could really get rich that way.

Josh wondered what was happening with his and Tanya's property in Westham, about as far from waterfront as you could get in the Boston area. Between the gigantic mortgage they'd taken on and the recent sag in the market, they'd be lucky to sell it for a profit.

Ollie had talked about *flipping* property. Josh liked that term. It conjured a picture of himself with superhuman strength, powerful enough to toss a five-acre parcel into the air like a square of turf.

Curiosity killed the cat
Old saying

Chapter 19.

That same morning, the Cat had jumped into the car ahead of Josh and climbed up to the back shelf. Spreading the toes of one white forepaw, he licked between his claws to help himself think about his situation. His assessment of the man Josh had slid back several notches last night, when Josh shut him out of the bedroom again. Did the Cat really have to settle for such an unsatisfactory patron?

The Cat paused in his grooming and stared out the car window, hardly taking in the view ahead: a house, a shed, a wire fence around a yard. How happy he used to be, when he returned from his midnight patrol of the house to the Girl's bed! Without waking up, she would lift the covers for him. He would crawl under and snuggle into the crook of her knees, the aura of his warmer, smaller body mingling with hers.

But that was his first life. As the Cat's mother had told her kittens, the Great Cat helped cats who helped—

Great Cat! As the scene flashed past, the Cat just had time to stare down into a pen teeming with large, plump birds. The Cat sat up, his whiskers quivering. The vision disappeared around a bend, but a cloud of chicken-scent floated into the car and hung there.

Josh's car pulled into the parking lot with the gas pumps, and the Cat's thoughts returned to his quest for a patron. Maybe the Great Cat meant for him to choose one of the people he'd already come across, none of them perfect. What was his best option, so far?

There was the man Josh. His good point: He was a bird in the paw, which was supposed to be worth two in the bush. Bad points: Everything else.

Longhaired woman. Good points: Excellent food. Well trained. Bad point (only one, but a serious drawback): Already marked by multiple cats.

Neil the fire station man. Good points: Friendly and protective. Bad points: Limited diet. Noisy and dangerous building.

Danielle the coffee woman. Good points: That purring voice. The gentle way she scratched the itchy spots under his chin and behind his ears. The doting angle of her head as she bent over him. Bad points: Only one. She didn't seem to understand what to do next—take the Cat home.

All this thinking was not getting the Cat any closer to his new patron. It was as useless as stalking a bird on the other side of a closed window. Hard to concentrate . . . need sleep . . .

The car turned into the dog-building's parking lot. The Cat noticed another car with its window down, and he decided to investigate. After his morning nap.

By the time the Cat woke up, ready to explore, the other car with an open window had disappeared. Lapses happened, during naps. Never mind; he'd stroll over to the fence and poke his paw through the slats. That should get the small dogs going.

The Cat's teasing was so successful that the yipping attracted the attention of the kennel woman, the stringy one with very short hair. She sprayed him with a hose, and the Cat retreated to Josh's car for grooming and another nap.

Later in the afternoon, the Cat roused himself from still another nap. He stretched on the backseat towel and flexed his claws. Now he was in a mood to explore again, and he was curious about the door where humans took dogs in and came out alone. This building couldn't be an animal shelter, because although the dogs barked plenty, they sounded cheerful.

Jumping out of Josh's car, the Cat trotted up the steps and leaped onto the railing of the small porch. Before long a shiny gray station wagon pulled into the half-circle driveway. The Cat watched the driver get out and climb the steps. It was a man he'd seen more than once, with silver hair and a stiff gait. His dog was not with him, but the Cat remembered the muscular brown creature, bouncy but harmless.

The man seemed amused to see the Cat. "You've got the wrong address," he said as he opened the office door. "The cat shelter's up the road." He tried to block the Cat.

Easily dodging the loafer-clad foot, the Cat slipped through the door.

You bit it—you bought it.
Sign on the chew-toys shelf at Coastal Canine

Chapter 20.

By three forty-five the humid haze over Mattakiset had dissolved, and the sky above the exercise pens was clear and fresh. In the stuffy exercise shed, Josh opened all the windows. Outside would be too distracting for the Beginning Obedience dogs. He arranged folding chairs in a wide circle and wrote the first lesson, WATCH ME, on the whiteboard.

Josh found himself smiling, and he realized how much he was looking forward to standing in front of a class again: that on-stage, show-opening excitement. My god, he missed those kids, in spite of the stress of trying to work with the principal from hell. Fortunately, there'd be no stress in teaching a few elementary training techniques to dogs and their owners. A piece of cake, compared with one of his lesson plans for, say, World Civilizations.

As the human/canine pairs appeared and Josh greeted them, he noted that only half of the owners had their dogs on a six-foot training leash, as requested. The pets strained to sniff and bark at each other and tangled their leashes around the chair legs, while the owners gave useless orders to the dogs and explained or apologized to each other.

The scene reminded Josh of the first day of the school year at Westham Middle School. Kids without pencils. Kids without notebooks. Kids with lots of excuses. Kids nervously checking each other out. Josh knew how to get them to focus, how to transform the chaos into a process of learning.

Promptly at 4:00 p.m., Josh introduced himself and asked each of the owners to introduce themselves and their dogs. There was Carol Harrison with Tucker, a ten-year-old boy and his mother with a Golden retriever, a Captain Ahab-bearded man with a Border Collie, a vague woman with a young chocolate Labrador retriever, two middle-aged sisters with matching Great Danes, and a paunchy man with a fox terrier. Tricia Harrison and Aodh/Murphy were missing.

In the middle of the introductions, a man in a suit and tie entered the shed leading a Chesapeake Bay retriever. He handed Josh his dog's leash and turned to leave.

Josh couldn't help laughing. "You thought you'd come back in an hour and pick up your nicely trained pet? No-no-no. I'm not going to train your *dog*. I'm going to train *you* to train your dog."

The man stared at the circle of chairs as if someone were trying to trick him into group therapy. "I don't have time for this." He hauled his dog out of the shed.

Seizing the teachable moment, Josh looked around the class. "Did everyone get that? The goal of this class is not to train your dog. It's for you to learn how to train your dog. Now, the first thing you need to get your dog to do," he went on, "is pay attention." He chose the chocolate Lab to demonstrate, counting on her to have the typical Labrador eager-to-please personality. "If your dog isn't paying attention, she won't know what you're asking her to do. So we're going to teach her the first command, 'Watch me'." Josh pointed to the words on the board.

Only one of out the eight human pupils, the boy, seemed to be listening to Josh, but he continued, "This is the process. You've got a treat." He held up a bit of jerky. "You say the dog's name. *Cleo*."

Cleo tried to jump up on him, and Josh turned sideways to deflect her paws. "You command. *Watch me*." He held the treat in front of his own nose.

Cleo's body wiggled, but she obligingly stared at the jerky and past it, into Josh's eyes. "And you *treat*." Josh dropped the jerky, which the dog caught in midair. "Good dog! See, you treat the instant the dog obeys, and you praise her. That connects obeying with the reward (treat and praise) in the dog's mind."

Josh had the class practice *Watch me* with their own dogs as he strolled around the room to give feedback. The boy with the Golden retriever got it right away. Of course, Goldens were notoriously motivated by food—but they also weren't the brightest mutts on the block. "Nice job!" Josh told the boy.

Carol Harrison was wary of Tucker, offering a bit of dried liver but then pulling it back as he jumped for it. Josh could see the problem here: Carol's reflexes were slow, but Tucker's were instant, like the reflexes of a lot of teenagers Josh had known. It could be exhausting, trying to keep up with them. "You can drop the treat," he suggested. "You don't have to give it to him from your hand."

Again, Carol held up a piece of liver. Tucker started to jump, she threw it over his head, and he whirled in the air to grab it. "You're getting the idea," said Josh, and he walked on before he added something sarcastic.

The owner of the fox terrier was offering the dog a biscuit with no success, repeating "Watch me" and waving the treat under the dog's nose. The terrier turned his head away in a "Not interested" gesture, and the paunchy man looked at Josh and shrugged.

"Try this," suggested Josh, giving the other man a bit of jerky. "Just a little bit of something delicious can work better than a whole biscuit." The terrier sniffed the jerky, sniffed Josh's shoes, and tried to squeeze under the folding chair.

"Hm. Did he eat recently?" asked Josh. "Did you read the instructions? *Bring your dog to class hungry.*"

The terrier's owner hitched up his pants defiantly. "Yeah, I did, but Calvin's hyper. I knew he'd be calmer on a full stomach."

Josh managed to nod and walk away before he muttered, "If you know so much, maybe you should teach the class."

As Josh continued around the room, an Irish setter thrust his glossy auburn head through the doorway. "Welcome to the second half of Beginning Obedience," said Josh. Tricia Harrison had Murphy on that damn retractable leash, in spite of the pre-class directions.

"I thought the class started at four-thirty," said Tricia, in a tone implying that someone—possibly Josh—had misinformed her.

"No, it started at four. As per Erica's message," said Josh. But he tried to bring her and the setter up to speed. It was pretty much hopeless, with the dog in constant motion from side to side, dragging Tricia with him. The high heels of her sandals clicking, she kept up a stream of orders: "Aodh, no! Don't do that. Aodh! Bad dog. Settle down. Aodh, I'm warning you . . ."

Deliberately Josh stepped away from Tricia and Aodh/Murphy. To the people nearby, who had stopped working with their dogs to watch, he remarked, "Fascinating, isn't it, how an owner and her dog can reinforce each other's attention deficit disorder?" The watchers seemed taken aback.

Josh moved on to the sisters with the Great Danes. One of them actually had her dog sitting for the treat. "That's the next step!" Josh praised her. "You're way ahead of us."

But the other woman exclaimed helplessly, "Oh shit!" as her dog suited action to words. "I'm sorry."

"Not to worry," said Josh drily. He grabbed a poop scoop. "I'm only sorry you have a Great Dane instead of a Shih Tzu. In spite of the name." He would have liked to hand the poop scoop to the dog's owner, but Erica had advised him not to ask the owners to clean up after their dogs until the class was a couple of lessons along, to keep their minds on the training. He supposed that was logical. Anyway, poop dropped in the exercise hall had to be more carefully cleaned up than poop deposited on the wood chips outside.

Still, Josh reflected, as he sprayed disinfectant and then swabbed paper towels with his foot, in all his years of teaching middle-school kids, he'd never once had to clean up their excrement. They'd given him plenty of shit, but only the figurative kind.

Had the obedience class as a whole, never mind Tricia, gotten the idea of *Watch me*? If they hadn't, it was their own fault. Josh went on to the next lesson, *Sit*, demonstrating again with the chocolate Labrador retriever.

As he worked with the other owners, Josh kept one eye on Tricia Harrison across the room. He wanted so much to medicate her. To pry her jaws open and drop a sedative pill into the back of her mouth, then stroke her throat to make her swallow, just the way he'd pill a dog.

"Aodh, no! Listen, I'm talking to you!" Her heels struck the wooden floor in syncopation with the Irish setter's claws.

Panting, the dog threw Josh a look that seemed like a plea for help. Against his better judgment, Josh strode across the room to Tricia. "Look, when your dog does something wrong, it works better to ignore the misbehavior."

Tricia only made a scoffing noise, but Josh went on. "What works even better is to replace the unwanted behavior with desirable behavior, something you *do* want the dog to do. Look." He took the leash handle from Tricia and faced the setter. "Murphy. *Watch me.* Murphy, *sit*." The dog's feathered butt touched the floor, and Josh slipped him a bit of jerky.

Tricia tossed back her glossy curtain of auburn hair. "Well, *I* learned something today, anyway. It's no wonder I can't get Aodh to do anything. You've trained him to be called 'Murphy'! I thought it was just the old wise guy at the desk."

Josh sighed. "See, that's another problem you have, the name. 'Murphy' is an easier name for a dog to recognize. Because it has some consonants, whereas 'Aodh' is all vowels. To a dog, it sounds like too many other words."

"Are you actually telling me how to name my own dog? I can't believe this." Tricia turned her head away in a gesture as clear as the paunchy man's terrier's: I'm not having any of that.

"Believe it," said Josh with a false smile. Glancing at the clock on the wall, he realized it was time to wrap up, anyway.

After encouraging the class to practice *Watch Me* and *Sit* at home, Josh ushered the people and dogs out of the hall. "You don't have to go through the kennel; take the short cut through this side gate. See you all next week."

Ignoring the short cut, Tricia pulled Aodh/Murphy toward the back of the kennel. "Excuse me!" called Josh, loping after her. "You don't have to go out through the—"

Tricia turned on him. "Oh, I'm going to the office, all right, and I'm going to get my money back. I don't appreciate you and apparently everyone else at the kennel undermining my relationship with *my* dog—and charging me top dollar for it!"

"What the *ph*," muttered Josh. Now he was going to have to explain himself to Erica. As he followed Tricia and the Irish setter into the kennel, the dog kept glancing back at Josh as if for guidance. Josh reached out a reassuring hand, and the dog hung back, unspooling the leash from Tricia's hand.

"Aodh!" She gave Josh a poisonous glare.

Josh started to explain that she was upsetting her dog, but then he felt a poke on the back of his thigh, and he turned to see Tucker. Behind her dog, Carol Harrison smiled apologetically. "I heard you say to go out the side gate, but Gardner's meeting me in the office."

Tricia had reached the back door of the office, and the Irish setter paused abruptly. With one forepaw raised, he sniffed the air ahead. Josh instinctively reached for the dog's collar, but Tricia jerked open the door.

At the same moment, Erica entered the front door of the office. She saw Tricia's face and had just time to ask, "Is there something wrong?"

Growling, Aodh/Murphy launched himself at the black and white cat.

"Tricia!" shouted Josh. "Hold your dog!"

The cat leaped up to the counter. Erica exclaimed, "How did that cat get in here?" The setter lunged toward the counter, and Tricia screamed and dropped the leash.

The cat soared over the computer and onto the safety of a higher shelf, jostling a silver trophy, which bounced off the counter and fell on the floor.

Murphy's front paws scrabbled on the counter, gouging the wood. Tucker, barking with sympathetic excitement, dragged Carol through the back doorway.

Edging past Carol, Josh grabbed for the Irish setter. "Murphy! No. *No*. Leave it." The dog twisted and snapped, but Josh held onto the collar at the back of his neck.

As Josh pulled Murphy down from the counter, Tucker bounded forward. Carol gasped, "Tucker, wait!" Out of the corner of his eye Josh saw her stumble over the fallen trophy, stagger, and crash to the floor, still clutching Tucker's leash.

"Erica, are you out of your mind? Letting a cat in here?" Tricia put a hand on her chest. "I thought I—I *know* I specifically mentioned that Aodh had cat issues." Her thin eyebrows drew together. "And did you hear him call Aodh 'Murphy'?"

Erica was on her knees beside Carol, but she looked up long enough to give Josh a laser stare and point to the front door. Josh hustled Murphy out, the handle of the retractable leash clunking behind them. As he stowed the Irish setter in the Lexus, Gardner Harrison stepped out of his car. "What's going on?"

Without answering, Josh hurried back inside, and Gardner followed. Carol was still on the floor, with Tucker sniffing her as if he'd no idea why she was lying there.

"Carol!" exclaimed Gardner. "What the hell?"

Erica bent over the older woman, touching her hair. "Carol, Carol, are you all right?"

"I think . . ." Propping herself on one elbow, Carol started to move her legs, but her face crumpled, and she sank back with a groan. "I can't get up."

Erica pointed at Gardner. "Call 911." She pointed at Josh. "Put Tucker in his car. And then get your damn cat out of here."

Cats virtually always underestimate human intelligence, just as we, perhaps, underestimate theirs.

Roger A. Caras, *A Cat Is Watching*

Chapter 21.

The Cat didn't like the hasty way the man Josh grabbed him from the shelf and carried him out to the green car. But he was glad to be away from all the shouting and snarling. Praise the Great Cat, for providing the office with a high perch! Stretched out on the back shelf, he groomed his puffed black tail.

One thing the Cat didn't understand: Where was the brown dog? Along with all the confusion in the office, the Cat had thought that one thing was settled, at least: Tucker was finally matched with the right patron. When Josh returned to the office after removing the killer dog, the brown dog turned to him with pleading eyes. Josh picked up his leash and nodded toward the door, and Tucker trotted off with him, pressing his shoulder against Josh's leg.

But to the Cat's surprise, when Josh dumped him in the green car a few moments later, Tucker was not in it. Instead, Tucker was staring at them from the long gray car. As Josh drove away from the kennel, Tucker barked *What about me?* barks through the window.

Josh also seemed discontented, his shoulders hunched over the steering wheel. Even with his deficient human ears, he must have heard the dog, but he did not turn back.

Never mind; the Cat had other things to think about. Spitting out a wad of loose tail hairs, he twisted to groom the fur on his spine.

If you ain't the lead dog, the scenery never changes.
Louis Grizzard

Chapter 22.

Josh drove away from Coastal Canine with Erica's words echoing in his ears: "Do not show up here with a cat ever again. If I wasn't so desperate for help, I'd tell *you* never to show up again."

Why was it all Josh's fault? How about putting some of the blame on Tricia and Mad Dog Murphy? Oh, wait—the customer is always right.

A global insight lit up Josh's brain: He'd been under the illusion that life was about becoming his best self: trying to make his marriage work, striving toward excellence in teaching, managing his moods with the List. When actually, if he had lots and lots of money, he'd be on a whole different plane. Other people would strive to please *him,* to keep him in a good mood, to make things work for him.

"That's it, old girl!" Josh called to the backseat floor. "Lots of money, fuck the List." If only he could get his hands on a chunk of money to invest. Because investment: that was the way to make money, not saving the minuscule leftover from each pathetic salary check.

Without thinking about what he was doing, Josh had driven as far as Old Farm Road. Now he realized it would make more sense to get some takeout before he went all the way back to the cottage. He made a U turn—no, wait! This was the evening he was meeting his sister for dinner. In the chaotic ending to his work day, Josh had almost forgotten. He swerved into a more sudden U turn, meanly glad to see the cat almost lose its balance on the back shelf.

Good thing he'd remembered, Josh thought a few minutes later, rooting through the bags in his car for his sport coat. But too bad he hadn't remembered earlier, because it seemed he was out of clean underwear.

Hurrying into the cottage, Josh scooped up a pile of clothes from beside his bed and dumped them into the cottage's rusty washing machine. He'd dry them when he got back from dinner—it was almost time to meet Vicky at the Harrison House Inn. The black and white cat was meowing in a demanding tone, in spite of all the trouble it had caused; he'd feed it later, too. Josh pulled on chinos and sport jacket, jumped into the car, and tuned the radio to the Red Sox station. He was just in time for the first pitch of tonight's game with the Tampa Bay Rays.

The Harrison House Inn, a historic nineteenth-century resort hotel, was the one semi-fancy dinner place in Mattakiset. Vicky had booked a room for herself, she'd told Josh, so she wouldn't have to drive back to Boston tonight. Josh climbed the steps of the inn's spacious front porch only fifteen minutes late, which he wouldn't count as really late, but probably Vicky would.

In the dining room Josh found his sister sitting at a table for two with a half-full martini glass, looking only slightly annoyed. He greeted her with a hug, and she hugged him back, although she remarked, "Time to get your sport jacket cleaned."

"You don't understand how I'm honoring you." Now *he* was slightly annoyed, but he tried for a light tone. "This is the first time I've worn a sport jacket since—" He was going to say, "since I left teaching," but instead he finished with "since June."

The waiter quickly supplied Josh with a glass of cabernet, and Vicky raised her glass. "So—Happy birthday, Josh!"

He leaned across the table to clink with her. "This is really nice of you, Vic." He meant it, in spite of the crack about his sport jacket. No point in explaining that any unwashed scent came from his underwear, not his jacket.

Studying the menu, Josh was glad to sense the wine melting the tension he always felt with Vicky: a mixture of wanting to please his big sister, resenting her authority over him, and being annoyed with himself that he even had these childish feelings. It *was* his birthday, and he should just relax and enjoy sitting in the dining room of the Harrison House with a linen napkin in his lap.

Josh asked how his nephew and niece were doing at their respective colleges. "*They're* fine," sighed Vicky. "Except I'm not crazy about Zach's girlfriend. She sounds very clingy. But Paul and I, paying two college tuitions at once—don't ask!"

Josh didn't ask, because his sister was smiling, and he was fairly sure that Vicky and her husband could afford their expensive offspring. In fact, Vicki could probably afford to stake him to a real estate investment, if he explained it to her the right way. "How's Mom?"

he asked. "She seemed pretty good when I visited her the other day." (Or was it two weeks ago?)

"She's about the same." Vicky's forehead creased, and she stabbed at her salad. "But give her a call. She'd like to hear from you."

Trying not to react to the implicit reproach, Josh nodded. The entrees arrived, and over their pan-seared bluefish and grilled bay scallops, he entertained Vicky with edited sketches of his current life. He got her smiling, then laughing, at his landlady's quirks, and a day in the life of a doggie day care attendant, and the social scene at Soule's Market, and the cat that colonized his car and almost lost him his summer job.

Josh paused to emphasize how glad he was to be in Mattakiset, thanks to Vicky, and she beamed at him across the table. "You look so much better than the last time I saw you."

That seemed like a backhanded compliment, but Josh went on with the entertainment, turning his brief fling with Rune into a humorous story, with the joke on him. The dog obedience class, too, was good for laughs. "The owners didn't have a clue. It was so frustrating, because *I* could teach the dogs in a heartbeat. Like Tucker, this big Lab mix. One of his owners likes him, but she's too timid in handling him; the other one is strict, but he doesn't have any kind of rapport with the dog."

Vicky smiled. "Maybe next class, you should bring treats to reward the owners, not the dogs." "You're right!" exclaimed Josh. "What do you think—Cheez-Its?"

“No, chocolate truffles, absolutely.” Vicky grinned at him. “You’re funny, Josh. You’re such a natural teacher, you know? You can’t help yourself. You try to quit teaching, and here you are again—teaching.”

Josh’s face warmed, as if he’d been caught doing something embarrassing. “I’m not *condemned* to teach, no matter what.” He thought of the property waiting to be flipped, for big bucks. He had an impulse to tell Vicky, but he decided to wait. “I’m looking into some promising business opportunities.”

Vicky shook her head. “Josh. I hope you aren’t thinking of risking your retirement funds. And why do you want to throw your teaching career away? Why are you even talking about ‘business opportunities’? Face it, you don’t have any head for business.”

For a moment Josh couldn’t answer. His head tingled, as if it were about to explode. “Wait a minute! What gives you the right to evaluate my business sense?”

“Other than spending my adult life analyzing stocks, you mean?” Vicky sighed. “All right, I’ll back off. You’re an adult; it’s your life, etc. Want to split a dessert?”

Josh had an impulse to stomp out of the restaurant, but decided he could last through one more course. They ordered the local specialty of Indian pudding with vanilla bean ice cream, with two spoons, and sought out their respective restrooms.

The men’s room was just off the bar. Coming out of the restroom, Josh paused to check the baseball score on the TV. Tampa Bay Rays 4, Red Sox 2, bottom of the sixth. He groaned.

The man on the nearest barstool looked over at him. "Yeah, what're we gonna do about those Sox?" He gestured at the empty stool next to him.

"I can't stay," said Josh, half-sitting. The Red Sox were up with two outs, the bases were loaded, and a power hitter was stepping up to the plate. He nodded toward the TV screen. "What happened? They were way ahead in the second."

The man shrugged. "Pitching, what else?"

"Oh shit—right over the plate," Josh told the Red Sox batter. "What're you waiting for?"

They watched the batter take another strike, then hit three foul balls. Out of the corner of his eye Josh noticed a couple of U. Mass. Dartmouth students coming out of the women's room. Vicky must be taking her time in there. Unless she'd somehow gotten past him to the table? He should go check. But the lure of a possible grand slam held him on the barstool until the batter finally flied out to right field.

Back at the table, Vicky greeted him with a stony look. Judging from the precisely divided half-full dessert dish, she'd eaten her share of the Indian pudding. There was a candle on his half. And uh-oh, she'd finished a cappuccino and started on a brandy.

"I'm sorry, Vic. The Red Sox caught my eye . . . I was watching for you, but—"

Vicky cut him off, waving a hand at the dessert dish. "I had them come out singing 'Happy Birthday.' I felt like an idiot."

"*I* feel like a jerk," said Josh. "Let me pay for dinner."

Vicky put up her hand. "Nope. Already done."

Of course, Josh thought. She'd had time to go to the restroom and come back, eat her Indian pudding, order coffee, order brandy, sign the credit card receipt, and get thoroughly pissed at him. Although she seemed more upset about it than he would have expected. "I guess this wasn't one of your better dates."

Vicky just stared at him.

Josh continued, hoping to get on better footing, "But not quite as bad as that 'date' Mom told me about? This geezer at Northport Commons asks her to go for a walk with him, so she gets her hat and her three-pronged cane and meets him at the front door. Then halfway down the front walk he says, 'Wait, I'd better go to the bathroom first.' And she waits for twenty minutes . . . but he never comes back." Josh ended with a chuckle.

Vicky didn't chuckle. "Yes. That's our mother's life now, what there is left of it. She tries to be brave."

Josh sighed and hung his head. "Vicky, I'm sorry I kept you waiting. And look, I know you spend more time with Mom than I do."

His sister looked at him soberly. "I'm just not sure you realize . . . she doesn't have that much longer."

"No, I do realize it." A vivid memory struck Josh, and he leaned across the table. "The last time I went to see her, this new feeling came over me. Like a wall on the horizon. I mean, I always *knew* my life wasn't going to go on forever, but now I *felt* it." In fact, he felt it again, right at this moment.

Vicky's eyes filled with tears. For a moment Josh thought they had really connected. Then she said, "So you thought death was optional, for you?" He flinched at her sharp tone. She continued, "This is not about *you.* This is about Mom. *She's* the one at the Wall, to use your poetic metaphor."

"I'm sorry," said Josh. Too late, it occurred to him that dinner with Vicky had been an invitation for him to pay attention to her. "Seriously, I know I've been pretty self-involved for the last year. But from my side, it was like being hit over the head with a two-by-four—three times. Molly dying, breaking up with Tanya, the year from hell at school . . . I felt like I was being crushed. Like I'd never get up again."

Vicky dried her eyes on her napkin. She looked at him as if from a distance. "Well, you weren't crushed. It's time to get back in the game." She tossed back her last sip of brandy. "I've had a really long day. I'm going to bed." Pushing her chair away from the table, she walked out of the dining room.

Oh, shit. As Josh dug into his half of the dessert, he was glad that at least he hadn't mentioned to Vicky his idea of borrowing cash to invest from her. Or worse, from their mother. And maybe it wasn't the best idea. Something Vicky had said about his savings . . . yeah, he should have thought of that. He could take the money out of his retirement fund.

On his way out of the restaurant, Josh paused in the bar. The other baseball fan was still on his barstool, and Josh squinted past him to read the score on the TV screen. The Red Sox were still losing.

Man and cat each have active ways of communicating that do not involve what we normally refer to as language.
Roger A. Caras, *A Cat Is Watching*

Chapter 23.

As the man Josh dropped into the driver's seat, clouds of seafood scent wafted from his clothes. The Cat jumped down from his back shelf perch and meowed in the man's ear, to remind him that a hungry cat was present. Maybe Josh had brought back a morsel for the Cat? Any halfway decent patron would have.

But the man merely turned and stared at the Cat. "Unbelievable. Didn't I leave it at the cottage?" Pushing the Cat back with one hand, he drove out of the parking lot. "Five minutes, okay? Can you just wait five minutes?"

The Cat sank onto the backseat, resigned that Josh was probably not going to feed him while he was driving. But at intervals, to keep the emergency fresh in the man's mind, he leaned on the front seat and meowed again.

Back at the cottage, the mustache man and his little dog were in front of the TV. The Cat tried to lead Josh to the kitchen, the place to get out the cat chow and fill the Cat's bowl. But the man slumped into the other armchair. The Cat rubbed against the man's ankles and meowed; he sharpened his claws on the upholstery and meowed. Josh's eyes stayed fixed on the screen.

Finally the man Josh said, "Well, it's always fun to watch the Red Sox lose." He stood up, stretched, and yawned. Then he frowned. "Shit. I almost forgot to put my stuff in the dryer."

Rick blew a smoke ring over his dog's head. "Doin' laundry? Did someone complain at the kennel? 'Hey, Josh—you stink.'" He chuckled.

The Cat followed Josh through the kitchen. Without even glancing at the cat chow cupboard, the man opened the door of the soap and water machine. "Ugh," he said, pulling out a soggy pair of underpants. "Not much of a spin cycle."

Meowing, the Cat dodged drops of water as Josh tossed his wet clothes into another machine. "Temp," he muttered. "Better set it on High."

With a screech that made the Cat leap backward, the dryer began to turn its inner wheel. The screech merged into a rhythmic *whoop-whoop-whoop*, but the Cat had already fled back through the cottage and into Josh's room. He crawled under the bed, next to the leg propped up by a yellow book.

"Sheesh!" exclaimed Josh.

"Didn't I tell you?" Rick called from the living room. "Oldest dryer on the planet." He added, "Hey. That investment deal Ollie mentioned? Gotta jump on it. If you aren't in . . ."

"Oh, yeah. Yeah." Josh's footsteps returned through the kitchen. "Yeah, count me in."

"I mean, you have to come up with the cash. If you're in."

"Well, I can start the process tomorrow, but it'll take a few days to get the money from my retirement fund. And I need to take a look at that property first."

"Ollie says tomorrow," said Rick. "Not 'a few days.' He might know a guy that would give you a loan on the retirement."

Josh grunted. "But tonight, I am fucking going to bed right now."

From under the bed the Cat watched the man Josh's feet appear in his room. The feet kicked off their sneakers, and the underside of the mattress sagged as Josh flopped onto the bed.

"Shit." The man sighed a deep, self-pitying sigh. "I can still hear it." Pushing himself out of the bed, he shoved the bedroom door shut. He flopped onto the bed again.

Creeping cautiously out into the room, the Cat saw Josh pull his backpack under his head. He turned it over as if searching for a softer side, finally wiggling his head into a hollow. The Cat waited for the man's breathing to slow and deepen. Then he jumped onto the foot of the bed and curled up, one forepaw over his head to muffle the *whoop-whoop-whoop*.

The Cat dreamed that the mustache man was blowing smoke in his face. With a sneeze, he woke up.

The smoke was no dream. The air was thick with it.

The Cat leaped off the bed, toward the door.

The door was shut. Besides, the source of the smoke was on the other side. And heat pulsed against the bedroom door.

Bounding to the half-open window, the Cat tore at the screen. Useless. He hurt his claws, but not the wire.

What to do? Get help from a stronger animal—the human sprawled on the bed. With a soaring leap, the Cat shot himself off the window sill and landed hard on the man's belly.

"Aagh!" The man Josh coughed and rocked from side to side, but he did not wake up.

Desperately the Cat cast his mind back to the days when the Girl had slept past first light. How had he awakened her? Climbing onto the man's chest, the Cat licked his eyebrows, first one and then the other.

"Uhh." Josh's eyes were still closed.

With claws tucked in, the Cat rapped the side of the man's face. He only brushed feebly at the paw.

The Cat stepped onto the man's throat with both front paws, leaned over, and nipped the end of his nose.

"Aagh!" This time Josh did wake up, so violently that he flung both the Cat and himself onto the floor. The man crouched there, wavering. So slow. So stupid!

The Cat jumped onto the windowsill and meowed to guide the man, but he turned the other way, stumbling toward the door. He grabbed the doorknob—and instantly jerked his hand away. He stared at the light flickering around the edges of the door.

"Josh!" It was the voice of the mustache man, outside the window. His dog was yipping, too. "Fire! Get out! You there? Fire!"

Finally—finally—the man Josh lunged across the room to the window. The Cat jumped down to let him work. But instead of tearing the screen open for the Cat, Josh shoved up on the wooden frame. It moved a little, unevenly. "Stuck," Josh muttered through a cough.

"Get out! Get the fuck out!"

"Shut the fuck up," grunted Josh as he struggled to push the window up. There was a shuddering crash somewhere in the cottage.

"You gotta get out," shouted the mustache man. "Roof's gonna go!"

Josh stooped under the window frame and heaved. It scraped upward, scattering flakes of dried paint. Now, surely, the man would rip open the screen.

Josh tugged at a hook at the bottom of the screen. The mustache man pried at it from the outside. "Fucking rusted. Cocksucker!"

The Cat meowed. The dog yipped. And now sirens wailed in the distance.

"Watch out!" Cocking his fist, the man Josh plunged it through the screen. He scraped his arm back through the jagged wire. "Aagh! You idiot!"

At last. An escape hole for the Cat. Leaping onto the window sill, he wiggled through and dropped to the ground.

A living dog is better than a dead lion.
Ecclesiastes 9:4

Chapter 24.

The ER nurse lifted the oxygen mask from Josh's face to check his lips and tongue. "Pink—good." She added, "Blue would mean there was cyanide in the smoke. Bad stuff."

Josh tried to come up with an adequate response. "I guess I could have died."

As the nurse wrapped a blood pressure cuff around his arm, Josh struggled to take in what had happened: He'd woken up with the cottage on fire. He'd thrown his backpack through the screen and plunged after it.

Dragging his backpack, Josh had stumbled away from the cottage and into the glare of headlights. Behind him, the fire roared and parts of the cottage fell in.

"Anyone else in there?" shouted a fireman.

Josh shook his head dumbly. Rick shouted, "Nope!" holding up his terrier for proof. EMTs lowered Josh onto a stretcher. And here he was in a hospital.

Through the curtain dividing the ER gurneys, Josh heard a familiar voice. "Pepper! What'd you do with Pepper? Where's my dog?"

"Your dog is safe, sir," said a female voice with a Middle Eastern accent. "The EMT's should not have allowed you to bring him here."

"Pepper is not a 'him'!" Rick's outrage dissolved into a spasm of coughs.

Josh was suddenly outraged, himself. "Hey, Rick," he called. "The fire— You *smoked in bed*. Didn't you?"

"Smoke in bed?" More coughing. "What kind of an idiot do you think I am?"

The ER doctor, a woman with the sober gaze of a Greek Orthodox icon, stepped into Josh's side of the curtain. "You, too, escaped a fire without burns?" She examined his hands and arms. "Oh, but many surface wounds here, and here."

"I had to crash through the screen," explained Josh.

"You are fortunate to be alive." The doctor gave him a tetanus booster shot and left, directing the nurse to admit both of the fire survivors "for observation."

But as soon as the medical personnel left, Rick's walrus mustache appeared around the curtain. "I don't know about you, but I'm fucking getting out of here before the charges go through the roof."

Startled out of his dazed state, Josh focused on the expensive high-tech equipment near his gurney. Now that he was off of Tanya's medical insurance, he had large deductibles for ambulance and emergency room treatment. And a hospital stay could dig even bigger chunks out of his funds.

Out at the desk, as Rick and Josh signed medical releases, Josh's smoke-addled brain circled back to the question of the fire. "If you aren't the kind of idiot who smokes in bed, how did the fire start?"

"Been thinking about that," said Rick. "Must have been the dryer, that piece of crap. Did you clean the lint screen?"

Josh was dumbfounded. "Clean the—"

"There must have been months of lint in there," Rick went on. "Just waiting for a spark from that broken-down excuse for a dryer."

Rick was blaming *Josh* for not cleaning months of Rick's lint out of the dryer? As Josh groped for a sufficiently caustic comeback, the receptionist managed to catch their attention: Did Josh and Rick have someone to pick them up from the hospital?

Pulling his phone from his backpack, Josh thumbed through his contacts. Who did he want to call for a ride at 2:17 a.m.? Not Vicky, certainly not his mother. None of his friends from Westham. As for contacts around Mattakiset: not his former landlady, Barbara; not his disgruntled employer, Erica; not his disillusioned romantic interests, Rune or Danielle. Josh wished he had an Uber account.

Meanwhile, Rick was talking to a balding man whose volunteer's badge rested on his slumped belly. It seemed that the EMT's had handed Pepper over to this volunteer, Warren, and he'd stowed the dog in his car. "Yeah, I guess I could give you a ride to the Dreamland. On Route 6, Mattakiset?"

In the volunteer's Chevy sedan, Pepper and Rick had a frenzied reunion while Josh pictured the Dreamland Motel, next to the Sincere Garden. It looked like a dump, but maybe it was the best choice for tonight. Then it struck Josh that he might still have a car. "Wait a minute, could we swing by the cottage first, to check something?"

Rick was all for checking on his truck, too, but Warren was getting the look of a Good Samaritan who hadn't intended to be *that* good. "It's kind of out of my way," he said.

"We appreciate that," said Rick. Tapping Josh on the shoulder, he rubbed his thumb and fingers together and nodded toward the volunteer.

Rick expected *Josh* to come up with money for the extra distance to the cottage? Josh hesitated, weighing how much he wanted his car, right now. He pulled a twenty-dollar bill from his pocket and tucked it into the cup holder. "We really do appreciate your extra trouble."

Half an hour later, the headlights of Warren's car shone on the blackened skeleton of the cottage, roofless except for the corner with the unharmed satellite dish. The hospital volunteer gave a long whistle. "You guys were lucky to get out of that alive. I'd think about suing your landlord, if I was you."

"You bet your ass," said Rick, opening the car's back door. Pepper scampered ahead of him to the landscaping truck, not a blackened skeleton but its whole self, complete with dried mud on the red paint.

"Thanks a million," said Josh, shaking Warren's meaty hand. "All set." The air stank of wet ashes, but Josh's Honda Civic waited beside Rick's truck, right where he'd parked it an eon ago. It, too, was undamaged except for its old injury of a dented left rear bumper.

"See you at the Dreamland," said Rick to Josh over his shoulder. "Where I should have gone in the first place, instead of renting from that prick Harrison."

"Wait a minute," said Josh, picturing an object: the disk of a wall-mounted smoke alarm. In Barbara's apartment? Yes, but also in the living room of the cottage. "Why didn't the smoke alarm go off? It should have gone off." Had Gardner Harrison carelessly—or cold-bloodedly—neglected to change the battery?

"Oh, that," said Rick, starting his engine. "I had to take the battery out. It was driving me crazy. Every time I lit up, *annh, annh, annh.*"

While Josh sputtered, Rick leaned out the truck window. "See you at the Dreamland," he said again. "Want to share a double?"

"No."

So *that* was the kind of idiot Rick Johnson was, thought Josh as the truck drove away. He opened the back door of his car and peered at the floor. There was no reason for Molly's carton not to be in the backseat, but he was reassured to actually see it. "Good girl. That was a close call, huh?"

Rick had rattled off down the lane, but the volunteer's headlights were still trained on Josh. Waving more thanks, Josh slid into the driver's seat and turned his key in the ignition. He'd assumed he'd follow Rick to the Dreamland, but as he reached the paved road, he changed his mind. It was hardly worth checking into a motel for the few hours left of the night.

Josh found himself driving his usual route to work, with a hazy idea of waiting in his car until the kennel opened. But by the time his headlights picked out the Coastal Canines sign, he'd changed his mind again. Even pulling into the parking lot would arouse the boarding dogs and worry the overnight caretaker, who might call the police.

And come to think of it, Josh knew of a place in the town where you could sleep undisturbed in your car: Mattakiset Neck. The Neck was a state park, but from what Uncle George said, it wasn't much patrolled. The town police considered it the state's business, and these days the state didn't have the resources to keep a close watch on one small spur of land.

Josh took a turn toward the river and drove across the bridge, along the marsh to the shore road, and over the causeway. There were a few other cars in the Mattakiset Neck parking lot: an SUV, a couple of sedans. The old pickup truck with a canvas camper shell must belong to the vet (Iraq War, according to Uncle George) who more or less lived on the Neck.

A small fire flickered on the bayside curve, and Josh heard laughter and the rhythm of traded insults. That must be the high school kids who gathered here to drink and mate. If they didn't bother him, he wouldn't bother them. He just wanted to recline his seat and sink into sleep.

But he couldn't recline, because the backseat was stuffed full against the upright driver's seat. In a way, that was lucky, Josh realized. If he hadn't been too lazy to take most of his stuff out of the car, it would have all gone up in smoke with the cottage. As it was, he'd only lost sheets, towels, his sport jacket—and oh shit, all his underwear except the pair he'd already been wearing too long.

Josh stretched out, as best he could, across the bucket seats and console. His head ached. The air was chilly here by the water; he wished for the warmed blanket that the nurse had draped over him in the ER. An expression floated through his mind: *You've made your bed; now lie in it.*

Josh had screwed up royally, in so many ways. His failings crowded him, as lumpy as his makeshift bed. How could he have been so thoughtless, so reckless, at the kennel? Erica's business seemed to be struggling as it was, and Josh's behavior in the obedience class might have pushed it over the edge.

And oh my god, what about Carol Harrison? Josh hadn't even thought about her until just now. How badly was she hurt? Much as Josh wanted to blame Tricia, that accident wouldn't have happened if Josh hadn't, in spite of warnings, brought a cat to the kennel.

Squirming, Josh tried to find a better fit between his back and the cup holder. No wonder Vicky thought her brother was a self-absorbed jerk. How could he have even considered asking her for money—a large amount of money—for risky business with some guy he'd just met?

Josh remembered the story he'd repeated to Vicky, about his mother and the fellow resident who'd asked her to walk around the grounds with him after dinner. She'd liked this guy, and she was really looking forward to the walk.

At the time Martha Hiller told him the story, Josh had been eager to go along with her humorous slant. "Didn't he even send you roses the next day, or something?"

"Actually . . ." His mother's smile faded. "He had to move to the nursing facility."

No, it wasn't so funny. Martha Hiller lived with daily reminders that she was sliding into "the wrong side of the grass," as Erica's Uncle George put it. The assisted living residents either got more and more decrepit and disappeared into the nursing wing, or they died suddenly, their departure announced by ambulance sirens in the middle of the night.

Josh wasn't even sure, any more, that Tanya owned 75 percent of the blame for their failed marriage. The women he'd met in Mattakiset, Rune and Danielle, didn't seem so impressed with him, either. And why should they be?

What kind of idiot are you? Josh had asked Rick. The real question was, What kind of an idiot was Josh? The kind of idiot who'd move in with an idiot like Rick. Who'd seriously entertain a "business opportunity" with a guy Rick knew. My god! Josh went cold, thinking of it. He'd actually intended to gamble with his retirement funds.

Why should anybody, anybody Josh could think of, think well of him? They shouldn't; they didn't. Except for one young exuberant black-nosed, flop-eared retriever mix. If only Tucker were here right now, licking Josh's face, curling up on the floor of the front seat with a contented sigh.

Josh must have slept at last, because he woke up to daylight. For a disorienting moment, he didn't know why he was blinking through his windshield at sunshine chasing morning fog. He was lying on his back, with his head pushed against the passenger door and his knees propped on the steering wheel. He'd slept in his car, like a homeless person. He *was* homeless.

Creakily Josh unfolded himself, stumbled out of the car, and ducked into the scrub oaks for a piss. He glanced down at his feet and did a double take. *He was wearing hospital slippers.* Holy shit, had anyone noticed that?

As Josh came out of the trees, he dropped the slippers in the trash barrel. Luckily there was only one other person in the lot who could have observed Josh shuffling around like an escapee from an institution. A man with an absent look sat in the pickup, smoking a cigarette. He nodded politely to Josh, as one homeless guy to another.

Josh nodded back but hurried to his car, desperate to get away from here. What time was it? Six-seventeen. If he arrived at the kennel on time and started the day as usual, he'd be back to normal.

Digging under the bags and boxes in his car, Josh found a pair of beat-up sneakers. His almost-new sneakers, of course, had gone up in toxic smoke in the fire. His Coastal Canine T-shirt was ripped and streaked with grime, but presumably the dogs wouldn't care.

Josh started the car. Once he reached Cumby's and coffee, he'd be back in his regular routine.

Half an hour later, in the kennel office, Uncle George looked up from a list on the counter. He gaped at Josh. "Jesus-Mary-and-Joseph. What happened to you?"

As Josh gathered himself to answer, Barbara Schaeffer and Lola trotted into the office. Barbara, too, gaped at Josh. "Oh, my goodness."

Uncle George pointed at Josh. "You were in that fire last night! One of Harrison's cottages, right? It was on the news feed."

Lola sidled up to Josh and began an extensive sniff-search. Barbara said, "That was *your* cottage? Oh, Josh."

Erica stepped from the kennel into the office, caught sight of Josh, and stopped short. "Josh! What happened?"

"He looks like he slept with a raccoon, don't he?" asked Uncle George. "With a raccoon, in a fireplace."

Josh was getting the message that he looked much worse than he'd thought. That explained the funny stares he'd gotten in Cumby's. "I guess I should wash up," he said to Erica. Talking made him cough. "If I can take a few minutes?"

"If you can— Of course, but do you think you're okay to work? What about smoke inhalation?"

"No, they checked me out at the hospital," said Josh. "Pink." He tried to smile. He wished they would let him start his work day as if nothing had happened.

Barbara was still standing by the office counter, staring at him. She took a breath as though she was about to speak, took a step toward him, and stopped, biting her lip. "Josh," she said. "You know, I'm sorry that— If you need a place to stay now, you could move back in."

Josh squinted at her. Was she kidding?

Barbara's light blue eyes squinted back at him, perfectly sincere. "As long as—you know: no pets."

"Well . . . thanks," muttered Josh. "I would like to. I definitely would." He managed a smile. "So—I'll see you tonight."

Handing Lola's leash to Erica, Barbara said, "Actually I might *not* see you tonight, because I'm going to the selectmen's meeting to speak up for the wind turbine. But you can let yourself in. You'll remember where the spare key is, this time?"

As Josh turned toward the staff bathroom, Erica said, "Wait a minute." She grabbed a new Coastal Canine T-shirt from the pile on a shelf and handed it to him. "Change your shirt, too."

In the bathroom, Josh leaned on the sink and looked into his bloodshot eyes. The kennel people were being so kind to him, it brought a lump to his throat. Even Uncle George had restrained himself from saying, "I could have told you what would happen if you roomed with Rick Johnson. A piece of work, always has been." Although that might come later.

Josh still had to face Rune, he realized as he washed soot off his face and arms and changed out of his ripped, dirty T-shirt. With her Tarot cards, Rune had pegged him as the Fool, feather-headed, not even looking where he was going. She was right.

But when he joined Rune in the exercise pens, she only shook her head sympathetically. "I'll put some aloe ointment on those scratches."

Again Josh felt overwhelmed with gratitude. The day care dogs milled around him, nudging, licking, sniffing. Tucker shoved the rest of them aside and began cleansing Josh's scratched arms with his tongue in a proprietary way.

i have had my ups and downs
but wotthehell wotthehell
Don Marquis, *archy and mehitabel*

Chapter 25.

The Cat crouched under a bush, stupefied and panting. Sirens wailed, close and unbearably closer. A long truck jounced down the dirt road, its roof lights flashing and headlights glaring. The Cat's ears ached; the pupils of his eyes contracted to slits, but still he could hardly see; he gagged on the smoke. Turning, he plunged into the dark.

Blinded, choked, and deafened, helpless as a newborn kitten, the Cat could only hope he was stumbling in the right direction. At least his sense of touch was still working: his whiskers, his eyebrow hairs, and the pads of his feet. He felt weedy stems as he pushed them aside, then vines and bushes as he squeezed through them. Finally, stepping onto a springy surface, he sensed a clear space.

The Cat sneezed, clearing ashes from his nostrils. Now he smelled pine trees. He blinked, and his pupils widened to take in the restful dimness. But his ears were still ringing, keeping the world eerily clueless of sounds.

Looking over his shoulder, the Cat was reassured to see how far he was from the fire truck and the burning cottage. The lights flashed and the fire pulsed and jumped, but at a safe distance.

Where had he gotten to? Gazing up, the Cat saw a ragged canopy of pine and oak branch silhouettes.

There was no moon. The sky above the black trees was gray, sprinkled with bits of light.

He was in the woods, then. The Cat felt a twinge of unease. He looked to one side, then the other. Dark columns of tree trunks, some larger, some smaller.

Off to his right, close to the ground, a shadow moved. Or did it? When he turned to stare, the shadows were motionless.

And what was that, to his left? Again, nothing? The Cat strained to listen for the cracking of twigs underfoot, or the rustle of a body brushing undergrowth. His ears gave him only the senseless ringing.

Then a rogue breeze, in the still woods, carried a message to his nose. It was a smell like a dog's, a mix of meat and plants.

But this smell was not a dog's. There was no overlay of human-connected scents, like collars or shampoo or car upholstery.

And this not-a-dog creature had one scent the Cat had never, ever smelled on a dog. He had smelled it on scat in the woods, on the first day of his second life.

The Cat froze in a crouch. Every hair on his body stood out. What he smelled now was the breath of a cat-eater.

A shadow on the left sprang at him. Another shadow sprang from the right.

Straight ahead the Cat leaped, to the base of the closest tree. With a second bound he launched himself upward. His claws dug into the bark; he scrambled up, up, up. Behind him, the monsters' paws scraped at the bottom of the tree. Clouds of that breath rose from their open jaws.

Reaching a high branch, the Cat paused to peer down. His ears were recovering, because he heard the shadows whining with disappointment while they circled the tree. One of them put its front paws up on the trunk, as if hoping it might be able to climb.

But it couldn't climb a tree, any more than a dog could. The Cat began to calm down. How, he wondered, had he managed to smell the coyotes? The air in the woods was very still, even up where he was, as high as the Girl's bedroom window in his old home. And yet he'd detected their dreadful breath when they were several bounds away, giving him time to escape up the tree.

The Great Cat. She must have stirred up a breeze with her magnificent tail, guiding the scent of danger right into his nose. *Praise to thee, Great Cat!*

The not-dog beasts waited under the Cat's perch for a long while. They crouched to rest; they sat up and gazed into the branches; they circled the tree again; they rested again. Finally one shadow rose, then the other, and they melted off into the woods.

In the morning the Cat clawed and slipped his way backwards down the tree. He started off in one direction, but where the trees thinned, he met a wet, scorched stench, and he slunk away from it at an angle. That direction led him to the sound of trickling water, and he followed the sound down a slope through ferns to a pool. He was so thirsty. Skimming dead leaves from the water with his paw, he lapped.

Refreshed, the Cat jumped from stone to stone across the brook, climbed the opposite slope, and found himself at the edge of a road. The scene looked familiar, like part of a route he'd seen while riding with the man Josh.

Great Cat! A ravishing scent flowed into the Cat's nostrils. His whiskers quivered. The chickens!

The Cat pattered along the side of the road toward the scent, as if pulled by a twitching, receding shoestring. The tantalizing aroma grew stronger, then almost faded, then grew stronger and stronger—

And there he was, outside that wire-fenced yard. Only now, the chicken yard was empty. The Cat examined a cooler near the road. He thought he smelled eggs, but it was tightly closed.

Squeezing under a loose corner of the fence, the Cat sniffed all around the pen. Stray feathers tickled his nose. He stole up the ramp leading to a chicken-sized door in the shed. The Cat could hear feathered bodies rustling inside, but the door was shut and bolted.

The Cat circled the shed twice, pawing at the door to make sure there was no way in. As he crouched beside the shed to see what would happen next, a man emerged from the nearby house. "Well, look who's here."

The Cat tensed, ready to leap away, although the man didn't seem angry. He didn't shout or stamp at the Cat as he entered the wire pen, swinging a bucket. "You like chickens, huh? Well, there's no baby chicks at the moment, so you can look all you want to."

The Cat's heart fluttered at a sudden thought: Had the Great Cat led him to his new patron—a *chicken farmer*?

Grinning down at the Cat, the man reached for the small door of the shed. "You ready for this?" He unbolted the door, and a rooster ducked through it into the sunshine.

The rooster strutted down the ramp from the shed to the ground, wattles flapping as his head jerked from side to side. A parade of hens followed his flowing tail feathers out of the shed.

Black chickens, brown chickens, white chickens strolled across the yard, pecking in the dirt. One dark brown hen lowered herself into a dusty spot near the fence, wiggling and fluttering lusciously.

The Cat licked his lips, and his jaw quivered. Up close, these succulent birds looked very large. The sight made the Cat salivate and tremble at the same time. His tail twitched with desire, but his ears flattened timidly.

Spotting the Cat, the rooster spread his wings, uttered a wrathful squawk, and rushed at him. The Cat shrank away from the outstretched beak. He had just turned to dash for the fence when the rooster flapped into the air to attack the Cat feet first. Clawed feet dug into the Cat's shoulder.

Snarling, the Cat rolled over to fight the bird with all four paws, but the rooster flapped into the air again, back out of reach. He spread his wings as if ready for a second round.

But the Cat was done. Where was the loose edge of the wire fence? He didn't see it. Instead, he leaped awkwardly onto the nearest fence post. His four paws barely fit on the top of the post, and he balanced for only an instant before dropping to the other side.

The rooster crowed, the hens cackled, and the farmer chuckled. "Way to go, Colonel!" he told the rooster.

Unfair! Chickens weren't supposed to fly. The Cat climbed onto a boulder near the fence and rubbed a paw over his face to groom away humiliation. Trying to reach his wounded shoulder with his tongue, he paid little attention to a car coming around the curve of the road.

The car slowed and stopped, and a plump young woman in pajama bottoms and a tank top climbed out. "Hey, Al," she said. She opened the cooler and started to take out a carton of eggs.

The farmer pointed a gloved finger at her. "Hey, *Jordan*. If you want eggs, I want cash. No more of this leaving a baggie of weed."

"But I need eggs! I am feeding nursing mothers." She gazed at him a moment before shrugging and letting the lid of the cooler fall. "You don't care." Then her eyes focused on the Cat. "Wait a minute!"

"What's your problem?" asked the farmer.

The Cat stared at the young woman. He'd seen *her* before, and it hadn't been good. He flattened himself against the boulder.

"That's my cat, Mr. Tux! What're you doing with my cat?" She pushed through goldenrod toward the Cat.

The Cat bounded from the boulder to the stone wall, pattered across the road, and squeezed through a hedge. The chicken farmer was laughing again.

The young woman didn't seem to be following now, but the Cat kept going into a great field of grass. He paused at the sight of several enormous black and white animals, but these creatures seemed interested only in eating the grass. Still, they were so huge, much larger than humans. Best not to be stepped on by one of them, even accidentally.

On the far side of the field, the Cat jumped onto another stone wall, and discovered that it ran beside a road. There was something familiar about this curving road—was that good or bad? Up and down the road, nothing to cause alarm. He began walking along the top of the wall, in the direction of a roof partly hidden by pine trees.

Closer up, the building under that roof turned out to be a disappointment. It was full of cats. The air vibrated with their cries and reeked of their smells. It wasn't the dreaded place where the Woman and the man Josh had tried to leave him; it wasn't the house where the young woman collected cats; it wasn't the vet's office. But it also wasn't a home with a prospective patron.

Anyway, now the Cat could see, farther up and on the other side of the road, a place he knew: the dog kennel. Ducking under the pines, he approached it cautiously. Among the cars in the parking lot, he recognized the small green one with a dented fender. It belonged to the man Josh. Even though that man was an unsatisfactory patron, he *had* fed the Cat more than once. He would *probably* feed him again.

Running across the road, the Cat sailed in the car's open window.

A tired dog is an obedient dog.
Sign above counter in Coastal Canine office.

Chapter 26.

By the time he took his lunch break, Josh was feeling the lack of sleep, but still buoyed up by his welcome at the kennel. Whistling "I Want to Be a Cowboy's Sweetheart," he crossed the gravel parking lot to his car.

A black and white cat was perched comfortably in the open back window.

Josh's whistling broke off, and he halted with the car keys in his hand. "How the *fuck*?" He looked all around, as if he were a car thief. For the moment, no one else—especially Erica—was watching. He had to get the cat out of his car, before anyone noticed. He lunged for the back door.

No. He pulled up short. First, get his car, containing the cat, out of here before anyone noticed. *Then* remove the cat from his car.

Josh drove jerkily out of the parking lot in a tense compromise between leaving asap, and not attracting attention to his back-shelf passenger by roaring onto the road. If he could just get as far as Soule's Market without being noticed . . . The brushy slope at the edge of Soule's parking lot would be the best place to release the cat. Then roll his car windows up and never, ever, roll them down again, no matter how hot the day.

Halfway to the market, Josh's phone rang. He glanced at it—Griffith Assoc.; that would be Ollie—and dismissed the call. Almost immediately the phone rang again. It was a Jordan. Josh didn't know any Jordan. Maybe Jordan was Ollie's assistant, calling to pressure him into throwing away his life's savings. He let the call go to voice mail.

But she called again, and now Josh was having second thoughts. Maybe he'd met a Jordan at one of the bars? Or maybe he knew someone who knew a Jordan? He turned into the Soule's parking lot and picked up.

"That's my cat!" Jordan's voice was shrill and quick. "Oh my god, I couldn't believe it when I saw the picture. Where is he? I can't wait to get him back!"

Josh couldn't believe his good luck, either, especially when Jordan explained that she was right there in Soule's Market, staring at his Found Cat notice on the bulletin board. He pulled his car up in front of the market doors, and a girl—a young woman? flip-flopped out, shading her eyes to peer in the rear window. "Yeah! That's Mr. Tux, all right."

The black and white cat, peering back at Jordan, flattened its ears. Odd, thought Josh. This cat had acted so friendly to him, and Danielle, and Rune. But he followed Jordan and parked next to her car. She must be old enough to drive, at least.

Jordan lifted a cat carrier out of her trunk and set it beside the Civic. "Wow, your car is full of junk. Get some of that crap out of the way for me?" As Josh pulled out several bags, she shoved the carrier onto the backseat and climbed in after it.

Standing beside his bagged belongings, Josh watched uneasily. The cat was hissing and growling, shrinking against the rear window, just as it had done when he tried to leave it at the animal shelter. Jordan wasn't even wearing gloves—her hands were going to get torn up.

Just before her fingertips reached the cat, it made a dash for the open car door. But Jordan, as expert as a calf wrangler, blocked it with her shoulder, seized the nape of its neck with one hand and both hind legs with the other, and popped the cat into the carrier. "There, that's better," she chirped, fastening the cage door. "Good kitty."

"Uh—" Josh felt impelled to say something. "You're sure that's your cat?"

Jordan gave him a cool glance as she stowed the cat carrier in her car. "What? You weren't expecting a reward, were you?" She plopped into the front seat, slammed the door, and was gone before Josh had re-stowed his bags in the Civic.

That afternoon, walking Smitty the German shepherd again (on leash, this time), Josh told himself that of course he'd done the right thing. After a lot of effort, and a *lot* of personal trouble, he'd succeeded in reuniting the black and white cat with its owner. And it was a huge relief to have the cat gone. In fact, it made him feel like bursting into song. "I wanna hear the coyotes singin'," he crooned.

Smitty gazed up at him, skeptical.

Walking Smitty back to Coastal Canine, Josh decided that he needed to really (not sort of) apologize to his sister. He took out his phone and started to leave a message. "Hey, Vic. It's your clueless little bro. Just wanted to say thanks for dinner—and I'm sorry it ended on a bad note last night."

As Josh took a breath, Vicky picked up. "Josh: I've been thinking about you some more. It's true, you did have a year from hell."

Josh started to say something appreciative, but she went on, "Obviously you had to get out of your marriage. But I hate to see you throw teaching away with the bath water." Vicky paused a beat, and then she said, "Oh, Josh. Stick to teaching!"

Couldn't his sister just treat him like an adult? "If you want to know, I am checking out new teaching jobs." That should shut her up, and he could always say later that he hadn't found anything.

"Really?" said Vicky. "Well, that's a start."

"I have to go," Josh said. "Thanks again for dinner."

"Yeah, yeah. And for God's sake, call Mom!" His sister's tone turned from bossy to worried as she added, "Ask her if she's taking her meds."

At the end of the day, on his way back to Barbara's farmhouse, Josh found himself glancing in the rear view mirror, unthinkingly expecting to see a black and white cat on the back shelf. That was one thing, at least, that he didn't have to worry about.

Josh felt suddenly exhausted. The fire, the hospital, his dark night of the soul at Mattakiset Neck—it was all catching up with him. By the time he drove between the stone posts, he was focused solely on hauling himself into the apartment and flopping on the bed. After tucking a sheet over the mattress, of course, to be considerate of his landlady.

But as Josh felt under the steps for the spare key, he remembered that his sheets had gone up in smoke with Rick's cottage. He supposed he could spread T-shirts out on the bed, instead. Feeling sorry for himself, Josh dragged a bag of clothes up the steps.

Inside the apartment, Josh first noticed the splash of color on the dresser: a pitcher full of fresh flowers. And the bed— The bedspread was pulled halfway back, and the bed made up with seashell-patterned sheets, one corner turned down invitingly.

Barbara, you are a sweetheart. Josh flopped on the bed, as initially planned. He was out in a moment.

Later that evening, Josh knocked on Barbara's kitchen door holding a bottle of Pinot Noir. She'd just returned from her meeting, so he intended to hand her the wine, thank her effusively, and leave. But she insisted that he share a glass with her. She looked at the label. "Oh, high class! This beats my usual Two-Buck Chuck. This calls for my mother-in-law's Waterford crystal."

While Barbara poured the wine into fussy little goblets, Josh surveyed the postings on her refrigerator door. Under a magnet advertising The Chimney Guy, there was a printout of an Internet page. It pictured a wooden-floored hall where rows of women in workout gear sat on pink exercise balls. A hand-lettered caption read, "The dangers of chewing bubble gum while doing aerobics."

Josh burst out laughing and turned to Barbara, who smiled demurely. "Someone in my aerobics class found that. Shall we sit down in the other room?"

Lola ambled into the parlor with them and sprawled on the carpet, her muzzle on Barbara's sneakers.

"Cheers, Josh!" Barbara raised her glass. "Tell me something about yourself. Melissa said you're a teacher, so we have that in common. I used to teach math at the high school."

Raising his glass in return, Josh nodded. "Me, social studies—middle school." He hesitated. "Do you miss teaching?"

Barbara smiled wistfully. "More than I expected. By the time I retired, I thought I'd had it with the students and their parents and the administration and the stupid state board of ed, the whole ball of wax. But since then, I keep remembering the good things. And sometimes I'll bump into one of my former students in Soule's Market, and they'll tell me how grateful they are that they were in my class. Ones I'd never suspect, like Neil Dickinson."

"I thought I was leaving teaching, myself," Josh admitted. "Now, I'm not sure. I came here for a breathing space, to figure things out. Some stuff in my life threw me for a loop: My dog died, my marriage broke up, my job went sour. . . . So, I thought I'd treat myself to a summer at the beach. Mattakiset seemed like a happy place to pause and get my bearings."

Barbara gave him an ironic smile. "A happy place for *you*, maybe. People who don't live here think Mattakiset is some kind of paradise, where nothing bad happens. I can tell you, a whole lot of bad things happened to me, just in the last few years." She ticked them off on her fingers: "First, my husband decided to leave."

Josh was startled; he'd assumed Barbara was a widow. "Oh, I thought—"

Barbara nodded again. "Yes. He left, just like that, after forty years of marriage. And what a cliché. He found someone younger and tanner." She bent back another finger. "Right after that, I came down with a very unpleasant case of shingles." A third finger. "And then, to top it off, the transmission in my car died."

"Seriously?" asked Josh. "I didn't even tell you about *my* transmission trouble." Their double litany of disasters struck him as funny, and he began to laugh.

Barbara laughed, too. She refilled their glasses. "Well! Here's to better times ahead, for both of us."

Pussy cat, pussy cat, where have you been?
Nursery rhyme

Chapter 27.

"You're so lucky I found you again. What am I going to do with you? You need to stay in solitary for a while, until you can make better choices." The carrier tipped, spilling the Cat down rough wooden stairs. He wheeled and gathered himself to rush back up, but the door at the top of the stairs clicked shut.

The Cat found himself in a strange place. The center of the cellar was as brightly lit as a veterinarian's office. But instead of one bare metal table under the lights, there were rows of tables covered with rows of potted plants. And while the vet's had smelled like disinfectant and medicine, the cellar was filled with a lush green odor, more intense than a freshly cut lawn.

Blinking, the Cat turned from the white glare to explore the dim edges of the cellar. There were white ceiling panels above the lights, but the rest of the cellar was unfinished, showing pipes and wires draped with dusty cobwebs. There was a sink attached to one wall, and an oil tank next to the wall behind the stairs.

Three high windows were set deep into the concrete walls. The Cat jumped up to each window ledge in turn and pawed at the glass, but it was securely fastened. And on the outside the windows were overgrown with vines, as if they were never opened. He jumped down, brushing off spider webs and the husks of dead insects, and investigated the concrete steps at the end of the room. They led to a bolted metal lid.

The Cat prowled around the cellar again, sniffing carefully. Other cats had marked the walls with urine, although not recently. They'd left dry turds, too. And behind the oil tank—

The Cat stiffened. He sniffed the bones. Every hair on his body stood out.

These bones had once been a cat.

The Cat forgot everything he knew about patience. A despairing cry burst from his throat. *O Great Cat! Help me!* Dashing up the cellar stairs, he scrabbled at the door. Yowl after yowl poured out of him.

After a time the Cat's throat hurt, his front claws hurt, and he was out of breath. Creeping down from the door, he crouched on the bottom step and fell into a doze. When he woke sometime later, panic seized him again. He ran back up to the door, and again he scratched and yowled, yowled and scratched.

Finally the Cat paused, exhausted. His shoulder, where the rooster had dug its claws in, felt tight and sore. He twisted his neck to lick the wound, but he couldn't quite reach it.

O Great Cat? A dreadful thought came to him. Was he being weaned for the second time in his life—in an even more final way?

He remembered the day his mother had weaned him and his littermates. She was resting on her side in a pile of laundry, while the kittens crawled and tumbled and tussled over the landscape of sheets and towels. *Listen up, kids. I'm only going to say this once: No more free lunch.*

None of them understood what she meant. A moment later, the Kitten saw her cuff his striped littermate away from her nipples. But he only thought she was annoyed with that particular kitten. And not surprisingly—he thought the striped kitten was annoying, too. He snuggled confidently up to her milky flank, little white forepaws stretched out to knead.

A blow sent him rolling off the laundry pile, onto the cold linoleum floor. The Kitten picked himself up and stared at his mother. She stared back. She really had struck him. The same bulwark of warmth and food, who had always gazed down on them fondly, purring as she offered herself, had flung him away.

Was the same thing was happening now, with the Great Cat? He had thought he was a favorite of Hers—but maybe She was through with him. The Cat imagined Her mighty haunches, Her indifferent tail swaying, as She strolled away from him.

Wait—what was that sound on the other side of the door? The slap of flip-flops coming closer. The Cat's muscles tensed, and his heart beat faster.

The flip-flops stopped on the other side of the door. The young woman was talking in a soft voice: "Hey. It's me. Haven't seen you for a while." A pause. "Busy? Hmm. So am I, but I'm not too busy for . . ." She giggled.

Another pause, and then she answered with an edge to her voice, "*Maybe?* Well, *maybe* I'll be here when you decide to come. And maybe I won't." A click. "Asshole."

A moment later, the door opened a crack. The Cat thrust his head into the opening, but a bowl shoved back against his nose. "*No*, Mr. Tux. Eat and be quiet." The door closed, almost catching his whiskers.

The Cat threw himself at the door again, yowling and scratching heedlessly. In the one-sided struggle the bowl of cat chow fell off the top step and shattered on the concrete floor. He was in such a state that the crash only startled him for an instant.

At last the Cat turned and crept back down the steps. He sniffed at the mess of broken pottery. He ate a few pieces of cat chow, but he was too upset to make a meal of it.

Actually, the Cat needed to relieve himself. He searched the cellar for a litter box he might have missed. Unlike those other cats, he had more pride than to defecate on a bare floor. *Cover your bits,* his mother had instructed her kittens, and they'd all learned to clamber over the hard plastic sides of the litter box and dig in the crumbled clay.

Jumping onto a table, the Cat discovered that the cellar did have litter of sorts, only it was in unexpected containers: the pots under the lights. Plants grew out of each pot, some of them so luxuriantly that the branches hung over the rims and their roots clogged the soil. But in one row, the plants were mere slips with a few baby rootlets. The Cat found it easy to scoop them out of the soil, leaving a receptive furrow over which to lift his tail.

Brothers and sisters I bid you beware
Of giving your heart to a dog to tear.
Rudyard Kipling

Chapter 28.

The following morning, Josh arrived at the kennel planning Tucker's next lesson. The smart pup already knew *Sit* and *Stay*. From there, it would be a natural progression to *Lie down* and *Roll over*, rewarded, of course, with a tummy rub.

The Large Dogs arrived for play group, all of them except Tucker. "Isn't this one of Tucker's day care days?" Josh asked Rune.

Rune shrugged. "They probably canceled. People do that a lot." Lola came wiggling up to her, and Rune bent to touch noses. "Whoa, my dream last night," she added. "I didn't realize it in the dream, but that animal must have been Tucker."

Rune and her paranormal drama. "A prophetic dream?" asked Josh.

Ignoring his frivolous tone, Rune stared at the back fence as if watching a dreamscape.

"But he wasn't *acting* like Tucker. His ears were down, and his tail was drooping." She turned suddenly to Josh. "Whoa, I bet Tucker's racked with guilt about causing Carol's accident. He probably felt too bad to come to play group."

Startled, Josh laughed. "What?"

Rune nodded to herself. "That's why I had that dream." She frowned at Josh. "You probably don't know that animals in distress can project their concerns over a distance. Maybe I should call the Harrisons and offer my services."

Josh had to ask. "What services?"

Rune launched into an explanation about how certain psychics, like her, had the ability to establish telepathic rapport with a disturbed dog, even over a long distance. She'd done that once before, with a Cairn terrier named Ethel.

It seemed that Ethel's owners had been staying at a campground in Vermont, at the same time as Kyle, a friend of Rune's, and his three-year-old daughter. Ethel bit the little girl, and Kyle called Rune for advice. Rune had already moved back to Massachusetts the year before, but Kyle sent her a picture of the little dog, and Rune was able to make telepathic contact. "Ethel was inconsolable. I could feel her reaching out for help."

"Wait a minute," said Josh. "What about the little girl? Did the dog have its rabies shots?"

"Oh, Kyle's kid was fine, just a flesh wound," said Rune. "She shouldn't have been teasing the dog, anyway. But poor Ethel! Her owners weren't very aware. They were really surprised when Kyle told them how much guilt and confusion she was suffering."

As Josh listened in disbelief, he thought Ethel's owners must have been even more surprised when Kyle suggested Rune's psychic healing services, for a reasonable fee. But they agreed, and Rune applied her special gifts in a long-distance session with the Cairn terrier. In the end, Ethel was still remorseful, but no longer conflicted, and newly aware of her responsibility for self-control. Ethel's owners sent Rune a check, which she split with her friend Kyle.

"Very interesting," said Josh. "Only in this case, the Harrisons are more likely to sue the kennel than write you a check."

When Josh had a chance, he ducked into the office to follow up on Tucker's whereabouts. Uncle George was at the desk, and he pulled up a schedule on the screen. "Yep, he was supposed to come in today. That's Harrison for you, no consideration. Carol, now, would have called to cancel, but of course she's laid up."

"How is she? Is she in the hospital?"

"She's home, but off her feet. I guess she sprained her ankle good." The old man added with satisfaction, "Next time it'll be a broken hip."

But since Carol was "laid up," why wouldn't Gardner be glad to dump Tucker at day care? Maybe Carol was keeping the dog home for company. Josh sure would, if he were injured and hurting. Anyway, Josh resolved to take Carol flowers tomorrow.

The morning passed in the usual round of hurling balls for the retrievers, filling water buckets, and raking wood chips, but Josh felt different. He was no longer drifting wherever the summer took him. It was time to start planning, not in a fooling-around *Small Business for Dummies* kind of way, but seriously. Where was he going to go? What was he going to do?

On his lunch break, Josh went to the library to check his email. Nothing more from Tanya about the dog bed, but—Ron! Good man.

Josh ran his eyes over Ron Watanabe's message: *No worries, feel free to rant.*" Ron gave the birth stats on his baby boy, and attached a picture of him and his wife at the hospital, beaming, cuddling a scowling infant.

It sucks that your principal had it in for you, Ron went on. *But isn't it a little extreme to leave teaching? You really love working with kids. Everyone says public schools are in the toilet, so why don't you look at private schools? You could check with Nancy Reston, remember her? I hear she's the new head of Kingstown Academy. If there aren't any openings there, she might know of other schools that are looking.*

Josh read this with mixed feelings. He was miffed that Ron didn't even comment on Josh's small business idea. Josh had thought he'd sounded pretty knowledgeable, even if he wasn't. And "You really love working with kids"—like Vicky, Ron was annoyingly sure about what Josh should do with his life.

But— Josh's throat ached as he remembered that exciting energy, when he was alone in his classroom with twenty-five kids. He remembered having nothing on his mind except working his strategies for luring the students into the subject, for teasing and challenging them just enough. And they tested him; they teased and challenged *him*. Teaching was like improv theater; the only way it could work was in attentive response to the other people.

Even when Josh failed to get a concept across, it was always interesting. And once in a while there was a big payoff. The year before last, one of the boys in his third period class had joined a discussion unexpectedly. It was March, as Josh remembered, and Zack had not yet volunteered in class. Zack, the coolest guy in the eighth grade, had better things to do, such as soak up furtive stares from the females in the class, and admire the decal tattoo on his arm.

Josh's question to the class was, "What do you personally know about the Vietnam War?"

The first answer came, predictably, from Brayden, a military history buff. "Nothing," he said with a smartass grin. "Because it was in the 1960s, and I wasn't born yet. My dad wasn't even born yet."

Josh acknowledged Brayden with a faint smile and nod. "In the sixties, right." *Zack was actually raising his hand!* "Zack?"

Zack rubbed his tattoo absently as he said, "So . . . my grandmother told me she went on a protest march. Against the war. She was pregnant with my mom, and there were TV cameras, so she thought it would help."

Several of the kids laughed, and one boy snickered, "Help how—if the baby was born right there on TV?"

Josh started to speak in support of Zack, but the boy spoke first, staring at the taunter. "*Help,* asshole, because babies are, like, the future. And the war was ruining the future. She wanted to show everyone that."

The class was suddenly quiet. Josh's throat tightened with emotion. He'd been so sure that Zack was paying no attention whatsoever the other day, when Josh talked to this class about the influence of the media. Zack not only got the concept; he'd offered an illustration from his own family's history.

"Good example," Josh said, letting the "asshole" go without comment. He went on to explain how public opinion had affected first President Johnson and then President Nixon. Zack had yawned and looked at the clock, as if to make clear that he was *not* sucking up to the teacher.

If Josh did go back to teaching, a private school might work. Of course he remembered Nancy Reston, another classmate from the long-ago MAT program, and he was intrigued. As a graduate student, he'd been in awe of her ambition.

In those days, Ron had teased her for wanting to reform American education. "What's wrong with that?" Nancy had said with one of her fierce looks. So it wasn't surprising that she was the new head of a good school like Kingstown Academy—maybe only surprising that she wasn't the new U.S. Secretary of Education.

It wouldn't hurt to give Nancy a call. Josh still had options—he was thankful that he hadn't let Principal Voss's report on his supposed insensitivity go uncontested. Carl, who was the president of the local teachers' union, had advised him to write a rebuttal and send copies to anyone who might care, including the board of education. Carl had also gone over Josh's draft to edit out the rage. "You can't call Voss a 'psychopath.'" (Josh had thought that was simply objective language.)

Looking over the Kingstown Academy website, Josh felt let down. Their only open faculty position was a coaching job. Was it worthwhile to pitch himself to Nancy, when the best she could offer would be a tip about some other school? To tell the truth, Josh had always been a little afraid of Nancy.

Still, Josh knew that word of mouth and people who knew people was the best way to find a teaching job. Clicking on "Contact us," he started, "Hi Nancy."

No. Composing a message would take a long time, and he had to get going. Better to call, anyway—if he really wanted to explore that possibility. Closing the email, Josh noted down the Academy phone number and Nancy's extension.

As Josh left the library, his stomach reminded him that he hadn't eaten, although he was due back at Coastal Canine in five minutes. He pulled into Cumberland Farms and dashed into the store. A poster beside the door urged, "Indulge your inner carnivore" and showed a meatball sub so enormous, it extended beyond the edges of the poster. Yes.

"I'm indulging my inner carnivore," Josh explained to Danielle at the counter.

She gave him a cool glance as she scanned the bar code. Josh added, "I'm really sorry about the other night. I was a jerk to forget."

Danielle only shrugged and dropped the change into his hand. Then she seemed to remember something, and her eyes widened. "Oh! By the way, I can take the cat now."

"The cat? You mean the one that was riding in my car?"

"Yes," she said impatiently. "Panda. I can take him home now." At his confused expression, she went on, "I know what I said, Ryan and his supposed allergies.

Well, last night I'm doing some wash, and I look down at one of his shirts—and it's covered with cat fur." She hit the side of her head. "Duh! If Ryan can pal around with Cat Woman, I guess he's outgrown those allergies."

"Too bad," said Josh. "I mean, I don't have that cat anymore. I found its owner."

"Oh." Danielle looked disappointed, more so than Josh would have expected.

"You should try the cat shelter, Fur-Ever," Josh told her. "Rune says they have so many cats, they don't know where to put them."

"Yeah, I know," Danielle snapped. "I wanted Panda." She began ringing up the next customer's iced coffee.

Josh paused outside the store to take a thoughtful bite of his sub. *Cat Woman.* Did he know who that was?

What! Lost your mittens, you naughty kittens!
Then you shall have no pie.
"Meow, meow, meow."
No, you shall have no pie.
Nursery rhyme

Chapter 29.

The Cat was losing track of time. In his prison, nothing seemed to change. The glare from the lights over the plant tables flooded the cellar, overruling light from the windows. Rising from an uneasy doze, the Cat jumped onto a window sill and strained to peer through the vines. With his whiskers brushing the glass, he could blot out the reflection, but he could see only the vaguest suggestion of black shapes against black.

After a time, the Cat began to make out a gray scene: a stretch of shabby grass, tires, and the bushes beyond. This was the same scene he'd dashed across, once before. His muscles tensed to bound toward freedom, and he meowed, scraping a paw against the glass.

The grass outside brightened from gray to brownish green. One bird, then three, flew over the grass and hopped around in the bushes.

As the Cat kept watching, a calico cat walked into view, trailed by a line of kittens. The Cat felt a pang of envy. But he wouldn't want a mother like this small, scrawny cat. *His* mother had been large and sleek.

The Cat wished his mother were here now, to lick his shoulder, which he couldn't reach with his tongue. He could feel heat from the swelling.

Jumping down to the concrete floor, the Cat made the rounds of the cellar again. He ate a few more pieces of cat chow, pawing it out of the broken crockery. But he was more thirsty than hungry. He jumped onto the edge of the sink and licked the faucet. A little rusty-tasting water ran out.

Each time the Cat jumped, his shoulder hurt, and now he hesitated to jump down from the sink. Luckily, just in that moment a cricket crawled out of the drain. He pounced and crunched. That was something, although not much juicier than cat chow.

As the Cat began to groom himself, spitting out the scratchy cricket feelers, the door at the top of the stairs opened. He rushed for it, but the woman called Jordan shut the door behind her before he was halfway up the stairs. He hissed, whirled, and ran under the oil tank.

The young woman's flip-flops slapped down the wooden stairs. "What's this, you broke your dish?" She sighed heavily. "Fine. Well, here's your breakfast, anyway."

As she crossed the cellar toward him, the Cat slunk farther into the shadows beneath the oil tank. She set down a saucer of cat chow. He hissed, and he added a growl.

"Is that the thanks I get, Mr. Tux?" She picked up the watering can, filled it at the sink, and began watering each of the pots under the lights. She sang as she worked: "Hmm hmm hmm, row by row, gotta make my garden grow, hmm hmm hmm . . ."

But at the last row she stopped, set the watering can down, and put her hands on her hips. "What the fuck!

Shit!” Over her shoulder she added, “Some bad, bad kitty messed up my seedlings. Do you know how much that’ll cost me? Cat chow doesn’t grow on trees.” Still muttering, she flip-flopped back up the stairs.

His head on my knee can heal my human hurts.
Gene Hill

Chapter 30.

The next morning, his day off from the kennel, Josh drove into the village to get a signal for his cell phone. Cool air flowed in the car window, and his mind felt marvelously clear. This must be his new life, Life Beyond the List. He could do better than dragging himself along a few percentage points at a time.

Josh had thought of making his visit to Carol Harrison this morning, but first things first: Starting today, Josh would man up and do his part to support his mother. He got it, now: It wasn't enough to just show up. And he already had a plan to do something she would actually enjoy. The day was September-bright, although it was only late July, and Josh imagined gallantly seating Martha on the patio of an upscale little café.

Parking at Cumby's, Josh took out his phone and dialed. "Bless you, Josh!" his mother answered. "It must be ESP—I was just thinking how wonderful it would be if you happened to call."

Josh started to ask if she knew of a restaurant near Northport Commons, but Martha Hiller interrupted, "No, no; I don't want to go out to lunch. Can you could drive me to the hairdresser? Apparently the Commons shuttle doesn't go there today." She added sharply, "I'm positive they changed the schedule without announcing it."

So why didn't she take a taxi, or book an Uber ride? Josh sensed that this was the wrong question to ask. "Sure, Mom. What time's your appointment?"

It wasn't until one o'clock, so Josh had time before he headed north to do his second most important thing: call Nancy Reston. With his thumb hovering over the Kingstown Academy number, Josh pictured Nancy as he remembered her, radiating benevolent energy. The picture of her on the Kingstown website had looked much the same, give or take a few creases and gray hairs.

But Josh's mental image of Nancy morphed into the smooth pink face and round blue eyes of Principal Voss during their last encounter. He'd walked into her office the week after the field trip to Washington. "Excuse me. Can we talk?"

Charlene Voss looked mildly surprised. "Oh. I'm in the middle of something, but if this is important . . ." She gestured at a chair facing her desk. As Josh started to close the office door, she said, "Leave that open, please."

Josh shrugged and sat down. Did she want Glenda, the office administrator, to be able to testify that she was not sexually harassing him? Or did she think he would try to strangle her, if they were alone together? Or did she say it just to throw him off balance?

Never mind. He held up a flyer titled "Creating a Safe Space in the Classroom." "Why did you put this in my mailbox?"

"Oh, yes. The sensitivity workshop." Her smile was bland. "Didn't I clip a note to it? I thought you'd find it helpful for personal as well as professional development."

"But why did you put it in *my* mailbox? And nobody else's." Josh tried to get more comfortable in the chair, which was low and wooden, with a seat tilting down toward the back. It folded his body, squeezing his already tense guts.

Pulling out a file drawer, Voss removed a manila folder with a tab labeled HILLER, J. Wow, that was a thick file. Either she was storing her junk mail in there, or she'd been taking notes on every single smart remark he'd made this year.

The principal opened the folder and frowned, as if it was hard to know where to begin. "Let's see. Well, you were the teacher in charge on the Washington, D.C. field trip. And I've noticed other indications . . . But I wouldn't recommend the workshop unless I thought you had the potential to benefit from it."

"The field trip. Oh. Are you talking about the incident with Kaylee?"

Charlene Voss nodded regretfully. "I have to wonder how you could have her in your class for most of a year and not sense how vulnerable she is. I could see that myself, in just one classroom visit last fall."

"I remember how sensitive *you* were that day," said Josh. "Aside from the fact that there was no reason for you to observe my class."

Leaning back in her high-backed, padded swivel chair, Voss said, "As the principal, it's my job to run this school."

"But not your job to harass teachers while they're conducting a class."

"So that was your interpretation." The principal regarded him for a moment, nodding her head. "Do you know that you have a serious problem dealing with women in authority?"

"What?" exclaimed Josh. "*That* came out of left field."

"Hardly," said Voss, tapping the "J. Hiller" folder. "The way you handled the post-field trip follow-up is just one example." She turned a page in the folder. "According to the docent at the National Gallery, you failed to model active listening for the students during the tour."

"I failed—" Josh began to get the picture of what a detailed dossier Charlene Voss had compiled on him. "You actually went to the trouble to hunt up that docent?"

As if he hadn't said anything, she went on, "And Amanda Gill noticed that you watched Kaylee walk over to the antique chair and sit down without trying to stop her."

That hurt—Josh had thought he was on good terms with Curtis Gill's mother. "I guess Amanda Gill was thinking the same thing I was: namely, that Kaylee wouldn't actually sit down on the chair. Because she didn't try to stop her, either."

"The worst part of it, of course, was the way you took advantage of Kaylee's distress with intimate touching."

"What! I did *not* . . ." Josh's voice trailed off as he remembered that moment in the portrait gallery. Kaylee with her head hanging like a scolded dog. His arm around her, his hand patting her head as if she were Molly. And Sarah Rothman's glare as she pulled the girl away. "If that's what Ms. Rothman told you, she completely misinterpreted what I did." He had a mental image of the principal with a phone pressed to her ear, making call after call, asking question after insinuating question, taking careful notes. The prosecuting attorney.

"That was not only insensitive," Voss was saying, "but highly inappropriate behavior. This workshop could help you understand that."

"I hope *you* understand that Sarah Rothman overreacted. Maybe she felt guilty about the way her own daughter picked on Kaylee."

The principal frowned. As if Josh's explanation was too far-fetched to even acknowledge, she continued, "Getting back to the authority issue. Our protocol at the Westham Middle School—and you'll remember I explained this to the faculty at the beginning of the year—is for a teacher to consult with me before discussing an incident of this nature with the parents."

"That's ridiculous," said Josh. "The important thing was for me to talk to Kaylee's parents right away, so that they understood why Kaylee came home unhappy. That they got the whole picture of the other girls, *including Margaret Rothman*, teasing her. Did Ms. Rothman mention that? Anyway, Kaylee's parents appreciated my call. We had a good discussion."

Charlene Voss was looking over his shoulder. "I think you're proving my point even as we speak. To be clear, the sensitivity workshop is not a suggestion. It's a directive. And then we'll re-evaluate in June."

"I see." Josh tried to jump to his feet, but getting out of the low, back-slanted chair was awkward, making him even angrier. However, he managed to restrain himself from saying, "Fuck your directive." He merely tore the flyer in half and dropped it onto her desk on his way out.

Now, on the point of calling Nancy Reston, Josh hesitated. Maybe the reason he hated Charlene Voss so much was that she'd pinpointed his weakness. If she'd been *Charles* Voss, would he have had as much of a problem with her?

Josh had resented his principal's authority so much that he'd given her cause to remove him from the classroom three weeks before the end of the school year, leaving his students to be babysat by a substitute. He shouldn't have done that to them. It wouldn't have killed him to sit through a sensitivity workshop. Much worse, in fact, to sit through three weeks of make-work in the superintendent's office, listening to "Take This Job and Shove It" through his earbuds.

As Josh fiddled with his phone, a school bus drew up beside him and stopped for the crosswalk. Such a golden yellow bus, against the bright blue sky. A boy leaned out a window, calling gleefully, "Help! They're taking us to an institution!"

Ah, middle school. That boy reminded Josh of Curtis. Curtis's decision-making center in his prefrontal cortex had a long way to go, and he'd tested Josh's patience many times. But he'd also given Josh the "World's Best Teacher" coffee mug.

Schools couldn't have started already—these kids must be in some kind of summer program. Still, Josh felt uneasy, as if there were a classroom in which eighth graders milled around, waiting for Mr. Hiller to show up. Josh wanted to walk into that classroom.

Josh picked up his phone again and called Nancy Reston's number. He only got her voice mail, which was a letdown. But he liked the way his own voice sounded—friendly, upbeat, and professional—as he left a message. Vicky was right; he wasn't entirely crushed.

As Josh headed north on Route 24, the phone rang: Kingstown Academy. His pulse sped up. "Nancy! Hey, thanks for getting right back to me. I'm on the road; let me pull over."

The sound of Nancy's voice took Josh back to his graduate school days. She still had that same force—not a bullying kind of energy, but a steady passion that made you want to grab a pike and follow her into the breech. "Of course I remember you, Josh. Anyway, you're famous—a runner-up for Massachusetts Teacher of the Year two years ago, right? I wish I had a place to offer you at Kingstown."

Oh. "I wish you did, too." Josh kept his tone regretful, but not as disappointed as he felt.

Nancy went on, promising to ask among her consortium of private schools for him. “What if a position’s out of the area—would you consider that?”

“I’d consider it, but I’d rather stick around Boston. My mother is pretty frail.”

They agreed to be in touch, and Josh sung back onto the expressway. Well . . . not the news he’d hoped for. Still, Nancy knew—Nancy *cared*—that Josh Hiller had a reputation as an outstanding teacher. She’d probably Googled him to find that out, but if so, he was pleased that she’d taken the trouble.

Another possibility was that Ron Watanabe might have been in touch with Nancy to let her know Josh was looking for a new job. If so, Ron had put himself out for Josh, and that was a heartwarming thought, too.

At Northport Commons Senior Living, Josh waited in the lobby while the receptionist rang his mother. He gazed up at the high ceiling, where whimsical mobiles floated. He looked over at the fern-banked entrance to the dining hall, where several residents sat slumped in wheelchairs. One woman slept with her mouth open.

In contrast, Martha Hiller looked almost sprightly as she stepped out of the elevator carrying a handbag, a lemon-yellow cardigan sweater over her shoulders. “Josh, you don’t know how much this means to me, getting my hair done. I couldn’t stand it a moment longer.” Pushing her white bangs off her forehead, she rested a hand on his elbow. “I don’t need my cane, if I can take your arm.”

As they drove out the gated entrance to the Commons, Martha gave Josh directions to the hairdresser's salon. "After you turn onto Endicott Street, it'll be on the right, past a Starbuck's." She chuckled. "The 'Mona Lisa,' it's called."

"So I should expect you to come out with a mysterious smile?"

At the salon, Josh opened the glass door for his mother and walked into a cloud of shampoo and hairspray vapor.

"Hello, Martha!" The woman behind the counter, who looked as if she used all the products available in the salon, beamed at her. "Diana will be right with you." She nodded toward the back, where a hairdresser wielded a hairdryer and brush over a customer. "Let's see"—she tapped her computer keys—"you're having a cut and perm, is that right?"

Josh felt his mother's grip on his arm tighten. He looked down in alarm—was she going to faint?

Martha Hiller opened her mouth, frowned, and shut it. She opened it again, seeming to make some kind of effort, but still she didn't answer. She shrugged, and her frown deepened.

The salon receptionist raised her sculpted eyebrows at Josh, and he wondered if his mother had heard the question. The earlier customer, her hair now as immaculately styled as a wig, stepped up to the counter and looked at Martha. Josh bent down and spoke distinctly into his mother's ear. "She's asking if you're having a cut and perm today."

Martha made a weak noise in her throat. She squeezed her eyes shut, then opened them. Finally she looked straight at the receptionist and nodded vigorously.

"Mom, are you okay?" asked Josh.

But before Martha Hiller could answer—or not answer—the hairdresser called Diana hurried up to them and took his mother's arm. "Martha, so good to see you! Let's sit down right over here."

Was his mother okay, or not? Josh watched the hairdresser settle Martha Hiller into a black swivel chair and fasten a black cape around her shoulders. His mother still wasn't talking, but she was smiling contentedly.

Josh sat down on a vinyl-covered couch in the waiting area. Maybe he should check with Vicky about their mother's odd behavior. He took out his phone and sent her a text, explaining what had happened. She didn't answer right away.

Josh connected with the Mona Lisa's Wi-Fi (security: weak) and checked a couple of news sites. He brought up Coastal Canine's website and admired his own pictures of the day-care dogs. He loved the one of Tucker showing his teeth just a little, as he did to emphasize some doggy demand.

A lot of the pictures included Tucker, Josh noticed, even though his goal had been to get one shot of each dog. Here were Tucker and Buster play-bowing before they threw themselves at each other in a wrestling match; Tucker shouldering Lola aside to plunge his muddy muzzle into a water bucket; Tucker shoving his snout right into the camera, a caricature of a dog with a huge head and tiny body.

Josh noted that the Beginning Obedience class was still posted, in spite of the disaster with Murphy and the cat and Tucker and Carol. Did that mean that Erica wanted him to continue teaching it, or did it mean that she hadn't gotten around to taking it off the site?

Looking up to check on his mother, Josh saw that she was now sitting under a hair dryer. She seemed all right, placidly turning the pages of a magazine.

Josh checked his messages again, but nothing from Vicky.

Maybe the hair dryer meant that Martha Hiller's appointment was almost finished. Josh got up to ask the receptionist.

She smiled tolerantly at him. "Not really. I'd say another half hour."

Sheesh. If he was going to wait that long, Josh might as well wait at the Starbuck's next door.

However, once he was perched on a coffee bar stool with a large latte and a pastry, Josh felt uneasy. He walked back to the salon and peered through the glass door at his mother, still under the dryer. He returned to the Starbuck's and checked his messages again. No Vicky text.

Josh Googled "loss of speech symptom." That search turned up "possible TIA," which stood for "transient ischemic attack." Which meant a mini-stroke.

Oh shit. Josh jumped down from the stool.

Back in the salon, the woman at the counter was welcoming another customer. Her eyes widened as Josh burst in.

"My mother's had a stroke. I need to get her to a doctor."

Martha Hiller was now lying with her head over a sink, as Diana removed curlers and rinsed the white curls. "I'm fine, dear," she said. "Oh, are you worried because of that little hitch when I first came in? That was nothing."

"You couldn't talk. You were having a mini-stroke. I'm taking you to a doctor."

"Josh, you're making too much of this. It goes right away." Martha sat up, with the help of the hairdresser, and allowed a towel to be wrapped around her head.

"We're just about finished here," said Diana soothingly.

Josh wondered for an instant if he were causing a scene about "nothing," as his mother called it. Yeah, it wasn't wise to diagnose an illness over the internet. But then he reminded himself of Martha's very peculiar behavior an hour ago. "We *are* finished. Mom, please get up before I drag you out of here."

Josh must have convinced them, because the hairdresser removed the towel from his mother's head and the cape from her shoulders and helped her stand up. "This is so unnecessary," said Martha crossly. She insisted on giving Diana her tip and paying at the counter before she let him hustle her out the door.

While his mother was fumbling with her credit card, Josh had checked his phone. Still nothing from

Vicky—he was on his own. Should he take his mother to a hospital emergency room? No. At an E.R., she might have to wait until she had a full-blown stroke.

Starting the car, Josh demanded, "Where's your doctor now? Are you still with the clinic in Peabody?"

"This is all so unnecessary," repeated Martha Hiller, but she sulkily directed him to a doctor's office in Northport. At the clinic, she apologized to the nurse for her wet hair as she was taken off to an exam room.

Josh sat down in the waiting room. He texted Vicky to let her know they were at the doctor's.

While he waited for Vicky to get back to him, Josh mused that his sister was right: Their mother tried to be brave. But compare her with Barbara Schaeffer, roughly the same age. Barbara could toss trash bags into the back of her S.U.V., while Martha Hiller needed support just for walking. It was as unfair as . . . as unfair as the way Labrador retrievers predictably gave out after age eleven.

A text popped up on Josh's phone, but it was from Nancy Reston. *Kingstown does have opening. Consider joining as coach? You'd love this school, + you'd be in line for something better.*

But Josh didn't want to coach. He wanted to teach history.

There was more: *Full disclosure: We'd also need you to lead the first scheduled field trip, because . . .*

Argh! thought Josh. No matter the reasons. No matter the destination of the field trip. Just, Argh!

In Josh's answer, he didn't mention the field trip. *Appreciate offer! But I'll keep looking for SS position.*

He pointedly thanked Nancy for promising to inquire about openings at another school.

Josh hardly had time to feel anxious about his employment prospects when he saw that Vicky was texting him back: *OMG. I was afraid of this. Keep me posted.*

She followed up immediately with another text: *I was in a meeting, no phones allowed. So glad you were with her.*

Never was there such a dog.
Jack London, *The Call of the Wild*

Chapter 31.

Later, in the car on the way back to the Commons, Martha Hiller admitted that she hadn't been taking her blood thinner prescription. "I was just tired of bleeding at the drop of a hat." She looked pensively out the window for a few moments, and then she cleared her throat.

Josh tensed out of habit, afraid she was going to change the subject to his worrisome life. Then he realized that would be okay—he could truthfully say he was looking for a teaching job and planning where he wanted to live.

"Frankly," his mother said, "I'm tired of the whole thing. It wouldn't be so bad to have a stroke—a real stroke—and never wake up."

Shocked, Josh didn't know what to say. But he remembered Vicky's words: *This is not about you.* Finally he nodded. He reached over and patted Martha's hair, now dry and extra curly.

Pulling into the Northport Commons driveway, Josh stopped the car in front of the entrance. As he started to open the door, his mother said, "Wait." She picked up her handbag. "Josh, I'm going to ask you a favor. It's something very important to me."

"Well, sure," he said, shrinking inwardly from her sober tone of voice.

"Don't say yes until you know what it is." She took a sheaf of papers out of her handbag. "This is a copy of my advance directive. I've already asked Vicky to be my health care agent, but I need an alternate, a backup in case for some reason she can't."

Josh stifled an impulse to put his hands over his ears. "You mean, if you— I'd have to—"

His mother was smiling wryly. "No, you wouldn't have to 'pull the plug.' You wouldn't have to decide anything. I've already decided what I'd want done or not done. You'd just have to make sure that the medical people know what's in here—" she shook the papers— "and that they don't decide for themselves." When he didn't speak right away, she added, "It wouldn't be like euthanizing a dog."

Josh flinched. Martha sighed. "Excuse me for speaking bluntly." She went on, "If you feel that you couldn't be my health care agent, I'll ask my cousin Susie to be the alternate."

"No, I'll do it," said Josh. He took a deep breath. "Of course I'll do it." Taking the papers from her hand, he looked straight at his mother. His throat ached, making his voice hoarse. "In fact, I'm honored that . . . that you have confidence in me."

Martha Hiller looked back quietly for a moment. Then she smiled at him, not a fond motherly smile, but as one adult to another. "Thank you," she said.

After walking his mother to the elevator, Josh sat in his car for a moment. He placed his set of Martha Y. Hiller's advance directive on the passenger seat. Running his right hand over the steering wheel, he stroked Molly's tooth marks. Life with a dog: puppy to ashes in twelve years. Was it worth it?

Yes.

I do want a dog, thought Josh. But first I have to get a job, so that I can afford a dog. As well as a place to live, in which to put the dog.

As Josh drove out through the gates of the senior residence, his thoughts spurted forward suddenly, like water from an un-kinked hose. Maybe he didn't have to wait until he had a job and a place to live before he got a dog. There was a dog, a special dog, who was already waiting for him: Tucker!

Carol Harrison was fond of Tucker, but even before her accident, she'd seemed overwhelmed by him. And now that she was hobbling around on crutches, she'd probably be relieved to turn Tucker over to a good home. As for Gardner, he didn't even like the dog.

Josh's car soon slowed to a crawl in the mid-afternoon traffic along Route 128, but his mind raced ahead. Tomorrow morning, when Gardner Harrison brought Tucker to day care, he'd offer to take the dog off their hands. After work he'd face Barbara Schaeffer with his lease violation. If he had to, he'd move out immediately. Yeah, the Dreamland Motel probably had a vacancy—not right next to Rick Johnson, he hoped.

It had been so clear, from the day Josh met them, that the Harrisons and Tucker were mismatched. Why had it taken Josh all this time to realize that, in contrast, he and Tucker were meant for each other?

It wouldn't be convenient. But screw the obstacles to true love! Josh smiled as he imagined murmuring into the dog's flapped ear, "Oh, Tucker . . . It was you, all along."

A green highway sign announced the exit for Westham. On an impulse, Josh moved into the right lane and drove down the ramp. Parked at a gas station, he called Tanya. Of course it was still his house, too, but . . . "I just wanted to give you a heads-up—I happened to be in the area, and I thought I'd stop by the house to pick up the dog bed." She didn't say anything right away, and Josh added, "Unless you've changed the locks."

"No, why would I do that?"

Ending the call, Josh wondered if coming back here so soon was a good idea. Especially to get the dog bed. The dog bed fight last Labor Day had been the beginning of the end for Tanya and Josh.

The trouble had begun about eleven o'clock on that sweltering day, when Josh returned from the store with 12-packs of beer and soda and bags of ice for the cookout. Tanya met him in the driveway as he opened the trunk.

"I thought you were going to take the dog with you."

What now? thought Josh. "Obviously I couldn't take Molly on a day like this—I couldn't leave her in the car, even with the windows down."

"Fine. Well, *obviously* she pooped on the lawn right in front of the grill. Please clean it up before you do anything else."

Josh had walked Molly earlier, just so that this problem wouldn't occur, but sometimes dogs had more than one poop per morning. "Shit happens," said Josh.

Tanya didn't laugh or smile. "I'll clean it up right after I put the ice in the coolers, okay?"

She turned and went back into the house.

Josh carried the coolers out of the garage to the patio in back and filled them with layers of cans and ice. Maybe once the party got going, everything would be okay. Maybe all they needed was more people around, to dilute the acid eating away at him and Tanya.

Josh cleaned up Molly's mess. By the time he came in the back door, his T-shirt was soaked with sweat under his arms and down his back, and his face seemed to be pulsing waves of heat.

Molly herself lay stretched out on the vinyl kitchen floor. She wagged her tail briefly for Josh, but she was too busy panting to get up. "Yeah," he told Molly, "black isn't a good color choice in this weather."

"Josh," called Tanya from the living room, over the sound of the laboring window air conditioner. That tone of voice meant she expected him to come and find out what she wanted. Josh didn't see why he should.

Grabbing a paper towel, Josh ran it under the cold water and mopped his face and the back of his neck. "Yeah," he called back.

Tanya stepped into the kitchen with the expression of someone who has been pushed past the point of endurance. "I don't think you understand how much there is to do. People are going to start showing up."

"What! What *is* there to do?" As Josh raised his voice, Molly got to her feet.

Tanya pointed toward the living room. "For starters, getting that dog bed out of sight. And the filthy blanket on the sofa. *I've* vacuumed up the dog hair from the floor."

"Tanya. You're losing it. The heat must be getting to your brain. This is a cookout, not a black-tie event. Nobody's even going to go in the fucking living room."

Molly whined, rolling her eyes from Josh to Tanya and back again.

"Yes, they are, because it's so hot that no one is going to want to stay out in the fucking yard." (Molly whimpered.) "Would you make your dog shut up?"

"You're the one who's upsetting Molly." Josh looked down at the dog, who was trying to wag her tail and tuck it between her legs at the same time. He stroked her flattened ears. "Poor old girl. I think the stitches in her mouth still hurt."

"Which is why we shouldn't have put her through the pain and suffering, when that *very expensive* surgery wasn't going to save her life anyway," said Tanya.

Josh stared at her. "You're still pissed about the money. What a big heart." He was aware that Molly was creeping under the kitchen table, but he couldn't lower his voice. "The bottom line—and it is literally the bottom line—is, you think it's more your money than mine. I'm not allowed to make money decisions, because your income is one point five times more than mine. Did you forget who put you through law school?"

"Let's get it right," said Tanya. "a) It was actually your father who put me through law school. b) My income is one point *seven* times more than yours. And c) you're on my health insurance, because yours is so pathetic. So would you mind very much putting the dog bed out of sight?"

"I'm taking a shower before I have heat stroke," said Josh.

But before he could even start for the stairs, the doorbell rang. Lugging the vacuum cleaner down the hall, Tanya gestured with her chin at the front door. "Happy Labor Day!" called their first guest.

Ever since that day, Josh had filed the incident in his mind as evidence that their breakup was Tanya's fault. He'd told Vicky the story of the Labor Day cookout from hell, and she'd taken his side. But now the memory only made him feel sad. Tanya cared so much about how their house looked, about having nice things around her. He hadn't respected that.

On his way to their house, Josh decided to take a detour into the business side of Westham, to the self-storage unit where he'd left his stuff. Liberty Self-Storage was located between a plant nursery and a Target store. The front had a cheery façade of faux shutters and gables, but around back in the parking lot, the access side was bleakly functional. Fittingly bleak, thought Josh. Storage units were for a death, or an eviction. Or a divorce.

It was daunting, when Josh unlocked the door of Unit 5C, to face his stuff jammed together like trash in a compacter. He didn't know where the Seth Thomas clock was in the tangle, or even who had last handled it. It might have been Carl, or it might have been Josh himself, with the unreal state of mind he'd been in that day. What if the clock was against the far wall—how long would it take him to move everything out and then move it all back again?

But Josh began, wiggling each item loose and setting it in the hall. Luckily the clock was only a few layers in from the door. Luckily he recognized its shape, bundled in a bathmat, on the seat of an office chair.

Josh had intended to pick up the dog bed before Tanya got home, but by the time he left the storage building, it was after five. Now he wasn't sure whether he hoped to avoid Tanya or hoped to see her.

At the house, Josh started to pull into the driveway, then parked at the curb instead. The yard looked startlingly cared for: the hedge was trimmed and clean, the lawn was an even green, and annuals made splashes of color along the walk. The walk itself was level, with the cracked flagstones replaced.

Tanya came to the front door when Josh knocked. She was still in business garb, a tailored skirt and silk blouse, although she was barefoot. She looked tired and pale, as if she'd spent the summer in the office. "Hey."

"Hey," said Josh, holding up the clock. "Can we trade?"

"Oh. I didn't think— It must have been a lot of trouble to dig that out of storage."

"Not really," said Josh. "It was only eight cubic feet into the unit."

It wasn't much of a joke, but Tanya smiled as she took the clock. "Well, thank you." She backed away from the door. "The dog bed's in the living room. I'm glad you're taking it. The more things get cleared out, the easier it is to get the house ready to show."

The dog bed was just inside the living room doorway. Josh's heart lurched when he saw it, and he braced himself as he folded the bulky thing and picked it up. But it didn't smell like Molly any more. Come to think of it, the color was a shade lighter than he remembered.

"I washed the cover," said Tanya.

"I can tell," he said. Was he glad Molly's scent was gone, or not? "Well, thanks."

Tanya shrugged. "You know me—compulsive."

Josh didn't know what to say, because all he could think was, maybe he *didn't* know her.

Tanya took a deep breath and added, "I thought it would be nice for you to get off to a fresh start, when you get a new dog."

"Thanks," Josh repeated, with more feeling. He had an impulse to give her a hug, but he wasn't sure it would be welcome. "So—enjoy the clock."

Reaching around the dog bed, Tanya gave him a quick, awkward hug. "Take care."

Back on the expressway, Josh felt his throat aching. Sad wasn't such a bad feeling. It was as if Josh had opened a closet, dreading to find horrors, but found only faded keepsakes.

There's more than one way to skin a cat.
Old saying

Chapter 32.

The young woman had taken his food, but the Cat was not hungry, anyway. His tongue was dry. He wanted water, much more water than the tantalizing drops from the faucet. As much water as Jordan had poured into each plant pot.

Creeping across the cellar to the plant table, the Cat lifted his head to sniff. There was more water here somewhere . . . in the watering can, under a table. He put his forepaws on the plastic rim and leaned in. He could see the water, but he couldn't lean down far enough to lap. He reached one paw down, then the other. They came up dry.

The Cat jumped to the top of the watering can, balancing on all four feet. Again he reached one paw down into the can. Ahh—this time, his pads met moisture, and moisture sank into the fur between his toes. Pulling the dripping paw up, he licked it dry. He dipped it in the water again and licked again.

It was a laborious way to drink, and he slid off the slippery plastic twice. But after his thirst was quenched, he felt more confident. He trotted back to the bottom of the stairs and searched out the last few pieces of cat chow, purring as he crunched. Praise to thee, Great Cat!

With fresh energy, the Cat jumped onto each window sill in turn, pressing his whiskers to the glass, and meowed for help. Climbing the steps to the bulkhead door, he pawed at the bolt. He tried to wedge his head into the crack of daylight between the metal and the concrete.

The Cat was getting angry. And every time he moved his left front leg, his shoulder hurt, which made him angrier. Had the woman Jordan seemed upset that he'd disturbed the plants on the table? All right, he'd disturb them some more.

Leaping onto a table, the Cat batted at one of the larger plants. He whacked the pointed leaves with one paw, then the other, whack-whack-whack, ignoring his swollen shoulder. Pulling a spray toward him, he tore off buds with his teeth. He attacked another plant, and another.

At first the Cat spit out the plant matter. But the more he bit, the more the taste intrigued him. Something about it reminded him of pizza, even though there was no cheese or (alas) sausage here. He nibbled buds thoughtfully, then rolled in the green wreckage he'd caused.

Now it must be time for a nap. Or at least a rest.

Stretching out among the pots, the Cat felt light and cheerful. He put one paw over his eyes to shield them from the glare. He didn't mind waiting, not at all.

Outside the dirty cellar windows, the daylight faded. The Cat's paws twitched; he dreamed he was leaping onto the Girl's bed, his pads sinking into the cloudlike comforter. She wiggled her toes under the covers, and he pounced on them. Giggling, she moved her toes to poke the covers on the other side of the bed, and he pounced again.

The Girl grew sleepy and stopped playing. She had changed somehow—now she was a full-grown woman, and she smelled like coffee. The Cat plucked the top edge of the covers with one claw. Drowsily she lifted the edge. He crawled under, purring.

Who touches a hair of yon gray head
Dies like a dog.
John Greenleaf Whittier, "Barbara Fritchie"

Chapter 33.

On the way to work the next morning, Josh couldn't wait to see Tucker. "Tuck!" he'd tell him. "Guess what? We're going to be together always!"

But Tucker was still absent from play group. And Rune was still imagining the dog as devastated with guilt and remorse; she'd called the Harrisons and left a message about her psychic therapy services. Josh decided he'd definitely visit Carol today, with flowers for her recovery, to explain that he wanted to take the dog off their hands.

"By the way," said Rune, interrupting Josh's thoughts. "Where's Ged? The cat who was riding in your car?"

"Oh, the cat—I found its owner! I meant to tell you," said Josh. "She saw my Found Cat poster." He searched for the name. "Jordan somebody."

"Jordan? *Jordan*?" Rune's mouth dropped open. "You don't mean Jordan, the cat-hoarder? I'm sure I told you about her. Young, pudgy, attitude? That Jordan?"

Of course it was that Jordan, Josh realized with a shock. Cat Woman, as Danielle had called her. He began to stammer an explanation, but Rune cut him off.

"You don't have the sense of a—a salamander! Giving a cat to Jordan is worse than giving him to the Mattakiset Animal shelter." She paused, blowing out breath like a dragon. "Not to insult salamanders." Those were the last words Rune spoke to Josh for the rest of the morning.

As Josh went about his day care duties, he felt increasingly uneasy about Tucker. Why hadn't he gone to the Harrisons' the day after Carol's fall? He hoped Gardner would be out when he visited Carol.

At noon, Rune let Josh do all the work of settling the dogs into their runs, while she made calls on her cell phone, in spite of the kennel rules. Rune's back was turned to Josh, but he caught "—can't let it go any longer."

Leaving through the office, Josh found Erica scowling at an accounting page on her screen. He asked, "Tucker just didn't show again today, huh?"

Erica raised her head. "Tucker? Oh, Tucker." She looked somber. "Mr. Harrison left a phone message early this morning. Apparently Tucker's not coming back to us at all."

"At all?" repeated Josh. "You mean they're taking him somewhere else for day care?" Poor Erica had lost another customer. "Erica . . . I have to apologize for the cat, for all the trouble it caused. It was stupid of me to ever let it ride along to the kennel."

"Yes, it *was* stupid of you," said Erica crisply. "But it was like a perfect storm that Gardner let the cat in, and Tricia brought Aodh into the office, and Carol couldn't control Tucker." She sighed, rumpling her cropped hair. "By the way, people liked your obedience class. I had several messages about it."

"You did?" After the disaster in the office with the cat and Murphy and Tucker and Carol, Josh had assumed the class was a failure. "But Gardner—Tucker?"

"He didn't explain. He just said not to expect Tucker for day care anymore." Erica pressed her lips together, grim. "But I can guess. I've seen this before, and I hate it. People go to a shelter and pick out a young dog because he's cute and friendly. Surprise—the dog grows up, and they can't control him. *Then* they bring the dog to obedience class, when it's a lot harder to teach him. And finally something happens, like Carol's accident, and they turn the dog back in. Now he's not so young and cute, and not so easy to place with a new owner."

"Turn him in?" Josh felt sick. "You think they turned Tucker back in to the shelter?" Without waiting for an answer, he bolted out the office door, got to his car before realizing that he didn't know where the Harrisons lived, and rushed back into the office, panting.

Erica hesitated before giving him the address. "Josh. I hope you aren't going to do anything stupid?"

Anxious as Josh was, he stopped at a farm stand long enough to buy Carol a bouquet, a bunch of hydrangeas. The flowers were big and showy, like oversized blue popcorn balls, and the farmer assured him that they were local, unlike the roses Rune had rejected. But when Josh arrived at the Harrisons' house on Riverview Lane, he saw that he'd made the wrong choice again. The flowers in his hand were "local," all right. The Harrisons' driveway was lined with profusely blooming hydrangea bushes; climbing stone steps, Josh noted the blue-globe-dotted hydrangeas framing the front door.

Should Josh have known that hydrangeas were the wrong choice? You don't have much imagination about what women want, do you, Hiller? Always trying to ply them with wine or flowers.

"Why, Josh," called Carol from a terrace to one side of the house. "Josh? Over here. How sweet of you to come." She was sitting under an awning, crutches nearby, with one ankle wrapped and propped up.

As Josh joined her at the glass-topped patio table, his heart sank. Tucker was not curled up comfortingly beside Carol's chair, as he'd hoped. He strained his ears for barking from the house, but he heard only bird calls and wind chimes. Pushing back his urgent questions, he said, "What a great view you have up here."

"It's quite a panorama, isn't it—the salt marsh and the river? It's supposed to rain today, but I thought I'd sit outside as long as I could." Carol accepted Josh's flowers as graciously as if she'd never seen a hydrangea.

Josh told himself, Apologize first, then ask about Tucker. He began, "I'm very sorry about your fall. I feel responsible for—"

Carol waved his apology away with her hand. "Don't think twice about it! An accident like that was bound to happen, sooner or later." She paused. "Actually, I thought you might have come to apologize to Gardner. He left a little while ago."

"Apologize to Gardner? For what?"

Carol looked as surprised as Josh felt. "For the damage to his cottage. At first, he was inclined to blame Rick Johnson, but Rick explained that you used the dryer without cleaning the lint screen. The firemen thought it must have caught fire from a spark."

Outraged, Josh opened his mouth to protest, but then he restrained himself. "I'll straighten things out with Gardner later, but I really came to talk about Tucker."

"Oh, Tucker," Carol said with a sigh. "You probably wonder what Gardner and I were thinking, adopting a dog like Tucker in the first place."

Josh smiled with relief. This was going to be easier than he'd thought. "Well, you could look at it that way. Anyway, I'm glad you weren't injured any worse. As for Tucker, here's an idea. What if *I* took Tucker? If I had him all the time," Josh rushed on, "I could train him, I know I could."

Carol was shaking her head regretfully. "Even if you trained him, I couldn't be confident . . . Gardner and I have pretty much decided to give him up. He's just too large and strong a dog for me to—"

"No-no-no!" Josh interrupted. "Excuse me, Carol, I didn't make myself clear. What I actually want to do is *adopt* Tucker."

"Oh." Shutting her eyes with a frown, Carol shifted her injured leg. "Well. That's easy, then. Gardner was on his way to the shelter, so he might be there by now. I think they're open until five."

"The Mattakiset Animal Shelter?" Josh pushed back his chair. "They aren't a no-kill shelter!" He was about to dash for the steps when he had a second thought. "Can I have Gardner's cell number?"

Carol looked puzzled and a little annoyed. "For goodness' sake. The shelter isn't going to euthanize a dog on his first day there! Anyway," she added, "Gardner's cell phone number wouldn't do you any good. He does have a phone, but he never turns it on. But— *Hm*. You might catch him at Soule's. He was going to pick up something to grill for dinner."

Before she finished speaking, Josh was halfway across the terrace. "Goodbye! Thanks, Carol. Speedy recovery!"

If man could be crossed with the cat, it would improve the man, but it would deteriorate the cat.
Mark Twain

Chapter 34.

The Cat drifted into another dream: It was light outside, which meant it was morning. Time for the Girl/the blond woman to get up and feed him. Squirming out from under the comforter, he leaned over her face and licked her eyebrows. But he couldn't lick very well. His tongue was dry.

The Cat opened his eyes, and the dream melted. He was lying on a table among potted plants. Overhead, purplish-white lights glared through the foliage.

The Cat rose to his feet and started to stretch, but he was stopped short by his shoulder. It felt big and stiff, and it throbbed. He still couldn't reach back there to lick it. But he was so thirsty, he couldn't lick anything, anyway.

Across the room, the window darkened, and rain beat against the dirty glass. Rain water ran down the window in sheets—outside the cellar.

But the Cat seemed to remember water down on the floor. Ignoring his sore shoulder, he dropped from the table. Yes, the watering can. Climbing clumsily on top of the plastic can, he stretched his right paw down toward the water. It came up dry.

Water glinted at the bottom of the watering can, teasing him. He stretched his other paw down. With his left shoulder swollen, that paw couldn't even reach as far as the first one.

Rising on his hind legs, the Cat threw himself into the watering can, squirming downward. His flailing weight tipped the can over, and he fell sideways, wedged in the top of the can with one forepaw in and one out.

Pain shot through the Cat from his sore shoulder, and he gave a forlorn cry. But then he felt moisture on his ear and whiskers. The water had rearranged itself. By turning his head, he could lap all he wanted. *Praise to Thee, Great Cat!*

There's no need to fear. Underdog is here.
Animated TV series, *Underdog*

Chapter 35.

As Josh drove the twists and turns of the road to Soule's Market, he couldn't help imagining Tucker as Rune had described him in her dream, with drooping head and tail. Josh had never seen the dog act listless, but now he could picture him that way. Gardner Harrison had probably dumped Tucker at the shelter already. Josh remembered the way he'd seen Gardner look at the dog. He'd heard Gardner say, "If my wife weren't so fond of you . . ." And that was *before* Tucker had caused Carol to fall and injure herself.

Heavy clouds darkened the day, increasing Josh's sense of emergency. If he could only catch Gardner before he turned Tucker in. Nip him in the butt, as it were, so that Josh wouldn't have to apply to the shelter to adopt the dog. For one thing, he'd have to pay a fee of several hundred dollars.

But that wasn't the main problem. By the time Josh turned into Soule's parking lot, fat raindrops splattering his windshield, he was obsessing over how to answer the questions that shelters asked. He knew them well, from reading dozens of application forms at the Westham shelter. **Employment**: *Occupation? Years employed? Employer?* He could try convincing them that he would soon be a re-employed teacher. Or maybe a business owner? Anyway, something more solid than a doggy day care attendant.

Your Home was worse. *What type of home do you live in? House? Apartment? Condominium? If you rent, does your lease allow dogs?* None of the above. If Josh took possession of Tucker, Barbara would lose all patience with him. *My home: cheap motel.*

He could lie, but he knew that shelters checked up on those things.

The parking lot of the market was almost full, so Josh had to find a place at the far end, near the Pooch Park car ports. Taking out his phone, he called the Mattakiset Animal Shelter. If Tucker was already there, no point in talking to Gardner.

A male person answered the phone, and Josh thought he recognized the voice of the rude youth who'd reached with leather gloves for the black and white cat.

Josh started to ask if anyone had turned in a Lab-terrier mix, light brown with a black nose, but the young man interrupted, "Can you hold?" Without waiting for Josh's answer, he transferred him to a recording about the shelter's current fundraiser.

Josh took a deep breath. All right, he could hold.

Five minutes went by while Josh watched rain slide down his windshield. Then the line went dead. Someone had hung up on him. "You jerk!"

Struggling to stay calm, Josh started to redial. Something he'd seen, but not taken in, tickled his mind: There in the Pooch Park was a silver station wagon like Gardner Harrison's car. Something moved inside the car, barely visible through the rain now falling steadily.

In an instant Josh was out of his own car and jogging toward the Pooch Park. The dog in Gardner's car began to bark, poking his black nose out the half-open back window.

"Hey, buddy!" As Josh reached the window, Tucker squirmed and whined, swiping at Josh's face with his tongue. Josh put his hands on the dog's ears and leaned down for a smooch.

Well! Gardner *was* in Soule's Market. "We're in luck," Josh told the dog. "I'll be right back." With a last rumple of Tucker's shoulders, Josh turned and plunged through the rain for the store entrance, followed by disappointed barks.

In the store, Josh checked the deli counter first. It was crowded, and several of the crowd were older men with gray hair and preppy clothing, but no Gardner. Check dairy, since Josh was now at the back of the store? Or wait, maybe Gardner was already in a checkout line. Why hadn't Josh looked there first?

Josh sprinted up the bread and peanut butter aisle, dodging around customers, muttering "Excuse me—sorry—excuse me." Just as he reached the front of the store, he spotted a man with silver hair, wearing a green polo shirt tucked into his shorts, pushing a cart out the exit. "Gardner!"

The clerks at the cash registers and several customers stared at Josh, but the gray-haired man didn't even turn his head as the doors closed behind him. Elbowing his way past the express lane customers, Josh dashed for the exit.

But even as Josh burst out into the rain, the man he was chasing opened the trunk of a Camry. Now Josh could see his profile, and it was that of an elderly cherub, nothing like Gardner's senatorial features.

"You clueless wonder," Josh told himself. He trotted along the front of the store and in the IN doors again, looking over his shoulder in case Gardner was sneaking out.

This time he searched the checkout lines first, then walked quickly along the front of the store, peering down each aisle. The trouble was, there was the possibility that each time he looked down an aisle, Gardner might have just stepped out of sight at the other end. Frozen vegetables, frozen dinners—no Gardner. Paper goods—no. Cleaning supplies—no.

Josh swung past a high stack of charcoal briquettes bags—and found himself only a few feet from a silver-haired man in polo shirt and Madras shorts. "Hey!"

Gardner turned from chatting with the butcher. "Josh. I have a bone to pick with you." The older man gave him a closer look. "Is something the matter?"

Out of breath, Josh rested his hands on his thighs. "No. No, fine." He tried to stop panting. "So, I just talked to Carol about Tucker."

Gardner frowned at him. "What?"

"I stopped by your house and talked to Carol, a few minutes ago. She said you'd decided to give Tucker up, and I offered to take him off your hands."

Without answering Josh, Gardner turned back to the butcher. "I'm going to have the lamb chops. Can you cut me two, double-thick?"

"Tucker and I are a better match," Josh went on. "I've had a lot of experience training dogs, and Tucker could be a great pet, if he had consistent attention and discipline. And of course—" Josh was about to finish, "of course I'm younger and stronger," but he thought better of it and said instead, "Tucker and I just have a special rapport."

"Really," said Gardner. "A match made in doggy heaven." He gave Josh an even stare. "To be honest, I'm not pleased that you bothered Carol this morning. Thank God she didn't break anything when she fell, but she sure bruised herself, and I know her sprained ankle hurts like hell."

Josh took a deep breath. "I'm sorry. She didn't seem— Look, we don't need to discuss this anymore, if you'll just let me have Tucker. Please."

Harrison accepted a package from the butcher and told him, "Give me a pork sirloin, too. That one." He turned back toward Josh. "You've been frank about my deficiencies as a dog owner, so I'll tell you something frankly. I'm not sure *you're* a great prospect to adopt a dog. From what I've seen, you don't have a steady job, you don't have a permanent address, and you sure don't have good judgment about choosing friends."

"Okay," Josh admitted. "But all that is changing."

Taking a second package from the butcher, Gardner shrugged. "You can explain it to the folks at the animal shelter."

"You're going to make me apply to adopt at the shelter, just out of spite?"

Gardner headed for the produce section without answering. Josh went on, "That would be cruel. And asinine!"

Josh stared at the older man's back as Gardner disappeared behind a display of potted chrysanthemums. Then he turned and walked out through the market into a downpour. Fuck you, Harrison.

Lightning crackled as Josh splashed in the direction of his car, and the following thunder booted him past the Civic, at a run, toward the Pooch Park. Tucker: thunderstorm phobic, thought Josh. The dog was ricocheting around the station wagon, letting out an eerie howl. As Josh reached through the open window, he felt Tucker shuddering.

Unlocking the door, Josh seized the dog's collar. There was a leash on the floor of Harrison's backseat, but it didn't seem right to take it. Josh and Tucker ran awkwardly toward his car.

Letting Tucker scramble into the backseat, Josh wondered how many illegal acts he'd just committed. His knowledge of criminal law was sketchy; he'd completed one semester of law school before deciding that he would not become an attorney, like his father. Breaking and entering? No, he hadn't *broken* into Gardner's car. Trespassing, maybe. What about stealing a dog—was that a felony? A free-floating quotation, "Possession is nine-tenths of the law," popped into Josh's head. That couldn't be right.

With his windshield wipers laboring to keep up, Josh drove past Cumby's, then the Fur-Ever Cat Shelter, then the dairy farm. Each time lightning crackled and thunder boomed, Tucker moaned and pushed his muzzle into Josh's neck. The dog's trembling shook the seat. The problem with dogs believing that humans were gods, thought Josh, was that they expected you to control the weather.

As Josh pulled into the Coastal Canine driveway, the storm seemed to be letting up. He looked back at Tucker, who promptly licked his face. He couldn't just leave the dog here in his car, in plain sight, in case Gardner came looking for him. He'd better park somewhere else.

Josh drove slowly back up Main Road, his eyes searching the landscape for an inconspicuous parking place. The ice cream stand? Too exposed. The dairy farm? He didn't know those people. Cumby's? Also too exposed, and a long way to walk.

The Fur-Ever sign, shaped like a house with a door that outlined a cat's head, caught Josh's eye. The cat shelter's driveway curved past a stand of pines. They must have a place to park there, and it was out of sight from the road. Josh turned in, his mind busy with explanations for the cat people: He only wanted to park for a few hours; he was a major—well, minor—donor to Fur-Ever; he was a personal friend of that cat champion Rune Borden . . .

On the other side of the pine trees, there were several parking spaces in front of a low building. Two cars were already there, one of them a white van lettered with FUR-EVER CAT RESCUE and one a yellow VW. Rune herself leaned against her car, talking with a dark-haired man.

Josh called, "Hey, Rune! Can I ask you—"

Rune glanced in his direction, but she held up her palm and kept on talking to the other man—Neil, the fireman.

"Okay, then," said Rune, "pick me up in the van at five-fifteen." Neil nodded and waved, and Rune stepped over to Josh's car. "Hey. What're you doing here? Did you change your mind about Pansy?" Her eyes widened as she caught sight of the dog. "Tucker! What're *you* doing here?"

Josh took a breath to explain. Behind him, Tucker panted and wiggled, his tail whacking the car seats as he leaned out the window toward his friend Rune.

Scratching Tucker behind the ears, Rune smiled sideways at Josh. "I didn't think you had it in you. You kidnapped Tucker."

"No, it's not like that." Josh laughed uneasily. "Carol said—it was fine with Carol for me to have him. Anyway, is it okay if I park here?"

"I can see . . . Oh, I can *see* why you and Tucker would be a good match," said Rune. "But are you sure you want to tangle with Gardner Harrison? He's the King of Swords type, you know?"

"Just tell me, yes or no," snapped Josh. "Can I leave my car here for the rest of the afternoon?"

The fog comes
On little cat feet.
Carl Sandburg

Chapter 36.

The Cat crouched on the edge of a plant table. He was thirsty again. He dropped slowly off the table, letting out a mew at the jolt to his wounded shoulder. He checked the turned-over watering can. It was empty, and the spilled water was only a damp spot on the floor.

The Cat crossed the cellar, jumped up on the sink with an effort, and coaxed a few rusty drops from the faucet. He sniffed the drain, but no cricket this time.

Back at the table, the Cat had to try twice before he could jump up. Crawling into his shelter among the plants, he sank into a feverish half-doze. Now and then he opened his eyes, just a slit, and saw his white front paws. In the glare of the overhead lights, they looked grimy. Shouldn't he be grooming them?

You don't really own a dog, you rent them, and you have to be thankful that you had such a long lease.

Joe Garagiola

Chapter 37.

"I'm going to leave early," Rune informed Josh that afternoon. "You don't mind handling the pickups, do you?"

Josh frowned at her across the chain-link fence. "Well, yeah, I do." He'd been wondering all afternoon how Tucker was doing, alone in his car up the street. The thunderstorm had cleared, but the dog might still need reassuring. "I already did all the noon work," he pointed out to Rune.

"It wasn't that much," she said. "Anyway, pickups is the least you can do now, to help us out with the raid. After handing a cat over to Jordan! You need to build up some good karma."

"I already banked good karma for today, by rescuing Tucker," said Josh.

"And you owe me for letting you leave him at Fur-Ever," said Rune. With increasing fervor she went on, "Do you understand how huge this is? The police actually decided to do something about Jordan's hoarding house! Well—they're more concerned about her supplying weed to underage kids, isn't that typical? Never mind dozens of innocent neglected animals. Anyway, Neil and I have to be there when the police show up, to grab all those cats."

Josh supposed he did owe her, so when Rune slung her hemp tote bag over her shoulder and left, he finished the work: wiping down each muddy dog; bringing the day care dogs to the office to be picked up; resettling the boarding dogs in their kennels; stowing the water buckets, throwing stick, and the other exercise yard equipment; and making one last round of the pens to scoop overlooked turds. In case telepathic communication with dogs was possible, as Rune claimed, he sent a thought message up the road: I'll be there soon, Tuck.

Finally done, Josh grabbed one of the kennel's leashes and a dog biscuit and loped up Main Road. As his feet crunched the gravel on the Fur-Ever driveway, he heard Tucker begin to bark: *Woof-woof. Woof-woof.*

A smile spread over Josh's face. Tucker knew Josh's footsteps, and Josh knew Tucker's bark. Or rather, his barks; that was a greeting bark.

Rounding the curve and the stand of pine trees, Josh caught sight of his car. "Hey, Tucker!" Then Josh stopped short, gaping.

The dog with his head out the back window had to be Tucker, but he was gray, rather than brown. The car windows were gray, too, as if a very small volcano had erupted inside.

"Sheesh! What did you get into?" Stepping up to the window, Josh slipped the leash over the dog's head while Tucker licked his chin and nuzzled his neck. He'd gotten into ashes—those were ashes on Tucker's head and shoulders, and now scattering over Josh.

When Josh opened the car door, Tucker seized something from the backseat before bounding out.

Making a play-bow, he shook the object—a tattered piece of cardboard—at Josh.

It was a remnant of what used to be . . . the carton of Molly's ashes.

Josh stood staring at Tucker. The dog grinned at him, giving the cardboard another shake. Josh felt— What did he feel? Fury? Deep outrage, at this act of desecration?

Instead, he had to repress a laugh. "Tucker. *Drop* it."

Tucker, his eyes on Josh, let the damp fragment fall to the gravel.

"Good drop!" Josh slipped him the dog biscuit. Then he stepped back, patting his own shoulders. "Tucker. Up." He braced himself as Tucker leaped on him. "Who's a lucky dog? *Who's* a lucky dog?"

Tucker slurped at Josh's face, his ears, his neck.

"*You're* a lucky dog. And so am I."

It took several minutes for Josh to wipe down the inside of his car windows with a beach towel. The result was not really clean, but clean enough to see to drive. He'd have to visit the car wash on Route 6 and use their heavy-duty vacuum on the whole interior.

But first, Josh needed all that usual dog stuff: chow, bowls, leash, etc. So first the pet store (also on Route 6), then the car wash. "You're costing me a lot of money already," he told Tucker in the rear view mirror. His stomach growled. No lunch except for a few stale peanuts from the staff room at the kennel.

Driving up Main Road into the village, Josh made calculations about how long he could afford to live on his savings. The rate at even a cheap motel like the Dreamland would add up.

Josh's focus shifted to a police car approaching from the opposite direction, and he felt suddenly ill. *What was he thinking?* Gardner was chair of the Mattakiset Board of Selectmen. If he reported the theft of his dog to the Mattakiset Police Department, they'd jump on it. Josh braced himself for a high-speed chase in his aging car. It'd last about one block . . .

The officer at the wheel of the police car looked straight at Josh's Civic, its criminal driver, and its stolen dog. He yawned.

Whew. However, Josh couldn't take the chance of staying in town. For that reason, and for reasons of income stream, he should suck it up and accept the coaching job at Kingstown Academy. And lead their field trip—aargh . . .

Coming up on the Cumberland Farms gas station and store, Josh noticed Danielle in the parking lot. She was pacing beside her blue Kia, phone to her ear. He wondered if she was trying to get hold of Ryan.

Then several things clicked together in Josh's mind: Ryan. Jordan's cat-hoarding house. Marijuana. Police/animal rescue raid. With a jerk of the steering wheel, he pulled into the parking lot.

Danielle lowered her phone. "Josh, thank God! Can you help me here?"

"Oh, shit," said Josh under his breath as noticed the flat right rear tire of Danielle's car.

He'd never been good at changing tires.

"Ryan *could* change the tire," she went on apologetically, "and he should, but he's not picking up or calling back." She offered a hand for Tucker to lick through the back window, then frowned slightly. "This dog looks just like the Harrisons'."

"Listen," said Josh. "I stopped to give you a heads-up about a raid on Jordan's this afternoon. I thought Ryan might get caught up in—"

"A raid? You mean the cat rescuers?" Danielle looked puzzled. "Well, it's about time. But even if Ryan's there--and there's a good chance he is, since he isn't picking up— Oh, you mean they might catch him smoking dope?"

"It's worse than that," said Josh. "Rune says the police are really coming down on Jordan. For dealing to underage kids. So for Ryan to be involved—"

"Oh, shit." Danielle stared at him. Then she ran around to the passenger side of his car, yanked the door open, and slid in. "Never mind the tire. I need a ride. Right now."

Again I must remind you that
A Dog's a Dog—A CAT'S A CAT.
T.S. Eliot, "The Ad-dressing of Cats"

Chapter 38.

The Cat seemed to be in a garden. Although his eyes were shut, he knew he was in the midst of plants, breathing in their moist green scent. Among the plants, the Cat sensed a Presence.

Opening his eyes just a slit, the Cat looked into an enormous eye, yellow with a narrow pupil. *Two* huge eyes in a face of shimmering fur, so close that the details blurred.

Somehow the Cat knew that he would not be able to see the Presence unless he was in great danger. But he was not afraid. He was filled with wonder.

Is this the end of my second life? asked the Cat.

The Presence did not answer right away, and the Cat wondered if he had a right to ask such a question. Or—a very strange thought—did the Presence, enormous and powerful as She was, not know the answer?

Finally Her whiskers twitched. *Perhaps. Perhaps not. It depends on a human.*

The furry vision began to fade, revealing the outlines of plant pots and leafy branches. The Cat thought that was the end of the answer. But then, so faintly that he might have imagined it: *It depends on—a dog?*

Outside noises reached the Cat's ears through the cellar windows. A car's tires crunched the driveway.

Human footsteps thumped the deck. Human voices talked back and forth, louder and louder, punctuated by barking.

The Cat's ears flicked. He started to raise his head, but the pain in his shoulder stopped him. Those voices—He recognized Jordan's nasal drawl, and the other two voices also sounded familiar. So did the dog's let-me-in bark.

The Cat felt a spark of hope. A cry burst from his parched throat: *Worlworl.* It should have been a piercing call for help. But the sound came out so faintly that surely the humans could not hear it.

Then the wail of sirens blotted out all other sounds. Louder and louder, almost as dreadful as the sirens on the fire trucks. The Cat needed to hide, right now. Forcing himself up, in spite of his throbbing shoulder, he crept farther into the greenery.

Cry havoc! and let slip the dogs of war.
William Shakespeare, *Julius Caesar*

Chapter 39.

"Um—" Josh didn't want to get anywhere near a police raid, himself. "I was on my way to the car wash."

"Please hurry," said Danielle, buckling her seat belt. "It's not that far." Her movement stirred up ashes, and she coughed. "Please. . . . What did you do, empty your shop vac in here?"

With a sigh, Josh decided he could risk dropping Danielle off close to Jordan's house, at least. He paused at the exit to the Cumby's lot. "Left?"

"No, right, right," said Danielle. "She lives off of Summer Street. . . . Here, left! Left in front of the fire station. Just keep going, it's a ways. A few miles."

Letting out a long breath, Danielle leaned back and closed her eyes. "I know he's there. That's why he isn't answering."

"You don't know that," said Josh. "Why would Ryan get involved in drugs? He's got so much to lose."

Danielle bit her lip, and her eyes shone with tears. "Damn right. He could lose his scholarship. He could even do time, if he's . . . if that fat little bitch talked him into—"

She hushed suddenly as a police siren wailed in the distance. Tucker whined and put his front paws on Josh's shoulders. "Get *back*," Josh told the dog. He hadn't taught Tucker that command, but the dog dropped down.

Slowing the car, Josh checked the ash-streaked rear view mirror.

"Go, go, go," pleaded Danielle. Twisting to look for herself, she came nose to nose with Tucker, and he licked her face. "*Aa*! Get away."

As the car swung onto a straight stretch of road. Josh's phone rang. "Ryan!" exclaimed Danielle, and she dug in her purse. "Pull over. Please."

"I think that's *my* phone," said Josh, but he pulled over. If it was Nancy Reston, he'd pick up. If it was Gardner Harrison, he wouldn't.

"It *was* your phone," groaned Danielle. "Never mind me, keep driving! See that beat-up mailbox ahead, on the right? Turn there."

Josh's call was from Nancy. His last chance to accept the coaching job before she hired someone else? "Listen, if that's Jordan's driveway, I'll drop you off there. I really need to—"

"We're almost there. Please!"

With a pang, Josh returned his phone to his shorts pocket and pulled into the road again. He swerved around the battered mailbox, and they jolted onto the crushed-shell lane. It flashed through Josh's head that if Ryan *was* mixed up in Jordan's enterprise, he, Josh, might be complicit in something or other by trying to help Danielle shield her son. Never mind the stolen dog. He checked his rear-view mirror again for police cars.

The end of the lane came in sight: a ranch-style house in need of paint and a new roof, and a car parked in front. Cats scurried around puddles and under the deck as Josh's car approached. Several cats watched them from the deck railing.

"Sheesh," said Josh. He spotted cats under the bushes, cats camouflaged in the moss on the roof. The whole scene was like one of those kids' puzzles: *How many cats can you find in this picture?*

Danielle un-cinched her seat belt. Josh swerved around a large puddle and pulled up on the grass. She jumped from the car without shutting the door and ran for the front of the house. Tucker was right behind her, trailing his leash, barking. Woman and dog dashed up the steps of the deck, scattering cats left and right.

"Tucker, wait!" shouted Josh. He jumped out after them.

Danielle and Tucker were at the sliding door, talking to Jordan through the screen. "Ryan?" the plump young woman said. "I might have seen him—a lot of kids come around . . . Oh, you mean Ryan *Ferreira*? Hm. Maybe."

"Jordan, do not give me that crap. I know he's here. Ryan?" Danielle shouted past Jordan. "Ryan!"

Tucker's ears swiveled toward the inside of the house, as if he'd heard something farther in. He whined, pawing at the screen door.

"Stop that!" Jordan kicked at his paw through the screen and glared at Danielle. "Are you just going to let your dog wreck my house?"

"It's my dog," Josh put in, "but look—"

"It's not my dog," interrupted Danielle, "and I happen to know it's not your house."

"Look," said Josh, "the dog knows Ryan, and clearly he can tell that Ryan's here."

"Oh, clearly?" said Jordan. She looked even younger than the first time Josh had seen her, almost young enough to be one of his middle-school students.

"Where *is* he, Jordan?" asked Danielle.

"I don't know." Jordan smiled sweetly. "Maybe I locked him in the cellar."

Josh stepped up to the screen. "Hey, Jordan." The stench of cat urine hit his nostrils, and he tried not to choke. "I'm Josh." His gaze shifted from her to the inside of the house, but all he could see was a small table overflowing with junk mail.

"Like I care?" Jordan said to Josh.

"I can see you're having a hard time," said Josh quietly. "It must be tough, living here by yourself. Taking care of all these cats. That's quite a burden."

Jordan didn't answer, but her puffy lower lip trembled as she dug a joint and matches from her pocket.

Danielle stared at him. "Josh, are you out of your mind?" She yelled into the house again. "Ryan! Get on out of here! The cops are coming!" She tugged at the screen door handle.

From the direction of the road a siren wailed. Jordan froze. "Cops?" she screamed. "You called the cops, you crazy bitch?"

A police car, lights flashing, appeared on the lane, with a second cruiser behind it. At the same time, Tucker began barking at a level of urgency that Josh had never heard before. *Gr-woof! Gr-woof!* He barked so hard that all four paws lifted off the deck on the *woof.*

Jordan struck a match, but instead of lighting the joint, she grabbed a catalog from the table and held the match to it. "Hey! I can be crazy, too."

The two patrol cars screeched to a halt at angles, trapping Jordan's car beside the house.

Josh put a hand on Danielle's arm and a foot on Tucker's trailing leash. He saw the dog pull back from the door. He started to say, "Wait, this isn't going to help."

But as Josh was speaking, Tucker launched himself at the screen, easily ripping the leash from under Josh's foot. Jordan shrieked and staggered back. The screen door fell inward, and the blazing catalog dropped from her hand. Tucker leaped over the screen and disappeared into the house, barking.

Danielle turned to yell at the police, "She's burning down the place down!" before she stumbled across the fallen screen and into the house. "Ryan!"

"Tucker!" Josh jumped after them. Flames licked at the legs of the hall table as he ran past.

Danielle and the dog passed an empty bedroom and paused at the end of the hall. The dog stopped barking. "Ryan?" Danielle called into a closed door. Tucker whined and threw himself against the door, making it rattle. As Josh dove for the leash, Danielle turned the doorknob and flung open the door. The dog tore down the cellar stairs.

Jupie said he was sure he would just *love* her, and he jumped right up in her arms and kissed her and started to purr.

Neely McCoy, *The Tale of the Good Cat Jupie*

Chapter 40.

The sirens stopped. Now the humans were shouting, and the dog barked harshly. Something crashed overhead. Footsteps thumped through the house.

Someone slammed into the door at the top of the cellar stairs.

"Ryan?" said a woman's husky voice. Was the Cat dreaming again? It sounded like the coffee woman.

There was a click, and the door flew open. "Ryan!" called the woman. "Where are you?"

Peering through the foliage, the Cat watched a dog with a loose leash scramble down the stairs. The Cat made an effort to think. He knew that dog: large, light brown, bouncy. But the dog didn't belong with the woman.

Leaping the last two steps, the dog paused. He turned his head this way and that, sniffing. He took a few steps in one direction—sniff-sniff-sniff—then another.

The woman paused, too, blinking at the tables of potted plants. "Ryan?" Shading her eyes from the tube lights, she turned slowly around to squint into the darker parts of the cellar.

The dog's black nose pointed toward the plant tables, sniff-sniff-sniff. He snorted. Stepping up to the closest table, he shoved his head between the pots, and several tumbled to the floor. Whining, he put his front paws up on the table, poked his muzzle through the leafy screen, and nudged the Cat in the ribs. Pain shot through the Cat's left shoulder. He tried to hiss.

The woman Danielle turned to someone coming down the stairs—the man Josh. "Nobody's down here," the woman said. She gasped and hit the side of her head. "Ryan's hiding in the *bedroom*! He's screwed." She nodded upward. "The cops are already in the house."

"Wait, look at Tucker," said Josh. "What's he up to?" He started toward the plant tables. Then a sequence of notes sounded, and both the humans pulled their little slabs from their pockets.

Danielle exclaimed, "Ryan! My god! *Where have you been?"*

The man slid his slab back into his pocket, muttering, "I've got to change my ring." He picked up the dog's trailing leash. "Let's go, Tuck, before the cops notice you."

"I *knew* you were there." The woman's voice grew angrier. "Uh-huh. I bet you were 'busy'."

The dog kept his front paws on the table. His black nose pointed to where the Cat crouched among the plants.

"Hmm, Tucker's after *something* . . . maybe an unregistered cannabis farm?" Josh snorted. "We don't need a drug-detection dog to see what's on the table."

The woman Danielle was still speaking into her little slab. "Stay. Right. There." To Josh she said, "He's in your car."

The man was intent on the dog, who whined and nudged the Cat again, this time at the base of his tail.

That was too much to bear, even from a friendly dog. The Cat snarled. At least, he tried to snarl. The sound coming out of his dry throat was a squeak.

"What was that?" asked the man. "There's something hiding in the plants—a mouse or something?"

Joining Josh at the table, the woman Danielle said, "Did you hear me? Ryan's—" As Josh parted the foliage, her eyes looked into the Cat's. "Oh my god."

The Cat thought he must be dreaming again. He was in a garden. Or he was at the dump, hiding in the weeds. He was dreaming that the special woman, the one meant to be his patron, had come for him at last.

"Panda, poor kitty, is that you?" whispered the coffee woman. "He doesn't look very good." She brushed her fingertips over his head and neck, but then her hand paused. "This shoulder's all swollen. And hot."

Although it must be a dream, the Cat opened his mouth to utter a greeting, *Rowr?* Again, only a squeak came out.

"Poor thing, he's dirty—cobwebs in his whiskers—" The woman Danielle turned on the man, and her soft voice became a snarl. "Josh. *Did you give Panda to Jordan?"*

The man Josh groaned. "Of course. *All* my fault."

At the same time, heavy footsteps sounded through the ceiling, and a male voice called down the stairs, "Anyone in the cellar?"

The Cat willed himself to rise out of the plants, twine himself around the woman's legs, slink into her lap. But he was so weary. Still crouching, he fixed his eyes on her and sent out waves of longing.

"Yeah, we're rescuing cats!" Josh shouted back. "We'll go out the bulkhead." Dashing to the other end of the cellar, he wrenched at the bolt of the metal door. "Out of my way, Tucker. Danielle, *come on*."

The woman leaned closer to the Cat, turning her head to one side. "Oh. He's purring." Her voice, soft again, rose to a higher register. "Come here, sweetheart, Panda kitty." She lifted him tenderly out of the plants.

It hurt the Cat's sore shoulder, but he let himself be gathered into her arms.

Love me, love my dog.
Latin saying

Chapter 41.

The bolt gave with a rusty screech. Shoving the bulkhead door open, Josh let Tucker pull him up the cement steps by the leash. "Danielle?" he shouted over his shoulder.

She was right behind him, cradling the black and white cat. "Very sick cat here," she called down into the cellar. "Have to rush him to the vet."

Outside, cats scurried away from the house as fast as they had run toward it a short while ago. A few paused to watch from the edge of the grass, while others slunk into the bushes.

Two police officers hustled Jordan, wailing, "My cats!" toward a patrol car, but they paused as a silver station wagon appeared on the lane. The car jerked to a stop in front of the house.

Josh froze, sure that Gardner Harrison would notice him and Tucker, guilty as hell, only a few yards away. But Gardner's eyes were fixed on Jordan.

"What seems to be the trouble, Officer Mello?" Gardner climbed deliberately out of his car. "That's my grandniece you're holding. This is my sister-in-law's property. Why wasn't I told?"

"As a matter of fact," said the older policeman, "we did notify the property owner." He cleared his throat and nodded at Jordan. "With all due respect, Mr. Harrison, this could be a felony situation here. There's some indication of an effort to destroy evidence. We had to put out a fire." He pursed his lips. "And with all due respect, this is the second time in one month that your family's been involved in a residential fire."

While Gardner was distracted, Josh hustled Tucker to his car and swung the back door open. But Tucker hesitated to jump in, and to Josh's amazement, something large and lumpy moved under Molly's towel. Some*one*, not something.

"I *told* you," Danielle whispered beside him.

In front of the house, as Gardner argued with the police officer, the white FUR-EVER van drove onto the grass. Rune leaned out the passenger window to wave to a third officer. He waved back, calling, "Stay out of the house! It's structurally unsound."

The driver of the van, Neil, pulled up to Josh's car. In a low tone he asked Danielle, "Was Ryan here?"

"Neil, thank God." Danielle jerked her head toward Josh's backseat. "If you back the van up to *there*, he can climb in."

Rune was already out of the van, and as Neil obeyed Danielle's instructions, she bore down on Josh. "What were you thinking, bringing a *dog* to a cat rescue?" Then she focused on the cat in Danielle's arms. "Is that—Ged?" She put a gentle hand on the cat's back. "He's burning up. You need to get him to the vet."

"I'm taking them," said Josh, ushering Ryan into the van and Tucker into his backseat. He hurried around to open the passenger door for Danielle and the black and white cat.

A man with a ponytail stepped in front of Danielle and Josh and pointed his heavy-duty camera at them.

"Nice. Can I get your names for the *Mattakiset Mariner?*"

"Get out of my face," said Danielle. She slid quickly but carefully into Josh's car. "This very sick cat is going to the vet's."

"Rune!" called Neil urgently from the back of the van. "I need some help here."

"Rune," added Danielle in an urgent whisper. "Tell Neil to drop Ryan off at Cumby's, okay? He needs to change my tire."

Josh had never seen Rune looking so confused, and it made him smile. As he drove around the cluster of cars, he wished he'd taught Tucker to lie down, but Gardner was still arguing with the police, and the officers glanced at Josh's backseat with no sign of recognition. "Good luck with that cat," Officer Mello called to Danielle.

While Danielle and the cat were in the vet's, Josh checked his phone. "One more try, Josh!" said Nancy Reston's voice. "I figured out a way to give you two history classes. So your job would be half history, half coaching, for the time being. I hope you'll consider it."

Josh exchanged looks with Tucker, who had been leaning over the seat back, listening to the message with his head cocked. "Tuck. Things are starting to go our way."

"Of course I'll need a resume from you," Nancy added, "and you'd come in for an interview with the dean. But we really want you to join us at Kingstown. Let me know!"

Of course, thought Josh soberly, there was also that field trip that she'd mentioned before. Not only did he not want to lead it—Kingstown might not want him to lead it. Or even to join their faculty, after they heard about his last field trip.

Don't be a wuss, he told himself. He called Nancy back and left a "yes" message.

Danielle came out of the vet's without the cat, but with good news: "Panda was dehydrated and he had an infected wound in his shoulder. They're giving him fluids and antibiotics." She sighed. "I hated to leave him. But they said he might be okay to take home by tomorrow."

By the time Josh and Danielle reached Cumby's, Ryan was in the parking lot, tightening the bolts on her Kia's spare tire. He looked over at them with a bland expression. "Hey."

Danielle swung out of the car, glaring at her son. "Don't give me 'Hey'! You really dodged a bullet this time, Ryan Ferreira."

As Ryan rose to his feet, Danielle threw herself at him, and for an instant Josh thought that she was going to punch him out. Instead, she hugged him. Ryan, still holding the wrench, looked over his mother's head to Josh and rolled his eyes.

Josh grinned and waved. "Good luck at U. Mass."

As Josh arrived at the stone posts of his landlady's driveway, the farmhouse windows reflected pink sky. Barbara was guiding her lawn mower over a last stretch of grass, but she stopped short at the sight of the large brown animal hanging from the back window of Josh's car. Her mouth opened and closed, and she shook her head.

Lola raced over to Tucker's window, barking vigorously. Tucker barked back.

"Don't worry," called Josh to Barbara over the barking. "I'm moving out."

Barbara turned off the mower and walked over to his car, still shaking her head. "I don't know what to say, Josh. Yes, you'll have to move out, if that's your dog." She added stiffly, "I thought we had an understanding."

"I know, we did," said Josh humbly. "I've been a lousy tenant. You should feel free to keep the security deposit." He explained, as simply as he could, the events of the last day or so.

As Barbara listened, her frown relaxed, and she suppressed a giggle when Josh told how he'd grabbed Tucker from Gardner's car. "Well. . . . Do you have a place to sleep tonight?"

Josh nodded. "I'm already booked at a motel on Route 6, the Dreamland? I didn't ask if they allowed dogs, but I don't think it'll be a problem."

"Not at the Dreamland," said Barbara. "The problem there is with letting the bedbugs bite."

Outside of a dog, a book is a man's best friend. Inside of a dog, it's too dark to read.
Groucho Marx

Chapter 42.

Early the next morning, Josh and Tucker emerged from Room 17 at the Dreamland Motel. The first thing Josh saw was the red pickup truck, loaded with landscaping equipment, parked next to his Civic. "Shit." The terrier in the front seat barked at Tucker, and Tucker barked back.

At the same moment, Rick emerged from Room 18. "Thought that was your car!" He pointed at Josh. "Hey, I heard from Ollie last night. He wants—"

"Give him my best." Josh let Tucker bound into the backseat of his car. The dog stirred up the ashes again, and he sneezed. "Yeah, it's still a mess," said Josh to Tucker, "and whose fault is that? Maybe we can get to the car wash this evening." It had been kind of Barbara to let him leave his stuff in her apartment for the time being.

Driving west on Route 6 from the motel, Josh passed a stretch of used car dealers, a donut shop, and a mini-golf course. Bearing south, he drove through a neighborhood of small, closely spaced houses and then past the Harrison Funeral Home, conveniently located next to the Mattakiset Senior Center. Barbara was right; there was much more to Mattakiset than an idyllic setting for summer people.

Josh turned onto Main Road, passed the high school and the Harrison House Inn. Farther down the road, the

Cumby's sign looked blurred. Coastal fog had drifted in, wrapping Mattakiset in protective batting. Like the "unsung gem" it was, thought Josh, remembering Melissa the real estate agent's phrase.

Before he went in the store, Josh checked his phone. Nothing from Kingstown Academy. Had he sounded too eager? Had Nancy hired someone else in the lag time before he returned her call?

In Cumby's, Josh took his coffee and snack to Danielle. "How's the cat? How's—" What had she called the animal?—"Andy?"

"*Panda* is ready to come home, thank you so much for asking," she said, handing him his change. "And I'm ready to max out my card with the vet bill."

"I'm sorry," said Josh. "I really screwed up." As the next customer set his coffee on the counter, Josh hesitated. He pulled out his wallet and handed Danielle his MasterCard. "Use this. You can drop my card off at the kennel afterward."

Back in the car, Josh's phone rang. It was Kingstown Academy, but the dean of the faculty rather than Nancy. "We're eager to fill this position, so can you come in for an interview sometime in the next few days?"

"Yes," said Josh. "I can do that. How about tomorrow? I'll email you my resume."

Ending the call, Josh blew out his breath. Now he was going to have to explain how he'd come to defy his last principal. Besides the resume, should he send the Kingstown dean his report on Charlene Voss?

No, not yet. He'd wait until the interview. If that was going well, he'd tell the story of his unhappy last year at Westham Middle School, including how he hoped to avoid going down the same path in the future.

At Coastal Canine, Josh greeted Erica and Uncle George in the office. Erica, shelving dog treats and toys, frowned at Tucker in a puzzled way. "Did the Harrisons ask you to bring Tucker in, after all?"

"I've got Tucker now," said Josh. The dog was straining at his leash, eager to get to his Large Dog playmates. "Tucker, *sit.* Good sit. *Stay.*" He went on, "Erica, a big favor: Can I hide Tucker here, just for today?" As Erica kept shaking her head in astonishment, he explained that Gardner would be after him for stealing Tucker. And that he probably had a new teaching job. And that in any case he was leaving town.

Before Erica could answer, Uncle George told Josh, "I wouldn't worry too much about Gardner hunting you down, if I was you. He's got enough problems: His wife's on crutches; his sister-in-law's house is a wreck, and his grandniece is in trouble with the law."

Josh went on to Erica, "But I wouldn't leave you in the lurch about the Beginning Obedience class. I could still do that, if you want. Only it'd have to be evenings or weekends."

At noontime, as Josh was leading the dogs into their pens, Uncle George shuffled into the back rooms smiling slyly. "Got a surprise. I'm going to make an honest man of you."

Fastening the door of a pen, Josh looked at the piece of paper the old man handed him. "Bill of Sale. Where'd you get this?"

Uncle George had never looked so pleased with himself. "Well, I got to thinking about what Harrison's rights were, with the dog. And then I had a suspicion about who really owned Tucker. Yep, so I called up Carol, and sure enough. And she faxed over this legal document."

Josh looked at the paper again, a sheet of personal stationery with the initials CRH. Carol had written the date and *Received of JOSH HILLER in exchange for the brown Labrador mix dog named TUCKER, the amount of $1.00 (One Dollar)*. She'd signed it. At the bottom of the paper she'd added *(All sales final)*.

"Uncle George, you're a prince! How can I thank you?" Josh had an impulse to hug the old man, but he thought better of it.

"Well, now that you ask," said Uncle George cheerfully, "I wouldn't say no to a reward. Erica doesn't pay me a full salary, you know." He seemed to have thought all this out. "And I'll do one extra thing: If you trust me with the cash, I'll deliver the sale price of the dog to Carol. You probably don't want to stir up more trouble, going over to their house."

Josh was glad to hand over a one-dollar bill and the three twenties in his pocket, and the old man seemed satisfied. "Of course I wouldn't take more money from Erica, anyway," he explained, tucking the bills into his wallet. "I know she's struggling to turn a profit here.

And I generally get along fine on my Social Security and my pension. I don't need much."

When Rune came back from her lunch break, she and Josh returned the dogs to the exercise pens. "What happened in your car?" she asked as she opened the gate. "I wondered why Tucker was sort of gray this morning, but I thought he must have rolled in something. But your whole car is polluted."

"Yeah, I know. I have to get to the car wash." Josh hesitated. "As a matter of fact, I wanted to ask you about this." He pulled an envelope from his pocket. "I scraped up some of the ashes, and I was wondering if . . ."

"*Wow*," said Rune. "Those are your old dog's ashes, aren't they?" As Josh nodded, she went on, "And you want me to help you with a farewell ceremony."

"That's right! I was sure you'd know—"

"Oh." She widened her green eyes. "I thought that New Age stuff went out with the Seventies."

Josh bit his lip. "I'm sorry. I wasn't very respectful of your beliefs. I apologize." No need to add that he still thought Rune's alternate version of history was laughable. "I would really appreciate it if you'd help me . . . It just seems like Molly deserves some last rites."

Rune's face softened. "Of course. She's waiting to move on. Let's see—we could do it at the beach tonight. The moon is waxing, so it's an auspicious time." She added, "I'll only charge you what I would for a Tarot reading."

That night Josh met Rune at the beach, outside the closed parking lot. Josh handed her the cash and started to let Tucker out of his car.

But Rune stopped him. “No, leave Tucker here. This is Molly’s hour.”

They ducked under the chain, and Josh followed Rune’s flashlight over the dunes, through wild roses and beach grass. Rune was wearing only a cloak that billowed gently around her. “I should have told you to come sky-clad,” she remarked over her shoulder. “But it’ll be okay if you just take your clothes off here.” She stopped at the high-tide line and shut off the flashlight.

Whoa! Josh hadn’t expected this, but he felt hopeful as he pulled off his shirt. It would be fitting, wouldn’t it, if the ceremony included a life-affirming bout of sex? He said only, “I can’t see anything without the flashlight.”

“Shut your eyes for a moment,” Rune told him in a non-seductive voice, “and then you’ll see better.”

She was right; after he’d closed his eyes and opened them, Josh could make out a grayscale scene. The surf was low, a line of foam surging forward and swishing back. In the clear sky, the half moon gave a surprising amount of light. Josh couldn’t help looking around for spectators as he dropped his clothes on the sand.

“Do you have the ashes?” asked Rune. “Bring them into the water.”

Josh bent to fish the envelope from his shorts pocket, then waded into the waves after Rune. The water was almost warm. “Aren’t you going to be sky clad, too?” he asked.

"Don't talk," said Rune. The wet cloak swirled around her body as she stretched out her arms toward the bay. "O Great Ocean, the water from whence life first arose, we thank you for the life of Josh's faithful companion Molly." She looked sideways at Josh. "Repeat what I say."

Josh repeated her words, suppressing a squawk as a crab pinched his big toe.

The ritual went on for several minutes, acknowledging in turn the air, the earth, and the hidden fire of the sun. "Now," said Rune, "before you scatter the ashes to the four points of the compass, let us meditate in silence on your most intimate memory of Molly."

"Intimate?"

"You know," said Rune, "the time when you felt closest to her. For instance, maybe she used to lick you off?"

"What!"

"Just a thought," said Rune. "Between people and animals, intimacy is normally some physical moment."

Now Josh was very aware of the waves lapping around his crotch. Trying to ignore that sensation, he searched his mind for an appropriate memory. "Okay, here's the intimate moment: We used to watch TV on the sofa together." As he spoke, he could feel the sweet weight and warmth of her body. "She'd lean against my side." He'd bend over and rub his cheek against her silky ear.

"TV?" said Rune, as if he'd brought up something distasteful. "Well . . . I guess that's all right." She bowed her head. Josh followed suit, and they were silent for a moment.

Finally, as Josh scattered Molly's ashes to the north, the south, the east, and the west, Rune pronounced a Wicca benediction. "So be it," she concluded.

"So be it," said Josh. He followed Rune out of the foam, noticing wistfully the way her damp cloak clung to her butt.

Back in his sandy clothes, climbing over the dune path, Josh felt a little foolish. At the same time, he felt peaceful. This must be what they meant by "closure."

As they neared the parking lot, a dog barked. It was the kind of bark that a large, healthy dog would utter, if he was impatient for his person to return.

"I'm coming, Tucker!" shouted Josh.

God made the cat in order that mankind might have the pleasure of caressing the tiger.

Fernand Mery, *The Life, History, and Magic of the Cat*

Chapter 43.

Three months later, in the bedroom of the Cat's new home, the woman called Danielle rolled away from the man called Neil with a deep sigh. The Cat, sitting on the night table, hoped they were through thrashing around. The breeze lifting the curtains was chilly, and he was waiting to go under the covers.

"Ahh," said Neil. Then he noticed the Cat. "Look at Panda. He was watching us. That's kind of kinky."

Raising her head to look at the Cat, Danielle laughed. "He's just waiting for us to finish so he can go to sleep." She stretched out a hand to the Cat.

He sniffed her fingers, although he could guess what they would smell like: Neil. The woman was getting off the track of their nightly routine. He meowed to remind her.

"He's filled out nice since you rescued him, hasn't he?" asked Neil. "He's one good-looking cat."

"And smart," said Danielle. "Want to see something cool? I taught Panda to do this trick." Propping herself on an elbow, she returned the Cat's gaze. "Good *night*, Panda."

At last. Stepping from the night table onto the bed, the Cat got in position, twitched his tail three times, and leaped at the wall switch. The light flicked off.

The humans still murmured back and forth, with pauses in between. Finally the woman said drowsily.

"I've got an early class tomorrow. Lock the back door on your way out, okay?"

Neil mumbled into his pillow. Their breathing slowed. Stepping across the woman, the Cat plucked at the top of the comforter.

The humans did not respond, so the Cat pushed his head into the space where the man's shoulder lifted the covers and wormed his way between the two bodies. There wasn't as much room in the bed as he was used to, but the warmth was extra heavenly.

Stretching out, the Cat began to purr deep, throbbing purrs. *O Great Cat, thanks be to thee!* He was, after all, her favorite.

About the Author

Beatrice Gormley has lived with cats, dogs, and other humans all her life. She has always been fascinated by our bonds with creatures who are so different from us—or maybe not so different?

Beatrice is the author of over thirty novels and biographies for young readers. *Second Lives* is her first novel for adults. She lives and writes in Massachusetts with her husband, Robert Gormley, and their Cat.

Connect with Me Online

Beatricegormley.com

Made in the USA
Columbia, SC
03 June 2021

38924639R00183